12/2017

D1565812

Illusions of Paradise

A novel by

Pat McKanic

This novel is a work of fiction.

Published by Brookgran Publishing Co. in 2017
Publisher contact: brookgranpublishing@gmail.com

Author Pat McKanic is available for book signings, book club events, speaking engagements, seminars, panel discussions and conferences. To arrange appearances, please contact us at: brookgranpublishing@gmail.com or via our website: illusionsofparadise.net

ISBN-978-0-692-85706-9

Dedicated to:

Jarrett—You are the motivation and inspiration
for everything. I love you.

My niece Robin—To Robin the little girl, thanks for listening to
my dreams, and believing. To Robin the woman, thanks for
remembering the dreams, and believing. I love you.

To Brooklyn—you changed my life more than I could ever have
imagined.

To Alexander Brooks—Thank you for "movin' me" to action. I
love you buddy.

To Cousin Duane—Thank you for sending the song that
motivated me to start writing.

Acknowledgments

Special thanks to Brittany Simmons, Jocelyn Donahoo, Dr. Gloria Perkins-Sellers, Janet Leigh Gibson, and Linda Wallace.

Limbert Fabian for your talent, patience and intuition, and the beautiful cover design. You are truly talented!

To everyone who helped, supported, nurtured and encouraged me throughout my journey. Thank you!

Feb. 2, 2018

Dream! Believe! Achieve!
Dreams do come true!

With much love and appreciation,

Gail

Enjoy!

PART I: Beginnings
CHAPTER 1

The sign on the door at police headquarters read *Do Not Enter*. Toni Jackson knocked, then entered the room. She looked around. The walls were lined with smart boards and bulletin boards. Some of the bulletin boards were covered with pictures, including mugshots, and crime scene photos. A man sitting alone at a workstation stood up as she entered.

"Good morning. I'm Toni Jackson, a reporter with the *San Saypaz' Chronicle*. I'm here to check the blotter," she said as she approached him, her hand outstretched.

He looked at her, but didn't immediately respond. She put her hand down.

"Good morning. Uh, was there a sign on the door? A sign reading *Do Not Enter*?" he asked.

Toni glanced back at the door. "I knocked."

"You *knocked*?"

"Yes."

"Did the sign direct you to knock and enter, or did it say *Do Not Enter*? This is a secure area. You're not supposed to be in here."

"The chief's secretary told me that Deputy Chief Baptiste is out today, and that Tolliver would have the blotter. Are you Tolliver?"

"I'm *Detective* Tolliver, yes. Did she also tell you to ignore the sign on the door?"

"I'm sorry," Toni said sincerely. "I can leave, if you want me to."

"Apology accepted," he said, coming from behind the workstation to stand facing her. "You're here now, might as well get what you came for," he added.

He smiled at her, and a giddy nervousness overtook her stomach. She took a good look at him. His eyes were brown—a shade of brown she had never known. His skin was a different shade of brown, a rich, deep brown. It reminded her of the chocolate squares in the gold foil wrapper her father used to bring home from work. She'd let each square melt in her mouth completely before unwrapping the next one, although they were so good she just wanted to shove them into her mouth all at once. And no matter how many she ate, she always wanted more. Looking at Tolliver now she could almost taste, and feel the sweet creaminess of that candy in her mouth. She licked her lips—it was involuntary.

He kept his eyes on her as he picked up a clipboard and handed it to her.

"The blotter, Miss Jackson."

"Thank you." She skimmed the pages on the clipboard. "Nothing newsworthy," she said, handing the clipboard back to him.

"I haven't seen you around here before. You new?"

"No. I've been here awhile. Most days I stop in to see Baptiste, get the information from the blotter, and head back to the office. Sometimes I just call."

"I see. So, did you move to the island with your family?"

"My family? You mean my mother and father?" she asked, trying not to laugh.

"I mean, is there a Mr. Jackson?"

"No, I'm not married, if that's what you're asking. I have to go," she said, turning to leave.

"Wait, wait a minute."

She stopped in her tracks and turned slowly toward him.

"I really need to get back to the office. And besides, I'm not supposed to be in this room. What if somebody finds out I'm here?"

"I won't tell if you don't."

"I really have to go."

"Will you be back tomorrow?"

"Probably not," she said, backing away.

"Well, here, at least take my card," he said, pulling a business card from his shirt pocket as he approached her. "My cell number is on the back. Just in case."

"Just in case of what?" she asked, reaching for the card.

"Just in case you figure out you need me," he answered, not releasing the card.

They stood face-to-face, staring into one another's eyes. That strange feeling radiated through her stomach again.

She tugged at the card. "Thanks." She walked quickly through the door, pulling it closed behind her. Feeling weak, she rested against the doorjamb and closed her eyes.

What just happened?

***

Toni quickly scanned the lobby of the San Saypaz' airport, then headed for the staircase in the middle of the lobby. *I'm sure glad Old Yeller gave me this assignment. After my encounter with that cop yesterday morning, I'm going to stay away from police headquarters for a few days. I can just as easily get the information from the blotter over the phone. Now if I could just stop thinking about him.*

Old Yeller was the nickname reporters at the paper had given Toni's editor, Jim, because he was ancient, and was always yelling. They reasoned that he'd developed the habit of yelling to be heard over the clatter when newspapers still used teletype machines. Today, he'd assigned her the task of meeting a plane carrying the cast of a reality show that pitted B-list celebrities against one another for a chance to win $1 million dollars. She was to get with their publicists and set up interviews for feature stories. She was three steps up the staircase when she saw Detective Tolliver at the top. He headed down. She froze.

"Hello Toni Jackson from the *San Saypaz' Chronicle*. I have your press credentials," he said, smiling at her as he pulled a lanyard from his pocket."

There he goes with that smile again.

"Why are you . . .?"

"The department is providing security for the cast and crew while they're on the island."

She watched his lips as he spoke. They were plump and inviting. *Those lips look like they know how to handle their business,* she thought.

"The plane is going to be late," he said, bringing her back to the moment. "Have something to drink with me while we wait," he added, leading her up the stairs. "So, do you like kids?" he asked as soon as they were seated.

"*Kids*? Who doesn't like kids? That's a strange question."

"It's a question a man who wants kids asks a woman he's interested in. If it's one of his deal breakers, and she says no, he knows to keep it moving."

She pondered what he'd said as she studied his shoulders. There was something almost expressive about his shoulders.

"Okay. I have a question for you, detective."

He raised his eyebrows.

"What's your first name?"

His first name was Jameyson, but everyone called him "Jamey," or "J." He'd always wanted to be a cop, had been married and divorced, served in the Army, and spent time as a big city cop before returning to the island. He was anxious to start a family.

When the plane arrived, the celebrities stopped briefly to speak with the reporters gathered as their publicists handed out business cards.

"Have dinner with me tomorrow night. Buttered Lobster House, say, seven?" Tolliver asked as he walked her to her car after the last limo had pulled away. "I want to know who you are."

"Good night, Jameyson," she said, unwilling to commit.

"I'll see you tomorrow. Good night, Toni."

She shook her head in resignation as she watched him fade from view in the rearview mirror. *Kids? I'm not looking to settle down anytime soon. This little island is just a stopover in my grand plan for journalistic stardom, travel to exotic locales, and adventurous lovers. If I mess around with him, things could go south. That could hamper my ability to do my job here, and hurt my career.*

She was good at her job because she was a triple threat—book smarts, street smarts, and killer instincts. She did alright in the looks department, too. Warm brown and thick, she had a small waist, nice butt and big legs. She was what the fellas back home called "a round honey." She shook her head again. *There's something different about this guy, that's for sure. But as much as I like him, and Lord God in heaven knows I'm feeling him, he doesn't fit into my plan!*

CHAPTER 2

Toni picked up Jameyson Tolliver's business card from her desk, and studied it. She'd memorized the cell number he'd written on the back. *It's been a week since I stood him up for dinner, and he hasn't even bothered to call to ask why. How interested could he really have been?* She laid the card down, and looked at the blank computer screen in front of her for what seemed like the millionth time this morning. She put her elbow on the desk, rested her chin in her palm and sighed.

"Jackson!"

She turned to see Old Yeller approaching.

What? She yelled back, in her head.

"Cops found a body on Sandset Beach, a homicide. Get out there ASAP. The body is still there."

Murder was big news on the island, guaranteed front page byline. Her excitement was dimmed by the prospect of running into Tolliver.

Maybe I can grab a piece of this story without going to the crime scene.

"Jim, why don't you send Danny out to the crime scene? I'll work the phones to see what my sources know. Besides, I'm in the middle of writing a story."

He looked over her shoulder. "Yeah, where's it at? There's not a damn thing on that screen. Now get out of here before they move that body."

Maybe I won't run into him, she thought, stuffing her notebook and cell phone into her messenger bag. She slipped Tolliver's business card in, too. *Just in case,* she told herself.

***

Toni took her place among a group of reporters standing behind crime scene tape at Sandset Beach. Just then a group of cops came from behind a cluster of trees, and formed a semicircle on the beach. She recognized Tolliver's shoulders. At almost the same instant, as if he knew she was looking at him, Jameyson Tolliver turned and looked straight at her. Her stomach fluttered. He didn't smile, nod, or even acknowledge her, just stared at her briefly before turning his attention back to the group. She looked around on the sly to see if any of the other reporters had caught the look.

Maybe it was just my imagination.

"What's up?" Toni asked a television reporter standing beside her.

"Don't know. Cops aren't talking yet," he answered. "Body is just on the other side of that group of trees," he added, nodding his head in the direction of the beach.

When the other cops dispersed, Tolliver stood talking with Deputy Chief of Police Mel Baptiste. When they were done, Baptiste headed toward the parking area. Toni backed slowly away from the other reporters. She was standing next to Baptiste's car when he got to it.

"Hey, Toni."

"Good morning, Deputy Chief Baptiste."

"Come on now, call me Mel."

"So what's with the body? Murder?"

He nodded.

"Killed here, or somewhere else?"

"Elsewhere."

"Male? Female?"

"Young woman, twenty, twenty-two, maybe twenty-four, somewhere in there."

"Wow! How did she die?

He made a gun with his thumb and index finger, placed it against his forehead and jerked it upwards to indicate she had been shot in the head.

"Any leads?"

"Nothing yet. It's early."

"Anything else?"

"I've said too much already."

"Thank you, Deputy Chief Baptiste."

She started to walk back toward the beach.

"Toni."

She turned but didn't say anything.

"I don't want to see my name in the paper tomorrow."

"I always protect my sources. You're good unless you change your name overnight to *a source close to the investigation*."

Baptiste laughed. "Come visit me soon."

She nodded. Shortly after she returned to where the other reporters were gathered, Tolliver approached them.

"Detective Tolliver, Detective Tolliver," several yelled as he approached. He held up his hands to quiet them. Toni kept her eyes on his shoulders to avoid making eye contact.

"Listen up," Tolliver said. "We received a call at 7:45 a.m. A couple walking on the beach discovered a body partially hidden in a stand of trees," he added, speaking slowly. "When we arrived on the scene, we found the body of a female. Probable homicide. Our investigation is ongoing. We will keep you posted."

The other reporters shouted questions at him as he turned and walked back towards the beach. Toni watched as the truck from the coroner's office made its way back to the paved road, and disappeared. She turned to take one last quick look at Tolliver.

He looks good coming and going.

***

She had the kind of beauty that made other women give their men permission to turn their heads and look—but just once. Her sun-painted, honey colored skin was crowned by a mass of wild warm brown hair, with golden streaks that didn't come from a bottle. Her hands hadn't known hard work. Sweetly curved hips led to shapely smooth legs, tiny feet, and cute little bunion-free toes. A small, simple tattoo on the inside of her left ankle read "Marie." She was absolutely gorgeous in every way—except for the small black hole in the middle of her forehead, made when someone touched a gun to her skin, and pulled the trigger.

"I believe she is from one of the French-speaking islands," Dr. Cornelius Randall, the San Saypaz' medical examiner said. "I estimate her to be between twenty-two and twenty-five. We haven't identified her yet."

Toni looked at the body laying on the morgue table again. *She was so young.* "Her tattoo says Marie, maybe that was her name."

"Or perhaps a child's name," Dr. Randall said.

"You think she had children?"

"She has given birth at least once, yes."

She was someone's mother. "How long do you think she had been dead before her body was discovered yesterday morning, Dr. Randall?"

"Five, six hours."

"Any scrapes, scratches, anything to indicate a struggle?"

"No. But," he said hesitantly, "someone had relations with her."

Relations? Toni thought about it for a moment. "You mean she had sex before she died, sir?"

"No, Miss Jackson. What I mean is, someone had intercourse with her . . . after," he cleared his throat, "she was deceased."

Oh my God! Feelings of disgust and sadness enveloped Toni. She focused on the rows of shiny metal doors on the opposite wall of the morgue, wondering how many of the drawers actually contained bodies.

"There was DNA evidence on the body, evidence that could help identify the anim . . . whoever did this?" she asked after a few minutes.

"Yes. It is in the custody of the police for processing, after which it will be returned to this office. That is a detail not known to many, Miss Jackson. If you disclose it, it will be apparent that it came from me."

"You have my word," Toni said quietly. She looked at the young woman's face one last time, trying to retain her composure. Dr. Randall covered the body with a sheet.

Never let them see you sweat, or cry.

"Thanks, Dr. Randall. I'll follow-up," Toni said, making her way quickly through the morgue's heavy double doors.

* * *

She rushed off the elevator and ran smack dab into Jameyson Tolliver. Despite her best efforts to restrain herself, she started sobbing.

"Hey, hey, what's wrong? What's wrong?" he asked, cupping her elbow.

She shook her head. He pulled her gently toward an exit sign, and through a door that led to a stairwell. He eased her down onto one of the stairs, reached into his pocket and pulled out a handkerchief.

"Here you go."

Taking a seat next to her, he placed his arm around her, and held her. She rested her head on his shoulder. When she was all cried out, she wiped her eyes and blew her nose. He rose and squatted in front of her, cupping his large hands over hers.

"What happened?"

"I saw the girl's body."

"Oh, Toni. Why?"

"I needed to. I needed to . . . I didn't think it would affect me this way."

"Is this your first time seeing a dead body?"

She shook her head. "I guess it's just that she was so young. Does this stuff ever get to you?"

"It gets to me," he said, sitting back down beside her. "I find ways to leave it behind at night, or I'd go crazy. Believe me, it gets to me, especially when, well, she *was* just a kid."

Toni rubbed his arm lightly.

"So, how did you get in to see the body, anyway? I don't remember getting a call from Dr. Randall asking permission to let you see the body? You're not a relative, are you?"

"I asked. He and I have a mutual professional respect for one another. I'm good at cultivating relationships."

Tolliver threw his head back and laughed. His laughter brought the sun in.

"*Is that right*? You couldn't prove that by me," he said, bending his body back and away from her so that he was facing her. "So why did you stand me up last week? Tell me what you're afraid of."

"Who said I was *afraid* of anything? I'm not afraid of you. I mean . . . look . . . okay here's the deal. I have a master plan for my life, and it doesn't include you. I'm just passing through this little island. I'm not trying to get married and stay here."

He chuckled. "Wow! Did I ask you to marry me, yet? I asked you to have dinner with me, and you've got me at the altar."

"Well, you asked me if I like kids."

"Where you come from, is that a marriage proposal? You Yankees do have strange ways."

She had gotten used to being called a "Yankee," or "Yunkee gull" since she arrived on the island. It was one of the nicer things she had been called by some of the island's territorial natives.

"When a man asks a woman if she likes kids, I mean, come on."

"He's saving time. If he wants kids, and she absolutely doesn't, then zip, zap, zop," he said, making horizontal chopping motions with his hand.

"Zip, zap, zop?" she repeated, laughing and mimicking his motions.

"Yep. Cut your losses, and keep it moving. On this job, I'm reminded everyday how short life really is. Besides, all things considered, I thought it was nice of me to ask you out."

"What things?"

"Cops generally don't like reporters, for starters. You make us look bad. There's a murder, and we don't have any leads, but instead of just being patient, you all keep reporting how many days it's been with no leads. Sometimes we have no leads because there are no leads, or we choose not to share. Sharing with you is sharing with the perpetrator. And, you," he said, pointing to her, "jeopardized my investigation by reporting that the victim was shot in the forehead. I never said how she died. Who told you that?"

"A source. And I'm just doing my job, officer," she said, suddenly feeling the giddy nervousness that always seemed to overtake her stomach when he was around.

"Now, when I get the perp in a room, because you, Miss Jackson, reported that the girl was shot in the forehead, he can claim he knows she was shot in the head because he read it in the paper. See what I mean, *Lois Lane*?"

She laughed and nodded.

"Yes, officer, I see. Our jobs are at cross purposes. You're the primary in this investigation, and I'm the lead reporter on the story. There's clearly a conflict of interest. Another reason not to have dinner with you."

She eyed his shoulders. *Character. That's it, his shoulders have character.* She had an urge to touch him, to feel those shoulders without the shirt, skin-to-skin. She wanted to slide her hands up and down those strong arms, to caress his face and slowly outline his lips with her fingertips. *I wonder if all that brownness feels as good as it looks.* She resisted the urge.

"So, how is it that you just happen to have a handkerchief in your pocket?" she asked, looking down at the handkerchief he had given her earlier.

"I always carry one. My father taught me that a gentleman always carries a handkerchief."

"Well, thank you, and please extend my thanks to your father," she said, holding the handkerchief out to him.

"I don't want that snotty thing," he said, shaking his head. "You can keep it."

"You are soooooooo silly."

"You like it," he said, staring deep into her eyes. "I make you smile."

Her smile grew wider.

"See."

"Gotta go," she said, squeezing past him to get to the door. "It smells like you," she added, pushing the handkerchief into her messenger bag.

"Yeah? What do I smell like?" he asked, turning to face her.

She looked into his eyes, tilted her head, and gave him a slow, sexy smile. "Trouble."

He laughed. "I'm harmless. I promise," he said, lifting his hands in a gesture of surrender.

"For the record, Detective Tolliver, are there any new developments in the case of the body found on Sandset Beach?"

"For the record, Miss Jackson, there are no new developments. We have not identified the victim. I am meeting with the medical examiner today to discuss his initial findings. That is, unless you'd like to share them with me, since you beat me to it."

"I just came to see the body," she said, reaching for the door handle.

"Sure you did. Anyway, you have my numbers. Call me when you've checked everything off that list. It's just dinner, the invitation is always open," he added as he started up the stairs.

"I'll keep that in mind," she said as she opened the door. "Take care." *Girl, you are so in trouble,* she thought as the door closed behind her.

She was steps from the front door of the morgue when she spotted San Saypaz' Police Chief Winston Frankland, Jameyson Tolliver's boss. *What is he doing here?* She stopped to wait for him.

"Good afternoon, Police Chief Frankland."

"Good afternoon, Miss Toni," he responded, smiling at her in his lustful way.

"This murder must be big to bring you, the chief of police, to the morgue."

"Oh, I'm not here for that," he said, hesitantly. "I was in the area, and just stopped by to say hello to Dr. Randall. He was busy, so I didn't stay long. He's an old friend. We go way back," he added, drawing out the word way.

She studied his face. Her gut told her he was lying.

Winston Frankland was one of the first people she met when she came to the island. Her dislike for him was immediate. It wasn't personal, it was instinctive. Her instincts simply didn't like the man. His face, his demeanor, and his very being screamed lustfulness.

He didn't like her either—that also wasn't personal. He had told her flat out during their first meeting that he despised reporters.

"You're a pretty girl," he'd said that day. "A reporter, of all things. I bet there are plenty of other things that you do well," he added, not even trying to be discreet about staring at her breasts.

Winston Frankland was a good-looking man, and he knew it. He talked a lot, had game, as they say. Toni was sure he'd talked a whole lot of women right out of their panties. He was always well groomed, and impeccably dressed. His nails were always manicured. He had beautiful teeth. When he smiled, which he did often, it reminded her of a villainous cartoon character. Every time the character smiled, those silvery star-like things would bounce off his pearly whites. With each bounce, you'd hear a chinking sound.

"So, you and Dr. Randall are old friends?" she asked.

"You leaving? I'll walk out with you," Frankland said, ignoring her question.

They must pay this clown pretty good, she thought as he climbed into a baby blue Bentley convertible.

"Always good seeing you, Miss Toni."

"Take care, chief," she responded. He tooted the horn and waved as he passed. He had dropped the top. She made a mental note of the car's license plate. It read "Big Win."

Big Win, huh? She threw her messenger bag onto the passenger seat, and climbed into her car. *Wonder why Big Win lied to me,* she thought as she backed her car out of the parking space and headed back to the newspaper office.

***

What a day, Toni thought as she stretched out on the bed, her head against the headboard. She stared at the musk-scented candle. The breeze blowing gently through the louvered windows made the flame flicker and dance. The breeze felt good blowing across her naked body. Twilight was her favorite time of the day—that time of day when the world is quiet, and she could reflect on her day, and her life. At least that's what she used to do. Lately it seemed that she spent most of her quiet time thinking about Jameyson Tolliver. The phone ringing made her realize that she had fallen into a light sleep. She cleared her throat.

"Hello."

"Good night."

"Good night," she responded. The islanders often said good night instead of good evening.

"I just called to make sure you're okay."

"Thank you, Detective Tolliver. I'm fine." She sat up and pressed her back against the headboard.

"Were you busy? Am I interrupting anything?"

"No. I was just laying here thinking. Usually at the end of the day I take a shower, light some candles, relax, and reflect."

"Sounds like you."

"You know me?"

"Better than you think," he said.

"How did you get my home number? Did you use your rank to cut through channels to get it? That would be an abuse of power, you know."

"I never abuse my power. We have this system on the island. You dial 7-1-1. Someone answers, you give 'em a name, they give you a number. It's called information."

"Detective Tolliver, do you know why donkeys aren't allowed to go to college?"

"No. Why aren't donkeys allowed to go to college?"

"Because no one likes a smart ass."

He laughed. "Girl got jokes."

"A few. I like to hear you laugh."

"*Yeah?*"

"Yeah." She could tell he was grinning.

"So where is the handkerchief? I bet you've smelled it since you've been home. Tell the truth."

Dang. "You said you called to check on me. Were you worried about me?" she asked, changing the subject.

"Yeah. You were pretty shaken up when I ran into you at the morgue today. I just wanted to make sure you're okay."

"And it gave you an excuse to call me."

"Yes, it gave me an excuse to call you. Is that okay?"

"Yeah. I was thinking about you before you called."

"So, you *do* think about me?"

"More than you know, and much more than I want to."

"What do you think when you think about me?" he asked.

"That you feel familiar. To be honest, I keep asking myself if I know you from somewhere else, although I know I don't. Do I?"

"You know me from that place where souls wait before being called for duty—the soul waiting room. Our souls were together there, and were destined to reunite here on earth. And here we are."

"Wow. How many times have you used that one, and did it work?" she asked through laughter.

"I just now made it up. *Did* it work?"

"No."

"Then I'll throw that one on the reject pile. But seriously, I haven't stopped thinking about you since that first day at the station."

"For true?" she asked, using an island phrase.

"For true," he repeated softly.

"Let me ask you a question."

"Okay."

"How did the dead girl's body get to the beach? If she was killed somewhere else, how did the body get to the beach?"

"Marie Doe?"

"Is that what you're calling her?"

"Yes, and I never said where she was killed. Who told you she was killed somewhere else?

"A source."

"Okay, Toni, let's establish some ground rules. We both value our jobs, right?"

"Right."

"So, let's agree that we won't do anything to compromise one another, okay? You don't ask me for inside information, and I won't ask you about stories you're working on, or when they'll be published. I won't ask you to sit on a story, or kill a story. *Agreed*?"

"Agreed."

"And Toni, stop changing the subject every time we start making some headway when we're talking about us."

"Is there an *us*?" She pulled her knees close to her body. The breeze was getting cooler.

"I'd like for there to be an us."

"I meant it earlier, when I said I'm not looking to settle down any time soon. But there's something about you, what you represent. I don't know why, and I can't explain it, but somehow, you're a . . ." she hesitated, "a threat to that. That's crazy, huh?"

"Toni, ask yourself if you'll regret it later on down the road if you don't take the time to get to know me. You'll always wonder what might have been. Me, personally, I think I'd always think that the person that I was supposed to be with missed me. Saw me, and recognized me, but was so busy chasing . . . whatever it is you're chasing . . . that she refused to stop long enough to see me. I mean *really* see me."

There was a long silence.

"You still there?"

"Just thinking about what you said," she answered.

"I'm a good guy, Toni. I pride myself on that. I live simply, treat everybody right, and I love my mother. I got good credit, too. And I usually get what I want. But then, I don't want much. A nice house with a really good sound system, and space to stretch out. A nice car with a really good sound system, or a mediocre car, with a really good sound system, nice vacations, good food and good wine. And I want *you*, Miss Jackson."

"You seem so sure of yourself."

"Look, have dinner with me. Let's talk face-to-face. How 'bout that?"

"Okay."

"Tomorrow night?"

"Okay."

"It's a date. I'll pick you up at eight, no seven."

"Tell me where, and I'll meet you there at seven," she said.

"Same place as before, when you stood me up. You remember?"

"I remember. Good night, Detective Tolliver."

"Good night, Toni. And stop calling me detective."

"Good night, Jamey."

CHAPTER 3

Toni chugged her soda, and set the can back down on her desk. *Ahhhhh, nothing like an ice-cold caffeine pick-me-up in the afternoon.* She adjusted the computer screen and read through the information about the murder again. *All I need to do now is call Dr. Randall for the DNA test results, and Deputy Chief Baptiste for an official update on the investigation, and I've got another front-pager in the bag. I'm stoked.*

"Medical Examiner's office, Dr. Randall speaking."

"Good afternoon, Dr. Randall."

"Miss Jackson, I presume."

She laughed.

"What can I do for you this fine day, Miss Jackson?"

"I'm following up on our discussion yesterday about the DNA. I wanted to check on the results of the DNA tests from the murdered girl. What did you come up with?"

Dr. Randall cleared his throat. "There has been a slight complication," he said.

"A complication?" She sipped her soda.

"Yes, Miss Jackson. It seems that the DNA has. . . disappeared."

The soda went down the wrong pipe. She coughed.

"Disappeared? What do you mean *disappeared*, Dr. Randall?"

"While in the custody of the police, it seems, the DNA evidence was somehow misplaced. No one seems to know what happened to it."

"How could that be? I don't understand. Who had custody of it?"

"It was signed out by a uniformed officer, only no one seems to know who that officer was, who sent him, or where the evidence went."

Holding the phone between her ear and shoulder, Toni made a note in her notebook: *Ask Baptiste about DNA.*

"How is that possible, Dr. Randall? I mean, don't you have, like, a chain of custody procedure, or something in place? Wouldn't the officer picking up the package have to show his I.D. badge, and sign for it?"

"Yes, we have a procedure. The person who picked up the package had on a uniform, flashed a badge, and scribbled a signature on the custody form. The clerk didn't recognize the officer, but because he had on the uniform and had a badge, well, you get the picture. This is quite a unique situation, Miss Jackson. It is all the more vexing because we were asked to turn over *all* of the DNA samples, with assurances they would be returned to us in a timely manner."

"*All* of the samples? Who made that request?" she asked.

"Yes, all of the DNA samples, including the semen samples that we took from the body. The request is another conundrum. The form was faxed from police headquarters on official letterhead, but upon further inspection, we find now that the signature is illegible. We're not sure who sent it, unfortunately."

Toni tapped her chin with her finger. *This is unreal.* "Dr. Randall, let me make sure I understand this. You're saying that you don't have *any* DNA evidence from the body now?"

"That is exactly what I am saying, Miss Jackson."

"Okay," she said slowly, her brain a whirlwind of activity."

"One other thing, Miss Jackson. I overheard several of the detectives discussing a car found on a beach early this morning. I wasn't able to ascertain much, but it seems they believe that the car is related to the murder. Apparently, the car was burned up. They seem to believe that that was done to hide the fact that the young woman had been in it at some point."

"Anything else? Did they say anything else about the car, Dr. Randall? Make, model, color?"

"Apparently, the car was so severely burned that the make, model, and color couldn't immediately be determined. One of the officers did say that it looked like a new-model Mercedes. And it was found on Southshore Beach, not the beach where the body was found."

"Thanks Dr. Randall. I appreciate the info."

"You are welcome. As always, your discretion is appreciated."

"Absolutely," she said. She looked at the clock on the wall opposite her desk. It read 2:15. Her front-pager had probably just fallen through. "Oh, one last thing, Dr. Randall. Yesterday, when I was leaving your office, I ran into Chief Frankland. Just out of curiosity, was he there about the murder? It just seems kind of unusual for the police chief to personally visit the morgue to get information about a murder."

"It is indeed quite unusual, Miss Jackson, that he would personally come to inquire about the murder. He asked a host of questions about the young woman. He wanted to know everything that I have learned about her, and the circumstances of her demise. I did not ask, but I assume that there is something very special about this case considering I have only seen the chief three times since I moved to the island."

"Only three times, sir? *Really?* For some reason, I thought that the two of you were old friends."

"No. I first made his acquaintance when I accepted this job. I met him again when we both participated on a panel discussion at the college, and once in passing at a restaurant while having dinner with my wife."

"Thanks again, Dr. Randall. I'll check back with you tomorrow."

"You're welcome, Miss Jackson."

Just as I suspected, Frankland was lying. Why is he taking a personal interest in this case? She took another sip of her soda. *I'll deal with that later. Right now, I have to try to salvage my story. If I can get Deputy Chief Baptiste to confirm that they found a car burned beyond recognition, and that it's connected to the murder . . .*

The phone rang, startling her. "Toni Jackson," she answered absent-mindedly.

"Listen up," a strange-sounding voice said. "I have information to share with you. This is major. There are some very bad people on this island. In telling you what I'm going to tell you, I'm putting a lot of people in danger. I'm going to *give* you the information you need to *get* the information you need— information that's going to blow the lid off this island. If you figure out who I am, you are never to tell anyone—ever. Do you understand?"

What the . . .?

"Do you understand?" the caller repeated.

"Who is this?"

"Do you want the information or not?"

"That depends."

"Don't have time for games. You've got thirty seconds. Decide."

Probably some crackpot, but I'll bite. You never know.

"Okay," she said skeptically as she flipped to a blank page in her notebook. She listened closely while taking notes, trying to pick up background noises. There were none. *They're using a voice modulation device.*

"You got that?"

"Yes."

"Now, about the car the police found on the beach today."

She listened closely.

"The cops will tell you that it was burned beyond recognition. That's a lie. It's a late model red Mercedes Benz SLS AMG."

"How do you know that?"

"I'll call you back in a week or so," the voice said.

"Wait, wait . . . the car, how can I confirm . . .?"

"Trust no one. Nothing is what it seems," the caller said before hanging up.

Toni placed the phone back on the base, and sat back in her chair. She felt her reporter's instinct kick in. Her instincts had a way of talking to her through her belly. She'd get a certain twinge in her gut when someone was lying to her, or something was off-kilter. She'd get a different twinge when she was on to something, like now. The feeling she got in her gut when she encountered Jameyson Tolliver was new, and she didn't quite have a handle on it yet. It excited, and scared her at the same time. She glanced at the clock again, grabbed her notebook and started for the newspaper's library. Her cell phone rang. She checked the caller I.D. before answering.

"Good afternoon, Detective Tolliver."

"I'm just checking to make sure we're still on for dinner. I'd hate to get all gussied up, and put on my good cologne for nothing."

She laughed. "We're still on. Wouldn't want you to waste your good cologne."

"So, how's your day going?"

"Taking a lot of interesting turns," she said. "And yours?"

"Must be a day for interesting turns. My day seems to be playing out the same way."

"Is one of those turns the discovery of a torched car—a car you all believe is connected to the murder? A car that might have been used to transport the body to the beach where it was dumped?"

"Who told you about . . .? We discussed this, Toni. If you have questions regarding an active investigation call Baptiste."

His reaction pretty much confirms that they found a car.

"Okay. Gotta go," she said. "I need to finish up so I can get out of here. I have a date tonight."

"I'll see you this evening."

"Bye." She laid the cell phone on her desk then dialed Baptiste from the land line.

"Good afternoon, Deputy Chief Baptiste."

"Toni, how are you?"

"Good, thank you. I understand that the San Saypaz' police have in their possession a car you believe is the vehicle in which Marie Doe was killed, and transported to the beach where her body was found? Is that true?

"We have a car, yes."

"Was it found on Southshore Beach?"

"Yes."

"Is it the car she was killed in?"

"We don't know. The car is burned beyond recognition. We're not even sure what kind of car it is."

"I understand that it is, or *was,* a late model Mercedes, is that true?" she asked.

"Who told you that?"

"I have my sources."

"The car is burned beyond recognition, Toni. We may never know what it is, or was."

"There's no VIN number, license plate, anything else that would help identify it? No paint left on it?"

"No. It was literally burned to a crisp."

"A new Mercedes. Sounds like a real nice car. Doesn't seem like it would be too hard to tap the DMV database to research late model Mercedes cars on the island. I mean, how many of those cars could there be on this island?"

"I have no idea."

"So, it *was* a Mercedes?"

"I didn't say that. You asked how many of a certain type of

vehicle there could be on the island, and I simply answered that I have no idea," Baptiste said.

This isn't going anywhere. "When do you expect to have something on the car?"

"Our crime lab techs are working on it. It may be awhile."

She shifted gears. "I understand the autopsy results are in. What did they reveal?"

"Not much more than we already knew. She died of a small caliber gunshot wound, and had been dead five or so hours when the body was discovered."

"Was there any DNA, carpet fibers, hair, bodily fluids, anything?"

"No. And even if there was, you know I can't give you that information, or any specifics."

To protect Dr. Randall, she decided to step away from the bodily fluids angle but pressed on the fibers angle, hoping Baptiste would let something slip.

"Since she might have been in that car before she died, wouldn't it be possible that she came into contact with carpet in the car, or maybe in the trunk? Maybe she was put in the trunk?"

"As I mentioned before, we don't know, and may never know if the car we have in our possession is even related to the murder."

"So there were no carpet fibers on the body, no other DNA, nothing?"

"No, there was no DNA on the body."

Let it go Toni.

"Okay. Have you made any headway in identifying her?"

"No. Definitely not local, or someone would probably have shown up to claim her by now. And she's not showing up on any missing persons databases yet. We've entered her picture in the UDP database in hopes of getting a hit."

"The UDP database? I'm not familiar with that."

"The Unidentified Deceased Persons database is an international log of Jane and John Does who died, whether by natural causes or foul play, but for whatever reason, haven't been identified, or claimed. Law enforcement agencies enter the deceased's fingerprints, a picture or artist rendering, or a list of identifying marks like tattoos or birthmarks, for other law enforcement agencies to access, with the goal of identifying these individuals."

"Interesting."

"There are literally hundreds of souls in the database."

"On another note, do you have any suspects, or a person of interest you're looking into at this point in the investigation?" she asked.

"No."

"Are there any other new developments in the case, sir?"

"No. And I don't like it when you call me sir. It makes me feel old. We should get together sometime for coffee, or dinner maybe."

"Thank you for your time, Deputy Chief Baptiste. I have some calls I need to make, but I'll be checking in."

"Call me again soon," he said.

"Take care." She hung up the phone, sat back in her chair, and replayed the conversations.

DNA that could help catch the girl's killer just mysteriously disappears after being picked up by someone who had a police uniform and a badge, and the signature on the request is illegible. That had to be an inside job. But without anything from the cops on that, I don't have enough to go with a story. Dr. Randall overheard the cops talking about a burned-up car they thought was involved in the murder. He said one of them thought it was a Mercedes. The anonymous caller says the car police found on the beach was a red Mercedes Benz they believe was torched to destroy evidence. Who the heck was that, anyway? Baptiste admits there's a car, but says they have no idea what kind of car it is, or was. The car, that's the lead for my story. She checked the clock. *Better start writing.* Twenty-five minutes later she hit the button to send the story to Old Yeller to be edited, and smiled. *I might make front page after all. Now, let's see if there's anything to the other stuff the anonymous caller told me.*

***

Saundra, the paper's officious librarian, was finishing up a conversation with another reporter when Toni entered the library.

"Saundra, can you run two VitaTrak reports for me?" Toni asked, handing the paper to Saundra.

Saundra looked at the paper, and handed it back to Toni.

"What?"

"I can't run a VitaTrak on those people, they're protected. You know that. We need an authorization code that we don't have."

"Let's just try it anyway," Toni said.

Saundra bowed her head and looked at Toni over the top of her glasses.

"Can we at least try? Please?"

Saundra rolled her eyes at Toni and lurched herself out of her chair.

"Okay," she said in an exasperated tone when she was seated at the research desk. She began to type, waiting for prompts in between typing. The words Enter Authorization Code popped up. Saundra gave Toni an 'I told you so' look.

"Put this in exactly as I say, then hit enter," Toni said before reciting a series of letters, numbers, and symbols.

Success!

Saundra gave Toni a quizzical look.

"I'll explain later. Can you print those for me?"

"Sure.

Thanks, Saundra."

Toni rushed to the printer and watched as it spit out the first report. It was five pages. She scanned it closely for red flags. *Average hardworking Joe*, she concluded as she placed it in a manila folder she'd borrowed from Saundra's desk. She glanced at the clock frequently while waiting for what seemed like forever for the second report to finish printing. It was the size of a novella. She thought again about what the anonymous caller said. *If what he said is true, it's going to rock this little island to its tropical core.*

She scanned the second set of documents. *This can't be right,* she thought as she read, and re-read the pages. She looked over at Saundra, wondering if she had somehow printed the wrong report. She rubbed her forehead, then checked the name and occupation listed at the top of the page again. She sat down in a chair next to the printer table. *Oh my God.* She laid the stack of papers on top of the manila folder, then quickly picked them up again. She flipped to page 11, and scrolled down the list of "Vehicles Owned" again. She re-read the description: "Late model candy apple red Mercedes Benz SLS AMG."

If Marie Doe was taken to the beach where her body was found in that car . . . but this could just be a huge coincidence.

She leaned back in the chair. Her eyes scrolled back to the top of the page to read the name again: *Winston Thomas Frankland.*

Occupation: Law Enforcement, Chief of Police, San Saypaz', United States Commonwealth. She went back to the income page: Annual salary $156,000. *In the scheme of things, $156,000 is a good salary, but there's no way he's financing this lifestyle, these houses, and all these luxury vehicles on a $156,000 a year salary,* she thought, scanning the asset page of Frankland's VitaTrak report.

She stood up.

Police Chief Frankland lied to me yesterday about why he was at the morgue, now this. It's pretty common knowledge that he has a penchant for PYTs, but could he be involved in a murder? He owns a car the exact same make, and model, as the one the caller said police found on the beach today. This could just be a coincidence, she told herself again. *The caller could be wrong, or maybe it's someone who's got beef with Chief Frankland. Baptiste said that they may never know the make and model of the car. Maybe they don't want to know.*

She shook her head and exhaled a whistle. *And all the DNA evidence, evidence that could have tied someone to the murder, just disappears. That's a little too convenient. Jameyson Tolliver is the primary on this case. He was responsible for that evidence. It disappeared on his watch. Ummm, another good reason to steer clear of him.*

CHAPTER 4

He was standing outside the restaurant smiling when she arrived.

"Hi."

"You look nice."

"Thank you, detective."

He took her hand and led her into the white table-clothed surf and turf restaurant.

"If you're ready to be seated now," the maître d' said, motioning for them to follow him.

Jamey moved in behind her, his hand on the small of her back as they followed the maître d'.

"And you smell good, too," he whispered in her ear as they made their way to the table.

Her face gave way to a smile.

A waiter appeared and took their drink orders as soon as they were seated. He ordered Campari, she asked for a glass of Moscato.

"So, how was your day?" he asked when the waiter walked away.

"A lost cause. I don't even know where it went." She had decided not to bring up the murder investigation tonight, she didn't want to tip her hand, or spoil the evening.

"Did you think about me?"

"Too much," she said. "How was your day?"

"Crazy. You wouldn't believe. Lot of distractions, including you. Good thing I didn't have to be out on the streets today. The worst thing for a cop on the streets to be is distracted."

"I'm a distraction?" she asked.

"You absolutely are."

She smiled. "In a good way?"

"Yes," he said, smiling back at her.

Wonder if he knows how much power that smile has? She needed to look at the menu, but couldn't stop smiling at him.

"Shall I order for both of us?" he asked.

She nodded. He reached for her menu and placed it on top of his. The waiter returned with their drinks and took their orders. She took a sip of wine.

"So you spent the day thinking about me? What do you think when you think about me, Detective Tolliver?"

He leaned in. "I spend a lot of time wondering why I'm spending so much time thinking about you, woman!"

She laughed.

"I want you *bad,* Toni Jackson."

"You seem so sure of that, detective."

"Let's cut the detective stuff, and just be Jamey and Toni tonight, okay?" he said as he slid his butter knife back and forth between his thumb and index finger.

He's nervous, too. "Okay."

"I am sure of what I want. The question is, what do you want?"

"Good question. I knew with some certainty until . . ." she stopped.

"Until what?"

"Until you came along."

"And now?"

She shook her head and remained silent.

"*What?* What does that mean?" he asked, shaking his head, imitating her.

"I'm not so sure anymore. I don't know. There's something about you. This whole thing is just . . . crazy scary."

"I'm scared too," he said.

"No you're not."

"I have no reason to lie to you, and I don't have to wine and dine a woman to get . . . I'm a cop. You wouldn't believe the propositions I get. Women can be very forward. This," he said, pointing his finger at her, and then back in his, direction, "is real."

She took a sip of wine to calm her nerves. "Something about you touches me," she said. "I don't know what it is. I can't quite put it into words, but it seems . . ."

"It seems right, like it was supposed to be," he said, finishing her thought.

She stared at him.

"I knew when I saw you that first time that you were going to change my life. Don't ask me how I knew it, and I know it sounds crazy, but it is what it is," he said.

The waiter returned with a basket of warm rolls. She studied Jamey's body language. *He's open. He'd be easy to love, hard to let go of.*

"But I realize you're very focused on your career. And you're afflicted with a serious case of wanderlust. I question whether there's room in your life for love right now."

She drank the last of her wine. She took her time sitting the glass back on the table before responding.

"Who says I suffer from wanderlust?"

"I see it in you. Am I wrong?"

"Wanderlust is not an affliction."

"But it can cause suffering," he said. "I don't want to pay to see the same show twice. My ex-wife was very career-oriented. There's a longing in you, you're searching for something."

She suddenly felt uncomfortable. She shifted in her seat.

"How do you know that? How *could* you know that?"

"I know it instinctively," he said.

"And what is it that you think I'm searching for, Jameyson?"

"I *don't* know that. Do *you* even know what you're searching for?" he asked, running his fingers lightly along the top of hers.

"Besides fun and adventure? Nope. But, I'll admit it, I'm searching for something," she said, leaning back in her chair. "Do you know how scary it is that you see that in me? I've never told anyone that. It's like there's this something out there somewhere waiting for me, summoning me."

She stared at the empty wine glass.

"Maybe I'm what you're searching for," he said.

"Maybe," she said softly, lifting her head to look at him again. The waiter reappeared with the wine bottle. She nodded her head and he refilled her glass.

"You've got good instincts, Jameyson."

"Cops and reporters, best instincts around. Another reason cops don't like reporters. I mean what I said, Toni. I want you in my life. Am I asking too much?"

"I don't know. There are a lot of things that have to be considered," she said, remembering her plan, the dead girl, the missing evidence, and the car. "Maybe we can just let things evolve naturally. What's meant to be, will be."

"Okay. But I don't want to be looking forward to the possibility of something developing, if that's not where your head is at. I don't want to take this ride alone, and I don't want to be blindsided. I've been hurt before. I'm not trying to see the same show twice."

Toni nodded. He lifted her hand to his lips and kissed the center of her palm. A wave of warmth swept through her.

Whew.

Their food arrived. The waiter refilled their water glasses and left.

"So exactly why did your marriage fail, Jamey?"

"My marriage . . . let's see . . . we hit a fork in the road, and it became very clear that we were headed in different directions. I wanted to nest, make babies, start a family, that whole thing. What she wanted, and what I wanted," he said, lifting his palms heavenward, "just didn't mesh, and I wasn't going to stand in the way of her dreams."

"Do I remind you of her?"

"Not at all. She had an almost ruthless ambition. You're funny and spirited, and beautiful. We'd make pretty babies."

He pushed a forkful of food into his mouth, not breaking eye contact with Toni.

There he goes with that baby making stuff again, she thought, watching him chew.

"This is good," he said after a moment, jabbing his fork in the direction of his plate. "Wanna try it?"

"No thanks."

"Try it," he said, moving a fork full of food in her direction.

She shook her head. "Uh, I don't know you like that."

He laid his fork down and reached for an unused fork laying next to her plate. He dug into an untouched portion of the spicy lobster polenta concoction on his plate, and held the fork in her direction.

She hesitated, then opened her mouth. He slid the food into it.

"Um, that *is* good," she said, trying to diffuse some of the sexual tension.

"So, Toni, now that we've confirmed that you're feeling me, and I'm feeling you, what are we going to do about it?"

She looked deep into his eyes. "I don't know, Jameyson. I . . . don't know."

***

He held her hand as he led her through the double glass doors that separated the restaurant from a lounge area. There were a few couples seated at high-top tables, and a few people sitting at the bar. A DJ was spinning soft jazz.

"Thank you again for dinner," she said once they were seated.

"It was my pleasure, believe me." He looked around. "I'll be right back." He walked over, shook hands with the DJ and talked for a few minutes.

"So, can you dance?" he asked when he returned.

"I've been known to shake my groove thing here and there," she said.

"Dance with me."

The first chords of the song, a haunting piano, held the promise of something special. The payoff was the husky voice of a woman singing about a man who loved her strong when he was down on his luck, but who left her behind, and didn't even keep in touch when his fortunes turned. The woman sang it as if she'd lived it, the sparse piano and a moaning sax underscoring her heartache.

Toni tried to keep space between their bodies as they slow danced. Jamey wasn't having it. His body was hard and sturdy, and felt good pressed against hers. She rested her cheek against his and let herself fall into the moment.

"I want you," he whispered, his lips so close to her ear that she could feel the warmth of his breath. It turned her on.

Out of the corner of her eye, she saw him make circular motions with his hand, signaling the DJ to play the song again. And he did, again and again. She wasn't sure if it was because Jamey kept signaling him, or if the DJ was just feeling them, but either way it was okay with her. She'd long since given up trying to resist what she was feeling. She let her body meld into his.

Noooo, she wanted to say when the lights came on, signaling that it was closing time. Jamey didn't resist the urge, letting out a groan so loud that it made Toni, the DJ and the few stragglers left in the club laugh.

"Can I see you home?" he asked, still holding her hand when they reached her car. He lifted her hand to his face and kissed the inside tip of her index finger in a way that made other body parts warm.

Nice move, she thought, *but it ain't gonna work.*

He stoked the fire, kissing her fingertips one-by-one, then gently kissed her forehead and her nose.

Don't do it girl, her slightly giddy head warned. She backed up before he reached her lips, and pulled her hand away. She reached into her purse for her keys.

"I could follow you home, to make sure you get there safely."

"I think I can make it home on my own," she said, still trying to regroup.

"It's no trouble."

Be strong girl. "That's what you say."

"What?" he asked, laughing because he knew that she knew that he knew exactly what she meant.

"Aren't you going to do something gentlemanly like take the keys, unlock the door and open it for me?"

"Now why would I do something like that? Help you make your escape?"

"I am so in trouble," she said, through laughter. "Thank you again for dinner, Jameyson. I'm going home now. *Alone.*"

"You're welcome, again. If things go according to *my* plan there will be a lot of dinners, and dancing, in our future."

Plan and future. Hearing him say the two words made her giddy get gone. "Good night," she said, climbing into her car.

He closed the door behind her, and waited for her to let the window down. She took her time, teasing him as she watched that smile of his through the glass. It was warm and inviting, and dangerous.

"Sure I can't see you home?" he asked when she finally let the window down.

"Good evening, detective."

"Back to that, huh? Okay. Good night, Toni."

***

The phone was ringing when she walked in the door.

"Hello."

"Hey."

"Hey yourself," she said. *He must live near the restaurant.*

"I just called to make sure you got home okay."

"I did. Are you home?"

"Yes."

"Where do you live? It dawned on me that I have no idea where you live, or who you live with," she said, taking a seat on the edge of her bed.

"I live alone. You want to come over?"

She stayed silent.

"I don't mean tonight. I meant one night soon, when you're ready. I'll cook for you. Unless you *want* to come tonight."

"Are you any good?"

"At what? Cooking?"

"Yes, *cooking*," she said, feigning exasperation.

"I'm a very good cook. I'd love to feed you," he said.

This guy is so good he's got me going over the phone, she

thought. "You make everything sound so . . . ."

"What?"

"Appetizing," she said.

He laughed.

"Thank you for calling to make sure I got home okay," she said, bringing the conversation to an end.

"My pleasure. By the way, do you like to fish?"

"Fish?"

"Fish, you know, take a fishing pole, put a worm on it, cast it out, reel 'em in."

"I like the pole, the reel and casting part, and especially the water. Not too keen on the worm part."

"I'll do it for you," he said.

"So, is this like, an invitation to go fishing?"

"Yeah, I'll pick you up at six," he said.

"Six a.m.? On my off day? I don't think so."

"The early bird catches the worm."

"We're not going worming. Pick me up at seven, and you've got a deal."

"Okay. Good night, Toni Jackson."

"Good night, Jameyson."

She thought about his statement about making pretty babies. It reminded her of something an old woman back home had said to her once. "I knew right off he was the one. That man just moved me," the old woman told Toni days after her husband's funeral. "One day, baby, you'll meet a man that will change the climate in the room every time he walks into it. You'll get warm all over, and you'll feel something in your belly like you ain't never felt before child," she'd added, patting Toni's hand. "You'll know him when he comes because you won't be able to think about nothin' else. That man will move you. You'll see your children in his eyes."

"See your children in his eyes," Toni said out loud. She laughed as she stood up and pulled her dress over her head. *That's beautiful. He moves me, and I definitely feel something in my stomach like I've never felt before when he's around, but making babies with Jameyson Tolliver is not in my playbook,* she reminded herself as she headed for the bathroom.

***

The sun was just coming up as they walked the half-mile or so through a canopy of trees to a clearing. His favorite fishing hole was secluded, and one of the most beautiful pieces of earth she'd ever seen. It had a waterfall at one end. At the other, where they settled to fish, the calm waters were a beautiful shade of turquoise. The grounds were lush with trees, flowering bushes, and wildflowers.

"Oh my God! This is amazing," she said.

He sat the picnic basket down, then spread a blanket out on the ground.

"Hope there's some good stuff in here," she said, squatting to rummage through the basket. "I'm hungry."

"All kinds of good stuff," he said as he fiddled with the blanket. "Got some brie and crackers, pâté, roasted chicken, grapes, pineapple, pineapple juice, and champagne for the Mimosas. And real glasses, too."

"Pineapple Mimosas?

"You're going to love 'em."

She eyed him suspiciously. "Uh . . . alcohol? This early in the morning?"

He held out his hand. She took his hand, stepped onto the blanket and sat down. He sat down beside her, reached into the basket and pulled out the two glasses.

"Hold these, please."

He opened the champagne and poured some into each glass. He did the same with the pineapple juice, then put both bottles back into the basket. He speared a chunk of pineapple with a wooden skewer, used it to stir the first glass, then plopped the pineapple into the glass. She handed him the second glass—he repeated the skewer and stir process.

"Cheers."

"Cheers," she repeated, touching her glass to his. She took a sip of her Mimosa. "That's good."

"Told you."

"Yeah yeah. Now, about that food?"

They cast their fishing lines out and forgot about them, talking nonstop as the morning slipped away.

"Huh oh," he said, rising from the blanket shortly after noon.

"*What?* What's the matter?"

"It's going to rain."

"It's a perfectly sunny day, the sky is clear," she said, looking around.

"Ever heard of a sun shower?"

"You mean when it's sunny and raining, like when the devil is beating his wife?"

"What?"

"That's what we used to say when we were kids—that when the sun is shining and it's raining, the devil is beating his wife."

He laughed.

"I don't know about all that, but it is going to rain, and we *are* going to get wet."

They were feet from the car when the sky opened up, soaking them.

"Ever caught a raindrop on your tongue?" he asked as he opened the car door for her.

"Nope."

"Try it. Just stick out your tongue, and catch the raindrops."

She shook her head.

"You know I'm not taking no for an answer, don't you?"

They stood smiling at one another.

"Try it. *Please.*"

She closed her eyes and stuck her tongue out. The raindrops were cool and sweet to the taste. She giggled. When she opened her eyes again he pulled her gently into him and kissed her slow, deep, and long. She felt dizzy. She pulled away.

I was right about those lips, she thought through her haze. *They do know how to handle their business.*

He pulled her back into him and kissed her again.

Oh Lord!

On the drive home, her head and her heart went to war.

Remember the three-month rule, her head kept saying. *You don't know this guy. It's only the three that matters,* her heart, and other body parts countered. *And this is technically the third date, if you count the time at the airport, dinner last night, and fishing today. Foolish heart!*

She waited for her gut to weigh in, but whatever it was saying was lost amid the racket her head and heart were making, and the feelings her body couldn't deny. *Come on, Toni, you've always been a sensible girl,* head said, scoring points, and taking a slight advantage.

As if reading her mind, Jamey pulled to the side of the road, stopped the car, leaned over and kissed her on the temple before brushing his lips lightly along her cheeks. His lips slid down to her neck for a soft and erotic nibble. He turned her face toward him, and pulled lightly on her lips with his teeth. He kissed her deeply, their tongues dancing, then pulled back and smiled at her.

She closed her eyes and laid her head on the headrest, praying the quiet would bring clarity. He brushed his slightly parted lips across her ear. She opened her eyes, placed her hands on his cheeks, pulled his face to her and kissed him with a hunger like none she'd ever known. The battle was over.

They entered her apartment hand-in-hand, without words. There was no reason to talk, nothing else needed to be said.

Their wet clothes were quickly discarded. He laid her down, stretched her out, and took her to another place. And she was oh so ready to go.

***

She looked at him laying asleep next to her. He was beautiful. She couldn't decide whether he was more beautiful asleep, or awake. He was just beautiful. She thought about last night, eating pizza, drinking wine, and making righteous love. She smiled to herself. *I need to wash my face, and brush my teeth before he wakes up,* she thought, slowly pushing the covers back. He grabbed her just as she was about to put her feet on the floor.

"Where you going, reporter girl?"

"To the bathroom."

"Come 'ere," he said, pulling her back. They made love again, and she fell back asleep. She was awakened by him planting little kisses on her face.

"Hey, sleepyhead, I've got to go," he said. "Some of us have to work for a living." He was fully dressed. She was still hazy.

"Call in sick," she said, reaching for him.

"If I do, who'll protect the citizens of this lovely little island paradise?" he asked, kneeling next to the bed.

"You mean, there are other people on this island?"

He laughed. "Made you forget about the world, huh? I guess that means I did my thang."

"Oh, you did your thang, buddy. Make no mistake," she said, sitting up slowly.

He looked deep into her eyes and touched her cheek with his

knuckle. It was one of those barely there touches that said more than words ever could. She knew in that moment that she loved him.

"I've got to go," he said quietly. "Come and lock your door, baby."

She followed him to the door.

"I'm going to miss you," he said, stopping at the door to turn and face her. He kissed her, and gave her a lingering hug. She felt safe and protected in his arms.

"I'll call you later," he said, opening the door.

"Be safe, Jamey."

They looked into one another's eyes, both recognizing the bond that had been built between them.

"I will."

He kissed her again and walked out the door, pulling it closed behind him.

She went to the bathroom, then back to bed. Self-doubt floated into the room like a cloud.

I totally blew the three-month rule. I gave it up before I really even got to know this guy. He told me that women throw it at him all the time. At least I didn't throw it at him. I made him work for it, well, a little, she thought, trying to reassure herself. *I need to have a sista-girl conversation.* She considered calling her mother. She reached for the phone, but quickly threw that idea out. *What would I say? Hey, Mama, I met this cop a couple of weeks ago, and yesterday we went fishing, and then I brought him home and totally acted like I had no home training? Maybe I'll just call one of my girls later.* She touched her cheek where he'd touched her. She fell back onto the pillow. *What the hell have I done?*

CHAPTER 5

"I'm headed out to police headquarters to check the blotter and shoot the breeze with Deputy Chief Baptiste," Toni said, sticking her head in Old Yeller's office.

"Bring back some news."

She thought about Jamey as she climbed into her car, debating whether she'd stop by his office. *It's hard to believe that we've been together four months already.* Despite her reservations, she had entered into a relationship with him. Things had progressed nicely. They spent a lot of time together, getting to know each other, and enjoying one another's company. Most evenings they picked up takeout, or he cooked at his place. They also spent weekends at his place. Saturdays were date nights, and Sundays were lazy and sensual. They usually had one another for breakfast, and pineapple Mimosas and omelets for brunch. They didn't try to hide their relationship, but didn't flaunt it either. To avoid the appearance of a conflict, she shared the cops beat with a reporter named Danny.

After a stop in Deputy Chief Baptiste's office, she headed to Jamey's office. He wasn't at his desk. She quickly scribbled a note: I was here, you weren't. Talk to you later. Signed ME. Walking out the front door of the station she spotted Jamey talking with Police Chief Frankland and Baptiste. Jamey immediately started walking toward her.

"Hey you."

"Hey. Come and say hi to Chief Frankland," he said, reaching for her hand.

"Hello, Miss Toni," Frankland said, smiling at her.

"Chief Frankland," she responded dryly.

Seeing Chief Frankland reminded her that it had been months since the Marie Doe murder, and the police still had no leads, or at least said they didn't. She nodded in Baptiste's direction.

Baptiste was the total opposite of Frankland. Where Chief Frankland probably spent too much time on his appearance—he took metrosexuality to another level—his second in command was pudgy, and messy. Baptiste always looked like he rolled out of bed, picked his clothes up off the floor, and came to work. He was taller than Frankland, but he slouched. There were always food stains on his shirt, and food between his teeth. His shirttail was always partially hanging out, sometimes exposing his gut.

Today, like most days, Toni thought, he could use a haircut and a shave. When Toni first met him, she thought that he was one of those men whose five o'clock shadow came home early, but soon realized that many days he simply didn't bother to shave.

Because Baptiste was the official keeper of the blotter, Toni spent a lot of time schmoozing him up. She was a great schmoozer. It was one of her best tricks for cultivating sources. His office was always a mess, with half-filled coffee cups and old food containers sitting on his desk. He often handed her official papers with grease stains on them. Once, he invited her to sit and talk, then spent ten minutes staring into two large Styrofoam cups.

"Is there something in your cups?" she had asked.

"Coffee."

"I mean a bug, or something?"

"No. I was just trying to figure out which one is from today, and which one is from yesterday," he said.

"Is one of them warmer than the other one, maybe the one with the steam coming out of it?"

He held the cups closer to his face. "Oh yeah, this one," he said, taking a sip from it. "Yeah, this is the one from today."

He ain't the brightest bulb in the chandelier, she thought.

Today she turned her attention to Chief Frankland. He was rarely around. She decided to take advantage of this opportunity to grill him about the car found torched on the beach—a car identical to one he owned.

"So, Chief Frankland, it's been months and still no positive identification on the girl, or the car you all found burned up on the beach. You know, the one that was supposedly used to transport her body to Sandset Beach."

"That's never been confirmed," Jamey interjected.

"What's your take on it, chief? I mean, the car was never registered with the DMV, or reported stolen. It just seems like someone would have seen a high-profile car like that driving around the island. Or, that the owner would have reported it stolen, if it *was* stolen. It's almost like the car, and the girl, didn't even exist before the murder. Does that seem odd to you?"

"It does, Miss Toni," he said, looking uneasy.

She watched Jamey and Baptiste for a reaction. *Nothing? Either they really don't know about Frankland's car, they're covering for him, or they're both damn good actors.*

"I have an appointment that I have to get to," Frankland said, suddenly remembering he had somewhere to be. "Good seeing you, Miss Toni," he added, backing away. "Bring her up to the house sometime, J. I'm going to throw a big blowout for my birthday. But you guys don't have to wait until then. You know the door is always open," he said, flashing his high-wattage smile in Toni's direction."

Why Jamey likes this guy so much is beyond me, Toni thought, remembering how often Jamey had expressed admiration for Frankland. "The man is like a father to me," he'd said. "I learned more about being a cop from him, than I did my entire time at the academy. I'd do anything for that man. The stuff he gave me saved my butt a whole lot of times. He looks out for his boys."

Frankland mostly looks out for Frankland, she thought as she watched the chief walk away.

"Later, Money," Jamey called behind him.

Money?

"I have an appointment, too, and then I'm out for the rest of the day. Hold down the fort, J," Baptiste said.

"Will do," Jamey said.

"I stopped by your office," Toni said as she and Jamey headed for her car. "I left a note."

"What does it say?"

She grabbed him gently by the collar of his Guayabera shirt, pulled him toward her, and whispered in his ear.

"Oooh," he said, stepping back. "Do you purposely try to drive me crazy, or is it that you just can't help yourself?"

"Both."

Jamey waved as Frankland passed. Toni took note of his car, another luxury car. She made a mental note to check to see if it was listed in his VitaTrak report.

"Give me a kiss, and stop teasing me. Right here," Jamey said, pointing to his lips.

"What about our no overt public displays of affection policy?"

He kissed her on the lips.

"Bad cop. Bad cop," she said.

His demeanor, starting with his eyes, moving down his face, and into his shoulders, changed completely.

"Do not ever again refer to me as a bad cop, not even in jest," he said.

"I was kidding." She could see the tightness in his shoulders through his shirt.

"Don't ever say that again."

"Okay," she said. "I'll see you later," she added, climbing into her car.

He leaned into the window and gave her a quick kiss on the cheek. It didn't ease what she was feeling in her stomach. *That was an awful powerful reaction to a totally innocent remark,* she thought, glancing back as she drove away. *Why would he react so strongly to jokingly being called a bad cop?*

***

I'm glad this week is almost over, she thought, looking down at her desk. *What a mess. I can clean it up now, or face this mess when I come in Monday morning.*

She picked up a stack of papers and sorted through them, her mind focused on Jamey. *That bad cop remark the other day must have cut pretty deep. That must be it, what else would explain why he's been so distant the last few days?*

Her cell phone rang. She didn't bother looking to see who was calling before answering. "Toni Jackson."

"We need to have a Come to Jesus," Jamey said.

"No hello?"

He didn't respond.

Come to Jesus? I know what that means when they use it in church but used in this context . . . "Look, Jamey," she said defensively, "I didn't mean what I said, the bad cop remark. I was just kidding. Why are you taking it so seriously?" She laid the stack of papers on her desk.

"This isn't about that."

"Then what is it about? And what's a Come to Jesus'? I mean, at church, they use the term to try to get sinners to sign-up with Jesus. Being that you're not Jesus, I'm not sure what's up?"

"We need to talk."

She sighed. "You know, relationship experts say that you should never say 'we need to talk.' It sets a bad tone."

"I'll keep that in mind. We need to talk."

"*About?*"

"About us. Where we're headed. This relationship."

Her stomach wasn't liking the conversation. "Okay."

"I'll see you later."

"Hey," she said quickly. "Are we okay?"

"I guess we'll see, huh?"

She didn't say anything.

"I'll see you about six." He hung up. She stared at the phone still in her hand.

"Come to Jesus," she said quietly, shaking her head. *This is not good.* She picked up the stack of papers and started sorting again. The land line rang.

Answer, don't answer, she debated, moving her head slowly from one side to the other. *Who would be calling this late on a Friday afternoon? God I hope it's not a breaking story. Lord knows I want to get out of here as soon as possible.* She decided not to answer it. Her instincts decided otherwise.

"Toni Jackson."

"Did you do your homework?"

"Homework?"

There was silence.

"Yes," she almost yelled, excited at the realization that it was the anonymous caller, whom she'd dubbed *Secret Island Man*.

"And what did you learn about our friend?"

"I've been waiting for you to call."

"I'm waiting for an answer."

"Makes about $156,000 a year. Lot of overhead—alimony, child support, private school tuition, bunch of expensive cars. Lives in a nearly $750,000 house, has probably another $500,000 or so in mortgages. Seems to do pretty good for someone at his civil servant's pay grade. Also seems to be in way over his head."

"So, the question is, how does a guy who earns so little, relatively speaking, live so large?"

"That's a good question," Toni said. "How does he do it?"

"You get an A on your homework assignment," the caller said. "For your next assignment, *you* find out how he finances that million-dollar lifestyle on a $156,000 salary. Here's a hint: Ray Braden and Crazy Q. When you find the connection to our friend, it will fascinate, and shock you. It will also put you in great danger."

She wrote: Ray Braden, Crazy Q, fascination, shock, DANGER, in her notebook.

"Be very careful."

"Trust no one," she said.

"Smart girl!"

"What kind of danger are we talking about?"

The caller hung up. *How does a guy who earns so little live so large?* That was one of the many questions she'd been pondering about Police Chief Frankland. She looked at her half-cleaned desk, then reached for her purse. *I'll deal with this crap, and those questions Monday morning. I need a shower, and maybe a glass of wine, or two or five, before my Come to Jesus.*

***

"You either want to be part of my life or you don't," Jamey said as they sat on his screened porch after a silent dinner. It was a nice evening outside—tropical breezes and clear skies. Inside, the weather between them was cloudy.

Toni tried to relax, aided by the sound of the porch's wind chimes tinkling in the breeze. *If peace had a sound,* she thought, *it would sound like wind chimes.*

Jamey cleared his throat.

"What are you talking about, Jamey? I am part of your life," she said, turning her attention back to him.

"My mother called today. She and dad are throwing a pig roast next Saturday. She ordered me to bring you."

"I don't know if I'm ready to meet your parents. I don't know if it's time yet."

"That's what I'm talking about. That's the problem."

"I didn't know until just now, in this very minute, that we had a problem," Toni said.

"We do. My mother said she sees women in the grocery store that she doesn't know, and wonders is that her, is that her?"

Toni laughed.

"You find that funny?"

"I thought you were kidding," she said, shifting her chair so that the breeze was blowing directly on her.

"Deadly serious," he said, walking into the house.

She took a deep breath and exhaled. He stepped back onto the porch and handed her a little silver box. She looked at it, then at him.

"Open it," he demanded. He read the look she sent his way. "Open it, *please*," he said with a smirk.

She held the box close to her ear and shook it. *This can't possibly be a ring. Lord, please don't let this be a ring.* Her stomach grew nervous as she opened it. It was a silver key.

"*Unlocks?*" she asked, holding it up.

"My heart, the front door, whatever you want it to unlock."

"*Seriously?*"

"Seriously," he repeated. "It's the key to the front door of this house. What you're holding in your hand is commitment. The question is, can you handle it?"

Commitment—there's that word again. She put the key back in the box, and laid the box on the little inlaid tile table next to her.

"Why now, Jamey? Because your mother is concerned that she hasn't met me?"

"Tip hasn't met you either. He's been threatening to come to your house."

"And do what?"

"Knock on your door and ask you what your intentions are?"

She tried not to burst out laughing but couldn't avoid it. It was clear he wasn't in a joking mood.

Tip was Jamey's best friend, and also a cop. She had miraculously managed to avoid running into him at the station, although she knew who he was, and had seen him moving around at crime scenes. She was pretty sure he had seen her, too. Now that she was sharing the cops beat with Danny, it had gotten easier to avoid Tip.

"Why now, Jamey?" she asked again. "Why is it suddenly so urgent for me to meet the folks?"

"Because it's time, Toni."

"Says who?"

"Says me."

"Meeting your parents is a serious step."

"I don't know about you, but I'm serious like a heart attack," he said. "We've been together for months."

"This key cost what, four, five bucks?" she asked, picking up the box and sitting it down again.

"What does that have to do with anything?"

"It's just a key. It doesn't determine or define anything."

"It speaks to your level of commitment, or lack thereof," he said. "You scare me, Toni."

"You scare me, too," she said.

"Yeah, what about me scares you?"

"I can't explain it."

"You use words for a living. I bet if you tried real hard you could."

He had a way of getting snippy when he was mad, or frustrated. They'd been together long enough that she could smell it coming. She changed the subject.

"So, what time are you leaving in the morning to pick up Tip to go fishing?"

He ignored the question.

"Baby, please, tell me what it is about this that scares you," he pleaded. "I just want to know where you're at, Toni. Your commitment issues aren't a reason for me to change my program. I've got my issues, absolutely. I know that. But I'm not a martyr. The trick is to figure out if there's a place for your issues, and my issues to co-exist, if not . . ."

"If not, what?"

He shook his head.

She yawned. "It's been a long week. I'm tired."

"Look, Toni, you're either going to be a part of my life, my whole life, and not just the part that happens between these four walls, or you're not. That's the bottom line."

She stood up. "I'm going to bed. Can we finish this discussion in the morning?"

"Good night."

"Good night, Jamey."

***

The gift box sitting on the dresser was the first thing she saw when she opened her eyes. She sensed that he was awake.

"Good morning."

"Good morning."

"Jamey, you know that I care for you, don't you?"

"Yeah. I know that, but there's a point in a relationship where you stop and evaluate where you are, and where you're going. We're at that point. If you don't think this relationship has the potential to be permanent, let's not waste any more time."

"We've been wasting time?" she asked, turning to face him.

"You know what I mean. I want a wife and a family. I've been honest about that from the jump. And I want it while I'm still young enough to enjoy it. He leaned back against the headboard. "Toni, do you ever think, I mean when we're not together, really think about this relationship?" he asked.

"All the time. I think about you all the time. You know that."

"I can't know what you think. I'm not a mind reader," he said.

"We agreed we would let this thing unfold as it unfolds," she said.

"Is it unfolding?" he asked, climbing out of bed. "We're not getting anywhere with this discussion. The key is on the dresser if you want it. I need to head out to pick up Tip."

He stood at the foot of the bed waiting for her to say something.

I should just take the darn key and end this discussion. But what if I'm not really ready? That key is a helleuva lot more than just a key to him. I'll deal with this later. She looked at the clock, at him, then back at the clock. *There's still time for a little bumpity-bump before he leaves.*

"Oh, now I suppose you want me to touch you up before I leave, huh?" he asked, recognizing the look.

She smiled.

"Oh, hell no!" he said. He walked into the bathroom and shut the door.

She laid back down, looked at the clock again, and waited.

"I hate you, you know that?" he asked, sticking his head out the bathroom.

"I hate you, too, Mr. I'm not a mind reader."

He ran and dived onto the bed. "I hate you more," he said, planting kisses on her body as he disappeared under the covers.

***

"You didn't take the key," she imagined him saying as she backed out of his driveway. She stopped the car, closed her eyes and laid her head on the steering wheel. "Do you even know what you want?" she heard his voice asking. She imagined him shaking his head the way he did when he was frustrated. She lifted her head from the steering wheel, backed the rest of the way out of the driveway, and headed for home.

The problem is I'm afraid of losing me, Jamey. I'm afraid of sacrificing my plan for my life, for a life with you. I'm afraid I'll miss something.

She let the car window down, and stuck her face partially out to catch the breeze. *Dogs know what's up*, she thought, enjoying the balmy island breeze blowing in her face. *One day I'm free as a bird looking to spread my wings and expand my horizons, and then boom, next thing I know, I'm rushing the minutes and hours of my day away so that I can get back to him. How did I get here?* She slowed the car. *Does committing to him mean that I have to sacrifice me? Maybe I can have it all, him, my career, travel and adventure. Maybe he is part of the plan. Maybe that's why the universe brought me to this particular island. Of all the gin joints . . .* She laughed as she looked for a place to turn the car around so that she could go back and get the key.

CHAPTER 6

Jamey's parents looked surprisingly young. *Guess that's what good loving does for you,* Toni thought as his mother hugged her like a long-lost friend.

"We are so thrilled to meet you," his mother said.

"It's very nice to meet you, Mrs. Tolliver," Toni responded.

Jamey had an older sister, Tina, who had four kids and a husband named Bertrand. His older brother Raymond, a big guy, was appropriately called Tank. Tank wasn't married, but had a long-term girlfriend, Yolanda. Everyone called her Yolee. Pig roasts and family cookouts, Toni learned, included aunts, uncles, cousins and friends that the family had claimed as kin over the years, and anyone else who happened to stop by. There was food for days. She'd heard that everyone was planning on coming today to meet "Jamey's girl."

She looked out at the sea of people filling Jamey's parents' yard. "Ready?" he asked, taking hold of her hand.

"As I'll ever be."

She beamed as they went from person to person, with him introducing her as "my girl."

"I think that's everybody," he said, looking around.

"Not so fast, cupcake," a voice behind them said.

Toni turned to see the tall man she knew to be Jamey's best friend Tip, wearing a big wide grin.

The two men fell into an embrace. The hug said it all. They had been best buddies since second grade. Toni smiled at the memory of Jamey telling her that he and Tip had decided early that they were going to be "crime-fighters" when they grew up. They had gone through the academy together, but weren't partners. "Partners need to be skintight, and we are," Jamey had said. "But we're a little too close, and too goofy together to be partners."

When they parted Jamey stepped aside, put his arm around Toni's waist and introduced her. "Baby, this is my bestest friend in the whole wide world. Toni, meet Tipton Manley."

Until now, she'd only seen Tip in passing, or from a distance at crime scenes. He was handsome, even better looking up close. He was slightly taller than Jamey, and a thin kind of muscular. There was something familiar about him. It was like she had known him before, too. *Maybe it has to do with the fact that Jamey talks about him so much*, she thought, extending her hand.

"It's a pleasure," he said, kissing her hand.

"Oh, Lord," Jamey said.

"Stay out of grown folks' bidness," Tip said, shooting his open palm in Jamey's direction, not taking his eyes off Toni. "Now, Miss Lady, let's just get right down to it. What are your intentions for my boy here?"

Toni burst out laughing. "It's nice to meet you, Tip."

"I'm sorry, I missed that. What was it you said? Your intentions are . . .?" he asked, leaning in as he cupped his ear with his hand.

"I've heard a lot about you, girl. And I've been waiting forever to meet you. You know I've seen you at crime scenes, don't you? We always notice the faces in the crowd. One of them could be the perp."

He has a big-hearted smile.

"You never acknowledged that you saw me," she said.

"I wasn't there to investigate *you*, now was I?

Toni laughed.

"But I am going to take this opportunity to interrogate you."

"I've heard a lot about you, Tip."

"Likely all lies," he said, narrowing his eyes. "Don't believe any of it."

"Most of it was good."

"That's the stuff you should really be cautious of," he said, laughing. "I don't have a decent bone in my body."

"Man," Jamey said, laughing and shaking his head.

"Hey! What did I tell you?" Tip said to Jamey, keeping his gaze on Toni.

Just then, a petite woman with an almost imperceptible baby bump walked up and placed her hand in the small of Tip's back.

"Hey, sweetness," he said, putting his arm around her. "Toni, this is my wife, Shannon. Some people might say she's my better half, but both she and I know the real deal."

She punched him.

"Ow. Shannon, this is Jamey's girl, Toni," he said through laughter. "Honey this one's real, she really does exist. She isn't just another blow-up doll."

Shannon, shaking her head at Tip, extended her hand to Toni. The handshake felt more like a joining of forces than a handshake.

"Nice to finally meet you."

"It's nice to meet you, too. Jamey talks about you guys all the time."

"Excuse us," an elderly woman said, walking up behind them. Shannon and Toni turned to see three elderly women standing lined up single file behind them, as if waiting for a bathroom stall at a sporting event.

"The aunties," Shannon whispered out of the side of her mouth.

Jamey had warned Toni that his father had not one, but three spinster sisters who lived together, and knew no boundaries when it came to other people's business.

"They're annoying, but harmless," he'd warned.

While two of the aunties peppered Toni with questions, the third one walked around her, silently touching and poking her.

Toni tried to answer the questions, while keeping an eye on the one that was prodding her.

"She'll do," one of the questioners said as she and the other one walked away.

"Yeah," the touchy-feely one said. "She got 'dem baby-making hips, shoal do. Shoal do," she repeated as she started in the direction of the others.

"Come on baby-maker," Shannon said to Toni, laughing. "Let's get away from here before they realize they forgot to ask you something, or missed a spot, and double back on you. They've been known to launch two ambushes in one evening."

***

The pig roast proved to be an eventful gathering. Jamey's parents announced that for their fortieth anniversary, they planned to have a big party to renew their vows. Everyone cheered. Jamey's brother, Tank, asked everyone to gather around, called his girlfriend Yolee to the front, fell to one knee, and proposed. Everyone cheered. Just as Yolee was about to respond, Tip's cell phone rang. Everyone booed.

Tip walked off laughing as Yolee accepted Tank's proposal. People gathered around them to offer congratulations. Out of the corner of her eye Toni saw Tip return and whisper something to Shannon. They headed over to where Jamey and Toni were standing.

"J, can you make sure my woman gets home safely?" Tip asked, rubbing Shannon's back. "There's been a break in the Marie Doe case. We got something solid on the car," he said, raising his hand to show that he had his fingers crossed. I'm headed to the station."

"You know I'll make sure she gets home safe," Jamey said.

"Let me talk to you for a minute, J," Tip said. "Excuse us ladies," he added, walking off with Jamey following.

Tip did most of the talking, Jamey nodded a lot. Toni tried to eavesdrop, but couldn't hear anything. When they returned, Tip whispered "I love you" in Shannon's ear, and gave her a kiss and a lengthy hug. He hugged Jamey, then grabbed Toni.

"Come here girl," he said, laughing. "You're family now," he whispered as he hugged her.

"Thank you," she whispered back.

"I'll say bye to mom and pop on the way out," Tip said, glancing around the yard.

"Be careful," Jamey and Shannon said almost in unison as Tip walked away.

"Always," Tip said, turning partially to give a quick wink.

"That's life as a cop's wife," Shannon said to Toni. "Cell phones going off in the middle of family gatherings, birthday parties, the middle of the night, weekends, and just about any other time you can think of. His phone even went off when I was in the middle of labor with our youngest child."

"Really?"

"Yes. I told him if he tried to leave that hospital, the crime they'd be investigating would be a murder in a delivery room. Pregnant woman goes crazy, beats husband to death with bed pan. I had my PPS, pre-partum stress, defense ready."

Toni and Jamey laughed.

"You get used to it, though. I'm going to get something to drink. You guys want something?" Shannon asked.

They both declined.

"So what's with the car?" Toni asked Jamey as soon as Shannon was out of earshot.

"You'll probably read about it in your paper tomorrow."

"Maybe not, so tell."

He smiled and shook his head. "And they say cops are never off duty. They've got what looks to be a real break in the case. That's all I know," he said.

"All you know that you'll tell. Do they know who the car belonged to?"

"Don't know."

"Come on, Jamey. Was it Chief Frankland's car?"

"Why would you think it was Frankland's car, Toni?"

"Because he has a red Mercedes AMG like the one found burned up on the beach," she said, regretting immediately that she'd let that cat escape the bag.

"How do you know that?" Jamey asked, turning suddenly serious.

"He was driving it that day at the morgue," she said, looking away from him.

"Nope. He wasn't." Jamey moved closer to her, forcing her to look into his eyes. "He was driving his blue Bentley that day. I saw you talking to him. I watched you from the window. Then he hopped in the Bentley, dropped the top and drove off. You waved at him as he passed you."

"You were watching us? You never told me that," Toni said, buying time. She wasn't about to tell him that she knew about the car because of the VitaTrak report. "I guess I must have seen him driving the Mercedes some other time."

"Not likely since he rarely drove that car," Jamey said, giving her a look that she couldn't read, but didn't like.

"*Drove*? You said drove."

"What?"

"You said drove, past tense. Why did you say drove, instead of drives? Have they determined that it was Frankland's car? What else do they know about it?"

"I only know what Tip told me," Jamey said, getting agitated.

"What did he tell you?"

Jamey gave her a slow smile. "You know this is not happening, right? You heard what he said. For anything else, you can go through official channels."

"Okay," she said. *Be smart, Toni, drop it.*

"I'll be right back," he said, "I need to go in the house for a minute."

She looked around the yard at the thinning crowd. *Now he knows that I know about Frankland's car. But I know that he knows about it, too. And he said drove, like he knew Frankland didn't have the car anymore. Maybe Frankland reported it stolen, and the cops kept it on the low, never put it on the blotter while they investigated it. But would someone have been dumb enough to steal the police chief's car? Maybe that's why they torched it. Maybe they realized after the fact that it was his car, and the only way to keep it from being tied to the murder was to torch it. Or maybe, my first theory was right . . . the dead girl*

- 89 -

was one of Chief Frankland's jump-offs, something went wrong, and he killed her in that car. Maybe that's why Frankland was squirming, and suddenly had to leave when I asked him about it that day at the station. I can't wait to find out what the solid lead on the car is. Maybe that will be the final piece of the puzzle. Maybe we'll finally know who the girl is, who killed her, and why.

She looked around the yard again. The aunties were walking, single file, toward Jamey's father. One by one they hugged him, then walked, still single file, toward the house. She hoped they wouldn't spot her. *If I close my eyes they can't see me.*

"What are you doing?" Jamey asked, interrupting her invisibility.

"Being invisible," she said.

"Oooohkaaaaa," he said. "You ready to go?"

"Yeah." She couldn't stop thinking about the car.

Maybe the cops already know what happened to that girl, maybe they're in on it, and maybe . . . maybe . . . Jamey . . . She remembered how he'd overreacted when she'd innocently called him a bad cop. *Trust no one,* she heard Secret Island Man's voice say in her head as Jamey took her hand, and led into the house.

CHAPTER 7

"So, what about the torched car, Tip? You guys never disclosed what the big break was," Toni said, cocking her head in his direction.

"It's," he hesitated, "we're still working on that, baby girl," he said, pushing Chief Frankland's presents aside so that he could slide himself to the middle of the backseat. He had decided to ride to Chief Frankland's birthday party with Toni and Jamey after Shannon decided she didn't feel up to going.

"It's what, Tip? What were you going to say? Do you at least know who the car belonged to?"

"Like I said, we're still working on it."

He's not going to give me anything. But I'll know soon enough if it was Frankland's car, she thought as Jamey turned onto the road leading to Frankland's house.

"What about the girl, still nothing on her, or where she came from?"

"Nope. It's as if she never existed before she turned up on that beach. Not local, doesn't match any missing persons bulletins, and none of the airlines have a record of her flying to the island."

"I don't understand how her fingerprints don't show up anywhere? I mean, you get fingerprinted, or have your footprint recorded when you're born, when you apply for a driver's license or a passport, or when you get arrested."

"Toni, we ran her prints through the FBI database and got notta. Even ran them through some international fingerprint databases, and got squat."

"How is that possible? No fingerprints on file anywhere?"

"A lot of people in the islands, especially the hill people, and Rastas, have their babies at home. Maybe she never got a driver's license or a passport, or got arrested. It is possible."

"And nobody saw her on the island before she died?"

"Somebody saw her, for sure. We just can't find anybody who'll say they saw her. Pretty girls fluster men. Women like that know their power. Even if she had raised some red flags, she probably just as quickly disarmed anyone who might have questioned her presence. But they wouldn't forget her."

"Then why hasn't anyone come forward, even anonymously?"

"Maybe they're afraid of the very powerful people involved. Maybe they're protecting someone."

"What very powerful people?"

"Who is everyone afraid of, Toni?

"*God?*"

"Yeah, him, and maybe, I don't know, law enforcement officials."

"Tip, are you saying. . .?"

"All of that is only speculation," Jamey said.

Toni looked in his direction. He kept looking straight ahead.

"So, what do you think she was doing here, Tip?"

"This is only speculation" he said, poking the back of Jamey's seat. "But I think she was either bringing dope, picking up some dope, or moving money for a deal. Probably fell in with the wrong guy. He used her to make deliveries because she was such a beautiful woman. She could use that beauty to bypass a lot of things. I also think she ticked off the wrong person."

"What could she have done to make someone mad enough to put a bullet in her head?"

"Maybe she mouthed-off. Maybe her man sent an underweight package—promised the buyer a certain amount of dope, but sent less than promised. Maybe she got smart, or thought she was being smart, and stole some of the dope. Maybe the buyer wanted to do a little side deal, if you know what I mean. She refused, and he killed her. Who knows? But you have to be a pretty cold dude to shoot a woman in the face with her looking you square in the eye."

"People don't just appear out of thin air. Somewhere, before she came here, she had a life. And there must have been people in her life, people who miss her."

Tip sat back. "Toni, we've searched and searched, and continue to search. I even check the milk carton when I make my kids cereal in the morning."

She wanted to laugh, but could tell by the sound of his voice that he was serious, and frustrated.

"We're here," Jamey announced.

"La maison de McMoney," Tip said.

"Why do you guys call him 'money' anyway?"

"You'll know when you see this house," Tip answered.

Jamey had told her that Frankland lived in the hills east of downtown, in a "nice house," with a view of the town, and the ocean. To say that Winston Frankland lived in a nice house was the very definition of understatement. She took it all in, looked at Jamey, then at Tip, before turning back to look at the house. Valets were either hopping in cars, running back after parking cars, or waiting to park them.

"*Wow.* Chief Frankland went all out," she said as they exited the car in Frankland's circular driveway. "And look at these cars."

They scanned the line of cars parked off to the side of the house. There were a few ordinary cars like Jamey's mixed in with Jaguars, new and vintage Mercedes, a Mercedes G-Class, a Lamborghini Aventador, a Maserati, a Ferrari, two Bentleys, Range Rovers, several Porsches, and other assorted high-end vehicles.

"I've never even seen most of these cars driving around the island," Toni said.

"Maybe, my dear, they're kept in storage only to be pulled out for very special occasions, like the police chief's birthday party,"

Tip said, laughing. He put his arm through Toni's as they headed toward the house.

The walkway just outside the house was granite, with Frankland's initials, WTF, carved into it. The front doors were giant, red and ornate. A man in white gloves and a uniform opened the door for them.

"Good evening."

"Good evening," Toni, Jamey, and Tip responded.

"We're here to see the wizard," Toni said under her breath.

Tip laughed. He placed the presents on a table piled high with gifts. A waiter took their drink orders.

She looked around. *Oh...my...God.*

The house was a series of floor-to-ceiling windows, with spectacular views of the town, and the ocean. The rooms were divided on either side of a long wide hallway. None of the rooms flowed into one another—each room was a self-contained compartment. Some had ornate, wrought-iron gates instead of doors. The library and bedrooms had beautiful mahogany doors with Frankland's initials inscribed in them. The sunken living room was tastefully done in an Asian motif, black, gold and red, with leopard print accents. It had a life-sized portrait of Frankland. Although she didn't like the man, Toni had to admit that the portrait was beautifully done, and framed just right.

Wonder who decorated this place?

The kitchen was all shiny stainless steel and granite, with a convection oven, a commercial oven, a pizza oven, and all of the other accoutrements of a professional kitchen. People in uniforms buzzed in and out as Toni, Jamey, and Tip took a quick tour of the room. They were just about to enter the game room when Frankland walked out.

"Greetings," he said like a ruler, dressed in fine silks, welcoming them to his kingdom. He slapped hands with Jamey and Tip, pulling each man into a hug.

"Happy birthday, Money," Jamey said.

"Happy birthday, chief," Tip said.

Toni moved in as close as possible to Jamey. She put her arm around him to discourage Frankland from touching her.

"Welcome to my home, Miss Toni. You like?"

"So far, so good," she said. "I'm eager to see the rest of it. Happy birthday."

"Thank you, Miss Toni," he said. "Why don't I give you a personal tour?"

Just the way he says my name makes me want to hit the shower.

"You have guests to tend to, chief," she said quickly. "Jamey and Tip can play tour guide."

"Jamey can play tour guide. I'm going to shoot some pool. See ya," Tip said, disappearing into the game room.

She poked Jamey in the side.

"I'll give her a tour, chief," Jamey said. "You enjoy your party."

"I'll see you later, Miss Toni," Frankland said, winking at her from an angle that Jamey couldn't see. "And remember, tonight you're not a reporter, you're a guest."

She gave him a half-hearted smile. *And you're not the boss of me.*

The game room had two full-sized pool tables, Ping-Pong and foosball tables, video game machines, a jukebox, and the biggest television screen she had ever seen. It was flanked by two smaller screens on both sides. The room was furnished with electric blue leather sofas, armchairs and barstools. A fully stocked bar flashed Frankland's WTF initials in blue neon. *WTF. What the f . . . indeed*, she thought as they exited the game room, and headed to the library.

"It's locked," Jamey said, turning the golden handle of the library door.

Frankland's fourth wife was in the dining room talking to some other women when Toni and Jamey entered. There was a three-foot long birthday cake on the dining room table. It had an amazing likeness of Frankland on it. Toni counted sixteen chairs around the dining room table.

"Hi Jamey," Number Four said, hugging him warmly.

"It's been awhile, Lisa. How have you been?" he asked, grinning.

Toni eyed him.

"Good."

"Lisa, this is my girlfriend, Toni," Jamey said, putting his arm around Toni.

Lisa was very young, and very pretty. She was advertising her assets in a skintight designer dress.

Baby got back, big boobs, and big hair. Wonder what's real, and what Big Win bought for her?

"Nice to meet you," Lisa said, giving Toni a girly half-hand handshake. "How long have you been Jamey's girlfriend?"

"Way too long," Toni said.

Lisa giggled. "She's funny, Jamey."

"You can't imagine, Lisa."

"How long have you been the chief's wife?" Toni asked.

"Since he married me. What did you say your name was again?"

"Toni. I'm sure the chief has spoken about me. I'm his favorite reporter."

"Noooo," she said, shaking her head vigorously. "Daddy doesn't like reporters."

Daddy? "Why?" Toni asked, playing dumb. *When in Rome . . .*

"He says they're nosy."

"Now, why would he say that?"

"Because he says they ask a lot of questions."

"A lot of questions about what?"

"About a lot of stuff."

Move on Toni. "This is a great house. How long have you lived here?"

"A couple of years. Daddy had it built."

"Where did you live before you lived here?"

"In his other house."

"Why did you move?"

"Because his other wife got it in the divorce. It was a nice house, too," she said.

"You lived there, with them?"

"Yep. I was his nanny."

"The nanny? Really?" Toni asked, suppressing a smile.

"Yep, I moved in, then she moved out, then we had to move out, and then she moved back in."

Jamey shifted slightly, trying to get Toni's attention. She ignored him.

"Isn't it something how when people get divorced, they have to split everything down the middle? That doesn't seem fair, does it?"

"Uh un. Daddy said that he's not going to go through another divorce. He said that there's only one way I'm getting out of this marriage."

"And what way is that?" Toni asked.

She giggled. "He never said what it was."

Toni thought about the murdered girl.

"We need to finish the tour, and get something to eat," Jamey said, reaching for Toni's hand.

Toni put her hand behind her back, and smiled at Jamey. "Lisa, I hear you have a collection of cars that's to die for. I love cars, can I see them?"

"Sure. They're in the garage. Follow me," she said, making her way past Toni."

Jamey tried to catch Toni's eye. She ignored what she guessed was a disapproving gaze, and quickly fell in behind Lisa, who she noticed had the muscled legs of a runner, or a pole dancer.

"Baby, Lisa has guests to tend to," Jamey said.

"I don't mind. A lot of these people are here all the time anyway. We have a lot of parties. Watch your step," she said, reaching for a light switch as they entered the garage.

The air-conditioned room was more museum than garage, with a black and white checkerboard-patterned floor. Toni scanned the cars until her eyes found what she was looking for. There was a classic Mustang, the blue Bentley, a Porsche Cayman S, a Mercedes G550, and four other expensive or classic cars, including a red Mercedes Benz SLS AMG.

"I like the red one," Toni said, looking directly at Lisa.

"That's Daddy's favorite car, too. He doesn't hardly never ever drive it."

Doesn't hardly never ever? "Really?"

"It was a gift."

That could explain why the car was listed among Chief Frankland's assets in the VitaTrak report, and why the purchase date box was left blank. He didn't buy the car.

"Someone must really like the chief to give him a car like that. So who gave it to him?"

Lisa made a sound, as if about to say a name, but stopped herself. "I don't know."

She's lying, Toni thought as Lisa smoothed her hair nervously. *At least now I know that the car found burned up on the beach wasn't Frankland's.*

"I'm hungry, Toni. Let's finish up, and get something to eat," Jamey said.

I've seen what I came for.

"Okay. Thank you for the tour, Lisa. Perhaps we can have lunch sometime," Toni said.

"I'd like that Lisa," Lisa said to Toni.

Toni didn't bother to correct her. She took a last look at the collection of vehicles. *How does a guy who earns so little, live so large? All these vehicles can't be gifts, and if they are, what did the chief of police do to so endear himself to the givers?*

"Thanks again," she said to Lisa as Jamey took her hand, and led her from the garage.

"I have to use the bathroom," she said, finally looking at him.

The bathroom, one of six full bathrooms in the house, was the size of the bathroom in a hotel. Not the bathroom in the guest room of a hotel, but the public bathroom of a hotel. It had multiple stalls. Everything was done in black marble with gold accents. All the hand towels, including the disposable ones, were black, with Frankland's initials in gold lettering. The room had a shower, a sauna, *and* a big sunken tub. There was a small clothes dryer built into the wall above the tub. Next to it was a rack of large fluffy white towels.

It would be nice to be in that tub with Jamey, she thought, *bathing one another, and sipping pineapple Mimosas. We could pop a few of those big 'ol towels in the dryer before we stepped into the tub. They'd be nice and warm by the time we got out.* She laughed to herself. *Or we could lay a couple of those nice warm towels on the floor, climb out of the tub, and have a little playtime.*

"You ever been in there?" she asked him as she emerged from

the bathroom. "You could live in there. What's over here she asked, heading toward another door."

"I think that's the master bedroom."

"Who has a fully stocked bar in their bedroom?" she whispered to Jamey as they entered.

"I guess the chief does," he whispered impishly, as if embarrassed by the excess.

The four walk-in closets, his, hers, and separate ones for their shoes and accessories, were all bigger than Toni's living room.

This is where Number Four earns her keep, she thought, standing at the foot of Frankland's bed. It was the biggest bed she had ever seen. His full name was stitched into the headboard. *Dude's ego is out of control.* She laughed as she pictured Lisa in the bed, Frankland riding her like a racehorse while shouting "Who's your Daddy, who's your Daddy?" Lisa, opening her eyes to read the headboard, responds "You are, Winston Thomas Frankland, you are."

"What's so funny," Jamey asked, looking at her curiously.

"I'll tell you later."

They made their way back to the front of the house, peeping in at Tip still in the game room. They loaded up on food, got fresh drinks, and sat at a table by the pool. Toni looked around. Aside from some cops and their wives and girlfriends, she didn't recognize many of the people.

Where are the usual suspects, the mayor and the police

commissioner? Where is Deputy Chief Baptiste? All the island's movers and shakers can't be off island. And who are all these characters? Some of these folks look downright unsavory, she thought. *There are more Rolexes and diamond-encrusted pinky rings in this room, than in a New York jewelry store.*

The women, except for most of the cops' significant others, looked like a variation of Lisa. One group of women sitting by the pool stayed to themselves, drinking champagne, and chatting.

Maybe it's my imagination running wild, Toni thought, *but if those women aren't pros, eggs ain't poultry.* She asked Jamey if he knew any of them, tilting her head up slightly to indicate direction. He took a half-hearted glance over his shoulder.

"Nope."

She stared at him. "Okay."

They finished eating in silence, and headed back to the living room. Toni was standing in the doorway talking to another cop's wife when the front door opened. Two enormous men walked through, followed by someone she couldn't see. He was surrounded by more massive men. Walking close to the opposite side of the hall, they headed straight for the library. Toni struggled to catch a glimpse of the person in the middle. She couldn't see the face, but he was short, with small feet, in expensive shoes. He had a pimp-daddy swagger—a walk that was a step with one foot, then a mean lean, a dip, and an almost hop on the other foot. She repositioned herself, but couldn't see the man's face.

Who is that?

One of the guys in front stepped forward to knock, in a rhythmic sequence, a pause, then another sequence, on the library door. When the door opened, the short man and two members of his entourage entered, quickly closing the door behind them. The other men stayed outside, taking up positions on either side of the door.

The woman Toni had been talking to hurriedly excused herself. When Toni turned back toward the interior of the living room to look for Jamey, everything was shifting. Some of the men headed for the library. A lot of people headed for the front door.

The "business women" who had been by the pool headed for the bedrooms. Toni was so engrossed with all the movement that the touch on her shoulder startled her. It was Tip, brushing past her as he quickly made his way over to where Jamey was standing. Jamey kept his eyes on the floor as Tip whispered something to him. When he looked up, his eyes met hers. He mouthed a stern "Let's go."

What's going on?

As they were leaving, she saw Chief Frankland rush into the library. He slammed the door behind him.

Jamey and Tip were unusually quiet on the drive home. When they arrived at Tip's house he gave Toni a kiss on the cheek.

"Night, baby girl."

"Good night, Tip."

Jamey got out of the car, and he and Tip talked for a few minutes. She strained, but couldn't hear what they were saying.

They hugged, and Jamey climbed back in.

"Is everything alright?" she asked.

"Yep."

They drove the rest of the way home in silence.

***

"Why did we leave Chief Frankland's house so abruptly?" Toni asked, taking a seat on the edge of the bed facing Jamey, who was sitting on a red chaise.

"*Abruptly?* Who says abruptly, Toni?" Did we leave *abruptly?*"

"Yes, we left abruptly."

"You'd seen the house, and the garage. We ate, and had something to drink. What else was there to do?"

"Who was that that came in with the bodyguards?"

"I didn't see any guy with bodyguards."

It's possible that from where he was standing he really didn't see the guy and his entourage. But he couldn't have missed all that shifting, and the mass exodus when they arrived. And Tip told him something that caused us to get the heck out of there in a hurry.

"I didn't say it was a guy."

He didn't respond.

"So, you don't know who that was?" she pressed.

"How could I if I didn't see him?"

"Tip saw him."

He swung his feet up onto the chaise, and laid back.

"Then why didn't you ask him who it was?"

"What was he whispering to you?"

"When?"

"*Stop it*. You know darn well what I'm talking about, Jamey. And that was some collection of characters at that party."

"I just went to share in the chief's birthday celebration. Beyond that, I try to mind my own business."

"We never even sang happy birthday, lit the candles, or cut that big-ass cake. What kind of birthday party is that?"

"Toni, you need to learn to turn off the reporter once in awhile."

"Even if I wasn't a reporter, as a thinking human being, I could see that the people at that party looked like a collection of . . . of people that you wouldn't expect to see at the police chief's birthday party. Frankland lives pretty good on a cop's salary, don't you think?"

Jamey inhaled deeply.

"I'm going to bed," she said. "And you wonder why I say that you act like he walks on water?" she added.

"Good night, Toni," he said, not looking in her direction.

"I'm beginning to wonder if I'm surrounded by a bunch cops playing both sides of the street," she said in a last-ditch effort to rouse him.

His shoulders tightened.

"Toni, how did you know about the chief's Mercedes? That's why you were so eager to see the garage, to see if *that* car was there. I asked you before, but you never gave me a straight answer. How did you know about that car?"

She stared at him.

You want answers from me, but you don't want to give me any. She laid back on the bed and replayed the evening in her head. *The extravagance of Frankland's lifestyle isn't lost on Tip. Jamey pretends not to see it. Hell, a blind man with a good sense of smell could see it. At least now I know the car on the beach wasn't Frankland's. But that means there was a car identical to his on the island, and whoever owned it probably had something to do with the murder. Tip's hesitation when I asked him about it tonight made it pretty clear that they know something about that car. But what is it? Even though Frankland's car was in the garage, things still don't add up with him. What's the likelihood that the chief of police would have a car identical in make, model and color, to one involved in a murder case? Frankland is somehow involved. I know it. I just need to figure out how. And I need to figure out who gave him that car.* She looked over at Jamey stretched out on the chaise staring into space.

"Good night, Jameyson," she said, as she climbed under the covers and turned her back to him.

***

Nothing, including a fight the night before, came between them and what Toni called *Sundays with Jamey*.

On Sundays, he served her brunch in bed. It usually consisted of omelets, bacon or sausage, sometimes both, croissants with honey brown butter, or French toast with warm, buttery caramel sauce and pecans, and always pineapple Mimosas with slices of fresh pineapple. They always made love on Sunday. The morning sessions were urgent, exhaustive, and messy. As morning morphed into afternoon, their lovemaking became tender and leisurely. Pineapple was always a willing participant in their Sunday sessions.

It's as though last night didn't happen, she thought as Jamey traced a chunk of pineapple down her chin, toward her breast.

"This pineapple is really sweet and juicy," she said, smiling at him.

"Nothing like some good fresh pineapple to get the day started right," he said, moving the pineapple chunk back and forth across her nipple. She giggled as the juice from the pineapple slid over her breast. He flicked his tongue from her chin to her breast to catch the juice. She squealed, laid back, relaxed, and enjoyed the ride. When they were spent, they showered together, then split a pair of his pajamas. He picked up the bathroom while she stripped the sticky linen from the bed.

Near the clothes hamper, in a far corner of the closet, she spotted a large picture frame that she'd never noticed before. It was his wedding picture. He was walking out of the bathroom as she was walking out of the closet carrying the picture. She sat down on the chaise, staring at the picture of him with the woman to whom he'd pledged his life. He had a huge smile on his face. She was attractive, tall and thin. There was a smile on her lips, but not in her eyes.

"What attracted you to her?" Toni asked.

"Karna? Her legs."

"*Her legs?*"

"My car was in the shop, and I had stopped by to talk to the mechanic. He was showing me something under the hood when I heard the sound of heels, muffled kind of, clicking on the floor. I looked through the space between the hood and the floor, and I saw a pair of legs. She had nice legs. I followed them up. She smiled at me, I smiled back." He sat down on the edge of the bed. "The mechanic talked to her about her car, and she left. I didn't even think about her again. She wasn't my type. The next time I saw her was in an ice cream shop. The clerk had handed her the ice cream cone before she'd gotten her money out. While she was struggling to get her money out, I paid for her ice cream. When I got outside she was standing by my car. We talked for a while, and I told her I would see her around."

"You didn't ask her for the digits?"

"Nope, didn't ask her for her phone number. A few days later she tracked me down at the station, and invited me out for coffee."

"She pursued you?"

"Yep. We went out for coffee, and then started seeing each other on a regular basis. I never thought I would fall in love with her, and I certainly didn't ever think I would marry her."

"Why did you?"

"Idealistic optimism" he said softly. "I thought that was the beginning of the future I always saw myself having."

"Why do you still have the picture?" Toni asked, gently. "I mean, women are usually the ones who hang on to the sentimental stuff," she added, laying the picture next to her on the chaise.

"When she packed up to leave she left it behind. She didn't want it. I'm not sure what to do with it. Throwing it away would be like throwing away a part of my life."

Toni moved over to sit next to him on the bed.

"You told me once that you weren't that little girl who dreamed about her wedding day. Well, I was that guy. Not so much planning the wedding, but I dreamed about making a family— like my parents. About a wife who would greet me at the door with a kiss, and kids who would run and jump into my arms screaming daddy, daddy."

He looked at Toni. She stayed silent. He put the picture back in the closet, and went into the bathroom.

How could she not love you?

He was standing in front of the mirror drying his hands when Toni walked into the bathroom. She moved in behind him, and put her arms around him with her lips close to his ear. "I love you, Jameyson Tolliver," she whispered, saying it to him for the first time. He laced his fingers through hers. His reflection smiled at her.

CHAPTER 8

"The wedding was beautiful," Toni said. "I love weddings, and I love wedding cake," she added, reaching over to steal a corner of cake off Jamey's plate.

"It *was* beautiful. They look so happy," Jamey said, looking toward the front of the reception hall, where his brother Tank, and his new wife, Yolee, were sitting. "I'm just glad it's over. It's funny how something like this takes months of preparation, then it's over in a few hours. Being the best man was stressful. I still can't believe I forgot the ring, and had to go all the way back home for it. I was almost late for the wedding. It's your fault."

"How is it *my* fault?"

"That sexy little dress. You had me all flusterated and stuff," he said, laughing.

Toni laughed. She was about to say something when Tip appeared.

"And speaking of being late," Jamey said.

"Let me holler at you for a minute, J," Tip said.

"No," Jamey said, taking a bite of his cake. "This cake sure is good."

Toni laughed. "So, Tip, why were you late for the wedding?" she asked.

"Toni, do you know none ya?"

"None ya?"

"As in, the reason I was late, is none ya business."

Jamey and Tip laughed.

"I can't believe you fell for that, baby," Jamey said.

"I'll be waiting for you outside, J," Tip said, winking at Toni.

"You *will* be waiting," Jamey said as Tip walked away. "Because I'm not coming." He took another bite of cake.

"You know you're going. Might as well go now so you can get back for Jumpy-Jumpo," Toni said. She loved Jumpy-Jumpo, a traditional dance done at gatherings on the island. Everyone was expected to join in—non-participation was taken as a sign of disrespect.

Jamey put his fork down with a clank. "I'm not sure who gets on my nerves more, you or Tip," he said as he rose, kissed her on the temple, and headed off behind Tip. Toni quickly finished his cake then followed them.

***

"So why was Tip late for the wedding, and what were you guys arguing about?" Toni asked on the drive home.

"How do you know we were arguing? Were you watching us?"

"Yes."

He shook his head. "You were spying on me?"

"No. Just watching you."

"And the difference is?

"Spying has a negative connotation. Watching is, like, like . . . observing," she said.

"Toni, you have a way of spinning things that allows you to go just to the line, but not actually cross it."

"I don't know what that means."

He looked over at her. "You know good and darn well what it means. Even that, playing dumb, pretending like you don't understand something, when you know darn well that you do."

"And you have a habit of trying to flip the script on me to avoid answering my questions. That's what you're doing now, but it's not going to work. It was obvious you two were arguing, even Shannon said that was unusual. Were you getting on him for being late?"

"Shannon was *observing* us, too?" he asked.

"She was ticked-off that he was late for the wedding anyway, so when she saw Tip heading for the exit, and you following him, she followed you to see what was going on. She was already watching you guys when I got there."

"I see."

"She said Tip is obsessed with the Marie Doe case. Were you guys arguing about that? Is that why he was late? Did it have something to do with the case?"

"Look. Tip is just . . . Tip is . . . idealistic. Nothing wrong with a little idealism, but it has its limits. Sometimes, you have to weigh the benefits of trying to fix something you don't think is right, against the potential costs to you and the people you love. Sometimes the cost is too high and . . ."

"And what?"

"Baby, some subjects are off limits between us. We've always both understood that, right?"

"Right."

"This is one of them."

"Oh, come on, Jamey, you can't start to say something that ominous, and then just stop midstream."

"Yes, I can."

"Jamey, it was obvious you guys were really into it. What's up?"

He pulled into the driveway and shut off the engine.

"We're home. This discussion isn't going into the house with us, Toni," he said, looking straight ahead.

"But Jamey . . . "

"No! No, Toni! Not doing it. Let it go. At the end of the day, all that's important is that Tip is still my boy, and always will be."

He entered the house first to turn off the alarm, and look around. She laid her wrap across the top of the couch.

"I've got a report that I have to review before Monday. I'm in court first thing Monday morning," he said.

"But you don't have to review it tonight, you can do it tomorrow."

"It's 200 pages. I need to start it tonight, or it'll take all day tomorrow to get through it," he said, stuffing his bow tie in the pocket of his tux.

"I'm going to take a shower. Come join me," she said, extending her hand to him.

He shook his head, and laid his tuxedo jacket across the couch.

"Tomorrow is Sunday, and you know what that means. If you don't let me get to this tonight, you won't get any of this good good tomorrow," he said, swiveling his hips.

"Go do your work," she said, laughing as she headed for the bedroom.

***

That shower didn't help, she thought as she dried her legs. *I'm still revved up. I need to dance some more.* She put on a pair of panties, then grabbed a pajama top from a drawer in Jamey's dresser. She buttoned the bottom two buttons, and went to find Jamey.

"Hey."

"Hey," he said, sitting at his desk in a guest bedroom that had been converted into an office.

"I'm still wound up. I'm gonna dance. I'll keep the music down so you can work."

He looked her up and down. "You're going to dance, in *here*, and I'm going to keep working, that's your plan?"

She popped a CD, one of his oldie but goody mixed tapes, into the CD player. She closed her eyes and let the music move her. She was feeling sexy, and let herself go with it. She could feel him watching her.

"Music too loud?" she asked, rolling her hips.

"Nah," he said. "Not at all."

"Thought you had work to do, reports to read or something."

He laughed.

"Join me," she said, extending her arms.

"Nope. But I will watch."

She stopped dancing.

"Stay right there," she said.

She ran to the bedroom and put on the sexy stilettos she'd worn to the wedding. She dragged a chair from the dining room to the middle of the floor in his office.

"Sit!" she said, in her best dominatrix voice.

Without hesitation, he came from behind the desk and sat in the chair. She went to the CD player and pushed buttons until she found the song she was looking for. She started to dance around the chair, slow and sensual. She danced with her eyes closed, peeking through periodically to gauge his reaction. A couple of times she moved in close, leaned over and shimmied the upper part of her body. She bumped and grinded her way around to the back of the chair. When he tried to turn his head, she quickly grabbed it with both hands and held it still. "Eyes forward," the dominatrix demanded.

She slid her hands down the front of his shirt, and rubbed the tips of her fingers roughly up and down his nipples. He moaned. She unbuckled his belt, unzipped his pants and slid her hands down his pants. She rubbed his lower stomach. She kissed his ears lightly as her fingers slid further down to comb through the carpet. She let her tongue dart lightly in and out of his ear as her hands massaged the tops and insides of his upper thighs. She worked her hands up and down in time with the music, careful not to touch his manhood.

He leaned his head to one side, slid further down in the chair, and relaxed his legs to make himself more accessible. She moved her hands in and out of his pants, and up and down his thighs, pretending that she was going for the gold, but stopping just short each time. She danced her way back to the front of the chair. He reached for her.

"Mustn't touch!" she said as she swatted his hand away.

He laughed.

She quickly turned her back to him to keep from laughing, too. She unbuttoned the pajama top and let it slide to the floor. Slowly, she backed up to him. She straddled him, and gave him a lap dance. She could feel his hardness as she grinded herself against him. She reached her arm behind her and wrapped her hand around his neck for traction, her face close to his. He nipped at her earlobe. She moved her bottom up and down, and around on him faster and faster. He let out a low moan. She stood up, and stepped back a few feet.

"Um . . . baby . . . don't," he moaned, reaching for her.

She grabbed his arms, holding them over his head as she looked into his eyes and resumed her lap dance, this time grinding herself into him while facing him. "Lover," she whispered, her lips brushing his ear.

He made a motion to pull his arms down.

"Do you want me to punish you?" she asked, trying hard not to laugh.

"You mean more than you're already punishing me?"

She let go of his arms and backed away. She snaked her body down into a squat in time with the music, rose, and did it again.

She turned her back to him and swiveled her hips. She turned to face him again. He leaned forward and made a grab for her. She jerked backward, lost her balance, and landed on her butt.

They both laughed.

I'm not going out like this. She positioned herself on all fours, lifted her hands off the floor and leaned back so that she was on her knees. She put her hands on her head, and starting bucking, humping and bumping as if riding a horse, alternating from slow to fast, and then slow again. She rode and rode faster and faster, round and round, up and down, eyes closed, panting and moaning louder with each movement. As the song came to an end she fell forward so that she was on all fours again. After a few minutes, she crawled over to him and pulled herself into his lap, nuzzling his neck as she caught her breath. He was breathing hard and fast, and his skin was moist to the touch. He remained silent. She lifted her head to look at him. Their eyes met briefly before he looked away.

Maybe I went too far.

He cleared his throat. "You know," he said, looking deep into her eyes as he scooped her up in his arms, lifted them both out of the chair and headed for the bedroom, "I think it's time for me to meet your mama, and your daddy!"

CHAPTER 9

"Mama, you're going to hurt him," Toni said as her mother heaped second helpings of food onto Jamey's plate.

Her mother had been cooking meals usually reserved for holidays and special occasions since she and Jamey arrived in her Midwestern hometown a few days earlier. Tonight, her mother was dishing up her world-famous smoked turkey and dressing meal with *"Oh my Gawd"* melt-in-your-mouth homemade yeast rolls, garlic mashed potatoes, collard greens with fatback, cornbread, five-cheese macaroni and cheese, turkey giblet gravy, and cranberry sauce, washed down with ice-cold sweet tea with lemon. And because her mother couldn't decide which of her world-famous desserts to make, she'd made a sweet potato pie, and a banana pudding.

"You went all out, mama."

"Yes, ma'am'," Jamey said. "Everything is delicious. Thank you so much. I can see where Toni got her culinary skills."

Toni smiled and looked over at her father sitting at the head of the table. He smiled at her.

"Does she cook for you a lot?" Toni's mother asked.

"She cooks sometimes, but because I love to do it so much I usually cook. She cleans up the kitchen—that's sort of our thing. One cooks, the other cleans. She's not as good as I am, but she's pretty good."

Toni's mother laughed. Her father didn't.

"I'm glad to hear that," her mother said. "I wanted her to be able to make a living and take care of herself, but I also tried to make sure that she knew how to take care of her home, and her man," she added, smiling in Toni's direction.

"What do you cook for her?" Toni's father asked.

"Lot of seafood dishes, fish and fungi, stew fish, and things like peas and rice, curry goat, plantains. I like to make up recipes, but I'm also good with things like gumbo and lasagna."

"I see," her father said.

"You would love his lasagna, "Toni said. "He makes it with a lot of different cheeses."

"I can make some for you while I'm here, sir," Jamey said.

"No thank you. I'll take Toni's word for it."

Toni's mother laughed. "Don't take it personal, Jamey. He's doesn't eat everybody's food. In fact, he pretty much only eats what I cook for him."

"Never know what people do in the kitchen," Toni's father said.

Toni bit into a fork full of dressing and thought about the time that she and Jamey were cooking and fooling around in the kitchen. One thing led to another, and before she knew it, they were using the kitchen counter for things it was never intended to be used for. She caught Jamey's eye then quickly looked away. The impish look on his face told her he was remembering it, too. She glanced at her mother, who was exchanging looks with her father. She turned just in time to catch a glimpse of her father's smile before he lowered his head, and focused his attention on his mac and cheese. It was the same rascally smile Jamey had just given her. Wondering if she'd misread the smile, Toni glanced back at her mother. Her mother gave her a conspiratorial wink.

***

"What's going on, Jamey? What's with all the texting?" Toni asked as she sat down on the stair above him on her parent's front porch.

He looked toward the horizon at the setting sun. "They arrested someone in the Marie Doe case."

"*Who*?"

"Guy named Reynaldo Brady. A dope-dealing thug they call Boppy."

"How do you know?"

"Tip texted me," Jamey answered, motioning his cell phone in her direction. "He thought you'd want to know."

"Love me some Tip."

His phone beeped, indicating he'd received another message.

"How did they get him?"

He held up a finger to indicate he would answer her when he finished reading the message.

"It's complicated."

"What does that mean?"

"It's code for they're not saying."

Her eyes scanned his face. "*They*? They is *you*! You're one of them. You playing with me? Give up the details."

"I don't know how they got him."

"Jamey, just this once, can we break the rule? Please tell me this, and I won't ask you ever again to break our rule. Pleasssssssse," she begged, clasping her hands together.

"First of all, I truly do not know. There are some really special circumstances at work here. Tip wouldn't even tell me. Second, breaking rules is a slippery slope. I work with people every day who were only going to cross the line once. Once you cross the line," he said, shrugging his shoulders, "there's nothing to stop you from doing it again. You start to believe that maybe you can get away with it again, since you got away with it once. So even if I knew, I wouldn't tell you."

"Seriously, Jamey?"

"Seriously, baby."

She searched his eyes.

"Okay," she said with resignation. Have they charged him with murder? Can you at least tell me that much?"

"Yep. They were able to link him to the car. Tip didn't say how."

"Wow. So, the Mercedes was his? Have they identified her?

"Yes. And no, they haven't identified her yet."

"Well, maybe now that they've got him, they'll be able to figure out who she is."

"*Was*," Jamey said.

"What?"

"Who she *was*."

"Yeah, who she was," Toni repeated. It made her sad to think of the girl's body still laying in a drawer in the morgue after all this time.

"I really like your parents," he said, shifting the conversation. "Think they'd adopt me?"

She laughed. "They like you, too. When we were washing dishes after dinner my mother said there's something different this time. I told her that this time *is* different, different than anything I've ever felt before. She said, 'you've found your movin' man.' I said yes, mama, he's my movin' man."

"Movin' man?"

"The one that moves you, excites all your senses, makes you feel more alive than you knew was possible. In every way— mentally, physically, spiritually, emotionally—you move me, Jameyson Tolliver."

He mouthed "I love you."

"I know," she mouthed back.

"Toni, while you and your mother were washing dishes I had a long conversation with your father."

"You mean you talked a lot, and he listened intently, don't you?"

"You'd be surprised. He asked me a million questions. I was surprised how talkative he was."

She leaned back and rested her elbows on the step above her.

"You know, Toni, this," he said, moving his hand in a sweeping motion, "is one of those rare moments when everything is right in the universe." He swung his body up so that he was sitting on the same step as Toni.

Her stomach suddenly felt shaky.

"What's going on, Jameyson?"

"I asked your father, this afternoon, you know, I asked him, I asked him if I could, uh, if I could, I asked him if I could have your hand in marriage."

"You did?" she asked, through laughter and tears. "What did he say?"

"He said, 'and the rest of her, too, son.'"

Toni took a moment to process what he said. She laughed.

"He really did. I told him that I would gladly take all of you, and take very good care of all of you. So, what do you say? Oh, wait, wait, let me do this right," he said, positioning himself on one knee." He held out a shaky hand with a little red box in it. "Toni Jackson, will you marry me?" he asked, fumbling with the box before he finally got it open.

"Absolutely," she said through tears. "Yes. Yes. Yes. I will marry you, Jameyson Tolliver," she added as he slipped the diamond ring onto her finger.

* * *

Toni took her seat by the window as Jamey put their carry-on bags in the overhead compartment. She peered out the window at the row of airplanes lined up next to theirs. She thought about her mother's reaction when she showed her the ring.

"You have to have the wedding here," she'd said to Toni, and then to Jamey to ensure that they both got the message. She hugged them both repeatedly. Toni's father gave her a big hug and a kiss on the cheek, then extended his hand to Jamey.

"A handshake, dad?" Jamey had asked.

She smiled to herself remembering the raised eyebrow look her father had given her before giving Jamey a hug so warm that it brought tears to her eyes. The hug confirmed that he approved of the man she was going to spend the rest of her life with.

"Take good care of her," her father had said to Jamey when he dropped them off at the airport. It wasn't a request.

Jamey closed the door of the overhead compartment and sat down next to Toni.

"You buckled in?" he asked as he buckled his seat belt.

"Yes sir!"

He laughed then kissed her.

"I love you," she mouthed.

"I know," he mouthed back.

She laid her head next to his. *I'd be flying even if I wasn't on this airplane*, she thought, closing her sleepy eyes as the airplane backed away from the gate.

CHAPTER 10

She had only seen him once, only the lower part of his body, but there was no mistaking the little feet and the pimp-daddy walk. Even in chains and leg irons, the swagger was evident. It was a grandiose kind of walk that overcompensated for something. Reynaldo Brady, aka Boppy, was the man who'd entered Chief Frankland's house the night of his birthday party, right before most of the guests made a beeline for the door. He was also the man charged with murdering Marie Doe.

Toni looked around the packed, wood-paneled courtroom. She spotted Chief Frankland in a far corner deep in conversation with a well-dressed man she didn't know. She looked away quickly, not wanting to make eye contact with him. *What's his relationship to this guy? First this guy shows up at his birthday party, now the chief shows up at his bail hearing?*

She looked around again and spotted Tip sitting with his partner, Stan, on the other side of the courtroom. Tip gave her a sly nod, she reciprocated with a slight smile. She looked at Stan again. Something was off-kilter about him—he always seemed to be uncomfortable.

The massive men that made up the wall of bodyguards surrounding Reynaldo Brady at the birthday party were seated a few rows behind her. Sitting with them was a woman dripping in gold and diamonds, dressed like she was going to the club to turn-up. *Probably Boppy's wife. Maybe she thinks showing all that boobage will sway the judge, and he'll let her man out on bail.*

Reynaldo Brady was seated between his lawyers at the defense table. He was in his late twenties, but had a hardcore look that said he'd done a lot of living in those twenty-something years. It was an open secret on the island that he was a big-time dope dealer, but his only arrests had been for juvenile offenses, including car theft and assault. He'd never spent any real time in jail. Toni learned from sources that he was high-level. He reportedly controlled the flow of drugs to and from the island, and had his hand in a number of other illicit enterprises, including renting girls and cockfighting. He had a reputation for being hot-tempered, merciless, petty, violent, and vindictive. If you got on his bad side, you could pretty much kiss your ass goodbye. He'd earned the nickname Boppy because of his distinctive walk.

She looked across the aisle at the prosecution table. The D.A.'s office had brought out the big guns: District Attorney Allen Murray, and Assistant D.A. Katherine "Kate" Marshall. Toni looked back at Boppy. *He's sitting there cool and calm like he doesn't have a care in the world. Probably has something to do with the high-powered lawyers he's got flanking him.* She recognized his attorneys as two of the most expensive on the island. Boppy hadn't brought a knife to a gunfight.

The bail hearing was long, and contentious. Boppy's lead attorney argued that the car found on the beach "did indeed belong to Mr. Brady, but, your Honor, the car was stolen in the weeks before it was discovered burned on the beach."

Boppy kept repositioning himself in his chair, making himself taller, or at least trying to.

"My client is a very busy man, and just never got around to reporting the vehicle as stolen," his attorney argued. "As to witness reports that the woman was spotted in the vehicle immediately before her untimely demise, that is entirely possible as my client was not in possession of the vehicle at the time, as, again, it was stolen sometime in the vicinity of the period in which the crime was committed."

Does this guy get paid by the word?

"It is improbable that someone wouldn't get around to reporting a nearly $200,000 car stolen. Unless, Your Honor, they had come into possession of the vehicle under less than honorable circumstances. Or, the vehicle itself had a criminal history," District Attorney Murray argued when it was his turn to make a case for keeping Boppy locked up until his trial.

"The district attorney is casting aspersions on my client's character your honor," Boppy's attorney countered.

"Continue, Mr. Murray," the judge said, ignoring Boppy's attorney.

"Mr. Brady should remain in the custody of the commonwealth because he has admitted that the Mercedes was his. We have proof that the victim, known as Marie Doe, was in the Mercedes the night before she was found brutally murdered."

I wonder what proof they have since that car was burned to a crisp.

"Your Honor, Mr. Brady, also known as Boppy, also known as Ray Braden, Ronald Brady, and by several other aliases, is a flight risk," the D.A. continued.

Ray Braden? Ray . . . Braden. Why is that name so familiar? She wrote "Ray Braden" in her notebook, and drew circles around it.

"Your Honor, Mr. Brady owns a cigarette boat, and has a valid passport. He has no job, and no visible means of support, but lives very extravagantly. We believe, that he has at his disposal the means to facilitate successful flight from the island. It is our contention, Your Honor, that Mr. Brady killed the woman in a drug deal gone bad. We believe also that if allowed to walk out of this courtroom, he will flee the island for good," the D.A. continued.

A chorus of grumbles rose from the area where Boppy's people were sitting.

"Order," the judge said, banging his gavel.

"Your Honor, we are prepared to prove, beyond a doubt, that Mr. Brady murdered the woman in a red Mercedes that he owned, and was in possession of at the time of the crime. And, that he subsequently burned the car to destroy evidence of the crime."

The D.A. returned to the prosecution table and sat down. Toni leafed through her notebook, the name Ray Braden echoing in her head.

Why is that name so familiar?

"Mr. Skelton," the judge said, encouraging Boppy's attorney to answer the prosecutor's accusations.

"Your Honor, Mr. Brady is a family man with ties to this community. He does not, except for a youthful offense or two, have a criminal record," Boppy's $500-an-hour mouthpiece said. "And who doesn't have a youthful transgression in their past? There is nothing in his history, Your Honor, to suggest that

Mr. Brady is capable of such a heinous crime, or anything to remotely suggest that he would flee the island that he loves, and has adopted as his home."

He asked the judge to set a reasonable bail to "allow Mr. Brady the opportunity to participate in the preparation of his defense." He also asked the court to place a gag order on the case, and restrict access to certain documents "so as to not prejudice the community from which the pool of jurors will be selected. We don't want his case tried in the media, Your Honor."

"Bail is denied," the judge said. He also denied the motion to seal the court documents, but did consent to blacking out "certain potentially prejudicial information" in lieu of sealing the records."

Boppy's crew grew loud.

Turning to look at them, Toni suddenly remembered how she knew the name Ray Braden. Secret Island Man had told her to find the connection between Ray Braden, something Q, and Chief Frankland, and when she did, it would shock her.

How does a guy who earns so little live so large? Oh my God! Trophy wife said the Mercedes in Frankland's garage, the one identical to the one owned by Boppy, was a gift. Was it a gift from him, a drug dealer who's being tried for murder? Is that why the chief has taken a personal interest in this case, and why she wouldn't say who gave him the car? Boppy is bankrolling Frankland's lifestyle! But what is the chief doing for him in exchange?

The judge's banging gavel made Toni jump.

"This court is dismissed." he said, rising to leave the courtroom.

"All rise," the bailiff ordered.

Boppy turned to his crew, smiled and gave them a head-up nod as he was led out of the courtroom. Toni waited until the courtroom was empty before leaving to avoid coming face-to-face with Chief Frankland.

***

Back in her office, Toni plopped down in her chair and cracked open a bottle of water. *That hearing was exhausting—all that back and forth.* She pulled two notebooks from her desk and thumbed slowly through one, then the other, searching for the references to Ray Braden and Crazy Q. When she was done, she texted Kate Marshall from the D.A.'s office. She'd just hit the send button when the land line rang.

"Toni Jackson."

"Is it becoming clearer to you now how a guy who earns so little, relatively speaking, lives so large?" the voice on the other end asked.

"Does it involve one Reynaldo Brady, aka Ray Braden, aka Boppy?"

"Jackpot!"

"Don't you find it interesting that Brady can afford such high-powered attorneys? They were pretty impressive in court today. Were you surprised he was denied bail?" she asked, trying to determine if her secret caller was at the hearing.

"You've done well," Secret Island Man replied, ignoring the questions. "Now go to the Clerk of the Court's office, and look at the documents that have been added to the file. Connect the dots. I trust that you can do that."

"What am I looking for? Help a reporter out."

"Look for names, dates, and Crazy Q's contradictory role in all of this."

More riddles, Toni thought, spreading her hand across her forehead to rub her temples. "Who. . .?" The line went dead. She quickly dialed *69 hoping just once her deep throat had called from an unblocked line. He hadn't. She made notes in her notebook, grabbed her messenger bag, keys and cell phone, and headed for the door.

***

"I need a copy of the Marie Doe case file," Toni said to the woman behind the counter at the Clerk of the Court's office.

The woman made a sucking sound. "You got a case number? We file cases by number here."

Toni reached into her bag, pulled out her notebook and started reading a series of numbers.

"Wait," the clerk ordered. "I have to get a piece of paper."

Civil servant alert. Civil servant, an oxymoron if I've ever heard one. Just be patient, Toni.

The clerk took her time getting the paper. She wrote down the number, and went to her computer. Toni looked at her watch, then took a seat. *Might as well make good use of the time, it's going to take some time for this straight out of central casting civil servant to get the file.* Her cell phone beeped. She had messages from Jamey, and Kate Marshall. She clicked on the one from Kate first.

"Can't meet tonight, have plans. Tomorrow, usual spot, 6 ok?"

"Ok," Toni responded, disappointed. "Our place 6 tomorrow." She hit send.

Our place. Toni smiled at the private joke she shared with Kate.

There were sources, such as Dr. Randall, that it was okay to hit up frequently. Others, because of their position, and what was at stake, she saved for special occasions. Kate Marshall was a special occasion source.

She had been immediately impressed with Kate's smarts, and her intensity. Kate had a great sense of humor, too. "Katherine Marshall," she had said, walking toward Toni with her hand extended on the day they met. She was the lead prosecutor on an assault case Toni was covering. "But please don't ever call me Katherine, I hate that name. It's so saintly, and heaven knows, I'm no saint. Kate will do."

She had become one of Toni's best high-level sources, and in another life, might have been one of her best friends. Besides Shannon, and a small handful of women she worked with, Kate was the only other woman she'd met on the island that she connected with. It was bad business for reporters to be too close to their sources, so Toni kept distance between them. That, and the fact that Kate was wildly unpredictable.

Toni stretched her neck to try to see what the clerk was doing. She had two stacks of paper in front of her, the Marie Doe murder case, and a copy of it, Toni assumed. The clerk was going through the two stacks, page-by-page, comparing the pages, then flipping them over onto two new stacks. She thought about asking the clerk how much longer it was going to take, but didn't want to annoy her, which would certainly slow the process even more. She rested her back against the chair, and was just about to check Jamey's message when the phone beeped again.

"Can we make it 7?" the text read.

"No prob see you at 7," Toni wrote back. *Classic Kate.*

Toni suspected Kate was involved with a married man. She had those flaky tendencies—standing you up, not bothering to call, cancelling at the last minute, or repeatedly changing meeting times. Women who messed with married men were always on call to accommodate their undercover lovers. The second time Kate stood her up, Toni went to Kate's condo and banged on the door. Her car was there, but she didn't answer. Toni's gut told her that Kate was there with someone. She took the episode as a sign, and kept Kate strictly in the source column after that.

She checked her watch again, then read Jamey's message. *Dinner plans? I don't even want to think that hard right now.* She put the phone back in her pocket, closed her eyes and rested her head against the wall.

"Your documents, Miss."

Toni opened her eyes. She looked around quickly, embarrassed, then checked her chin for drool. She glanced at her watch. She had only been asleep a few minutes. She stepped to the counter and handed the clerk her company credit card. She skimmed through the stack of papers as the clerk processed the payment. She sniffed. *Felt tip marker?* She moved her head close to one of the pages on the sly, and sniffed again. She looked around, then back at the documents. She turned the stack upside down, and lifted one of the pages discretely so that she could look at it from the underside. She quickly put the papers in her messenger bag, making sure to close the clasp.

"Sign here," the clerk said. She handed Toni a copy.

"Thank you," Toni said, heading for the door as quickly as possible.

***

Toni took a sip of wine and sat the glass on the table. She rubbed her eyes and looked at the clock on her living room wall. *Oh shoot.* She grabbed the phone.

"Hey."

"Hey. I thought you forgot about me."

"I'm sorry I forgot to call you back. I just got so caught up in my work. I can't believe it's as late as it is. Are you in bed?"

"Yeah, come join me," Jamey said.

"I'd like to, but I really have to finish this."

"What is it that you're working on so hard that it kept you from me this evening?"

"It's a secret," she said slowly.

"You can trust me."

"Can I?" She took a bite of brie, then broke off a piece of cracker and threw it into her mouth to catch up with the brie.

"I'm gonna let that slide," he said.

She took a quick sip of wine. "You'll know soon enough."

"Okay. But you know I don't sleep so good without you no more."

"That's grammatically horrible, but sweet."

"I wasn't trying to be sweet."

"Baby, I'd love to talk you to sleep, maybe even have a little pineapple over the phone. But if I don't get back to this I'll be up all night."

"Is that your way of saying good night?"

"Good night, sweet prince."

He laughed.

"Good night, baby. I love you."

"I love you, too, Jamey. Good night."

She hung up the phone, stood and stretched. She was eager to get back to the case file she'd gotten from the clerk of court's office earlier. She had hit pay dirt three pages into it.

The people in the clerk's office are apparently new to the concept of blacking out information, she thought as she reached for the stack of papers.

The information the judge ordered redacted had been blacked out by hand, using a felt-tip marker. The clerk had given Toni the original blacked-out documents, rather than a copy of the blacked-out documents. By holding the pages up to a naked lightbulb, Toni could easily read a lot of the information that had been crossed out. She lifted her eyes heavenward, and said "Thank you" for the umpteenth time. She rubbed her temples and turned the page on her notebook. She looked over the notes she had taken.

DEA Agent Qui . . . something something red Mercedes??? Agent Qui identified as . . . something . . . Qui, what could that be . . . Qui? Qui…? Brady . . . something missing . . . for weeks; whereabouts unknown. What's missing? What, or whose whereabouts are unknown? Is that a reference to the car? She put her elbow on the table and rested her chin in her hand. *Qui. Qui,* she repeated over and over.

She picked up the wine glass and put it back down. *If I drink any more wine tonight I'm gonna feel it in the morning, and it ain't gonna be pretty.* She yawned. *DEA Agent Qui . . . what's missing?* She tapped her pen on the table. *Qu . . . Q . . . Q . . . Crazy Q? Is crazy Q the DEA guy? What about him and the red Mercedes?* She flipped back through the pages of her notebook.

"Names dates Q contradictory role," she read aloud from the notes she'd made when Secret Island Man called after the bail hearing. *Contradictory role?* She yawned again. *It's been a long day, my brain is fried.*

She headed to the kitchen, emptied the wine from the glass into the sink, and rinsed the glass. She leaned against the sink and stared at the papers stacked on the table. *Contradiction . . . contradiction . . . a DEA agent working with a drug dealer, that's a contradiction, just the opposite of what he's supposed to be doing. Bingo!*

She rushed back to her desk and scribbled furiously in her notebook. She looked over her notes one last time, closed the notebook and stacked the papers neatly in a pile. *I'm gonna shake the source tree hard tomorrow,* she thought as she switched off the lamp.

CHAPTER 11

Dr. Randall was sitting at his desk, playing with a puzzle similar to a Rubik's Cube when Toni walked in.

"How's it going, Doc?"

He looked up, removed his glasses and smiled. "It is going well. Well indeed," he said.

"What's the latest on the Marie Doe case?" she asked, getting right to the point.

"Nothing new. Still no identification," he said.

Toni sat down. "Dr. Randall, have any DEA agents been here to ask questions about the case?"

"Yes, they have. Three agents are working the case."

"Three DEA agents?"

"Ah, I must clarify," he said. "Three were initially assigned to the case, and came to see the body the first time. But upon the second visit, only two came. When I inquired about Agent Quinnterro, they informed me that he was no longer assigned to the case."

"Quinnterro," Toni repeated, leaning in to encourage him to continue. "Dr. Randall, how do you spell Quinnterro?"

"Let me pull the file to ensure that I am giving you the correct spelling," he said, pulling out a drawer. "Q-u-i-n-n-t-e-r-r-o," he spelled slowly. "Reechardo Quinnterro. His first name is pronounced ree-*CHARD*-doe, like Chardonnay. He is called Reek."

Yes! Quinnterro. Okay. "Dr. Randall, are there any other DEA agents on the island whose names start with the letter Q, or whose names have a Q in them, that you know of?"

"I don't think so. I have paid special attention to his name because of its similarity to the word quinine, which is a drug made from the bark of the Cinchona tree. It is used to treat malaria. It also provides the bitter taste in tonic water. Another similarity," he said.

"How so, Dr. Randall?"

"The bitter taste. It leaves a bad taste in one's mouth, much in the same way I am left feeling after each encounter with young Mr. Quinnterro."

"What is it about him that leaves you feeling that way?"

"He is curt, vulgar and ill-tempered, and there is a nervousness about him. I suspect that he is a bad egg."

A bad egg?

"I cannot go so far as to say that the man is crooked," he continued. "But I do not believe that he walks the straight and narrow."

"Do you know why he was taken off the case?"

"No, but I gathered from the body language of the two agents that it was more than a simple reassignment. Their body language led me to believe that whatever caused the change was of a serious nature."

"What *was* their body language?"

"They both grew tight when I mentioned his name. And there was a look passed between the two of them."

"What was it?"

"It's hard to explain. Vexation, perhaps."

"Did they give *any* indication of what might have happened?"

"They did not offer, and I did not question it further."

"What are the names of the two agents assigned to the case now?"

"Agents Teig and Thornton."

"Thanks, Dr. Randall. I have to run. Please call me if anything develops."

"Certainly, Miss Jackson."

***

"Katherine, so good to see you," Toni said, greeting Kate Marshall at their place, an out-of-the way, source-meets-reporter hole-in-the-wall honky-tonk bar. Toni had discovered this place when Kate suggested they meet here for their first source meeting.

"We aren't likely to run into anyone we know there," Kate had explained.

It tickled Toni to no end to learn that there was a honky-tonk on the island. She had grown fond of the place. The people were warm and friendly, the burgers and onion rings were to die for, and the crinkle fries were fried hard, just the way she liked them. Regulars at the bar had taught Kate and Toni a line dance that Toni liked to do—it was a modified version of the Electric Slide she and her girls used to do back in the day.

"How have you been girl? How's that cop, soon-to-be husband treating you, and why do you insist on calling me Katherine?" Kate asked after they were seated.

"Good, very good, and just for the helluva it," Toni answered. "You hungry?"

"And thirsty," Kate responded.

They ordered burgers and onion rings, with a Coke for Toni, a beer for Kate, and an order of fries to share.

"So, what's up?" Kate asked.

"Tell me about a DEA agent named Quinnterro."

"Bad news," Kate said. "Ballsy bastard had the nerve to show his face in court today."

"In court? What happened in court today?"

"Emergency bail hearing for Reynaldo Brady. I was wondering where you were."

"Wait, there was a hearing today?"

"We got a call to get to the courthouse for an emergency hearing. Brady's attorney asked the judge, the new judge, to reconsider bail for him. Said he needed to go and be with his mother, who is 'making her transition.' We had twenty minutes to get to the courthouse."

There was sarcasm in her voice.

Toni shifted in her chair. "And?"

"He's out."

"He's out?"

"And gone."

"Gone where?"

"He headed straight to the airport, got on a plane and got the hell off this island. At least the judge made him hand over his passport," Kate said.

"Where did he go? And how come you didn't text me?"

"Somewhere in the states, Arizona, Colorado . . . I didn't have time to text you."

You don't know exactly where he went? And how long would it have taken to text 'get 2 courthouse NOW?' "A new judge? Why?"

"Don't know."

"You don't know why a new judge was assigned to the case, Kate?"

"Nope. It happened so fast..."

"Okay," Toni said hesitantly. "He handed over his passport, but did anyone consider that he might possibly have another passport, or two or twenty?"

The waitress returned and placed their food in front of them. "Need anything else?"

"We're good. Thanks," Kate said.

"He's gone," Toni said as the waitress walked away.

"Yes."

"No, I mean *gone*. He's not coming back."

"I know," Kate said.

"How much did his freedom cost?"

"Ten percent of $500,000—$50,000 cash."

That's what was on top of the table. How much did he have to spread around under the table? Somebody, maybe a lot of somebodies, got paid off, Toni thought, looking at Kate over the top of her glass.

"I'm missing something, Kate. How come his lawyer didn't raise the dying mother argument yesterday?

"We asked that question," Kate said. "Lawyer says the mother took a sudden turn overnight."

Toni shook her head, not wanting to believe what she was hearing. *Took them all this freakin' time to arrest him for the girl's murder, and they turn around and just let him walk.*

"Kate, the judge didn't find it strange that a guy who has no job, and no visible means of support, is able to produce $50,000 cash?"

"We raised that argument, too. Judge said that his job is to set the bail amount, not track where the funds to make bail come from."

Noooo, why should it matter to the judge where a known drug dealer, implicated in a murder, gets $50,000, cash, no less, to make bail? Toni could feel her stomach getting jittery as she watched Kate devour her burger.

"Why didn't they send a federal marshal with him?"

"Come on, Toni. You know that's not how it works. Bail is designed to make it detrimental for people to skip. Some are going to skip regardless of what's at stake. For him, it was simply a matter of forfeiting some money, and we figure he has plenty more in offshore accounts. We're just a few steps removed from being a banana republic. We can't afford to send federal marshals across the globe."

More bull, Toni thought as she bit into a light and crispy onion ring.

"I learned a long time ago, Toni, that in this game, I can only fight the good fight. And when it's time to let go, let go. Otherwise I'll become my boss, subsisting on antacids."

"Yeah, right. Back to Quinnterro, the DEA agent."

Kate leaned in. "Between you and me, you know that Quinnterro is the trump card, right?"

"What do you mean?"

"He gave the cops the final piece of the puzzle they needed to tie Boppy to the murder."

"Was Quinnterro working undercover in Boppy's operation or something?"

"Undercover? Yeah, sure," Kate answered, nodding her head. "No! He was playing both sides of the street. DEA agent on one side, drug dealer's henchman on the other."

"Tell."

"He helped dispose of the body, *and* the car that the girl was killed in," Kate said, squirting ketchup on her onion rings.

Toni thought about the case file, and the missing words. Kate had just filled in another big blank.

"Did he help commit the murder?"

"No. Well, he says he didn't. He says he just helped dispose of the body."

"*He* says?"

"Yes," Kate answered, taking a swig of her beer. "He knew that the police were getting close, so to save his ass he started talking. They had another witness, but they needed someone more believable."

"*Who*? And what do you mean *more* believable?"

"Boppy's daughter. You know, kids really do say the darnedest things. Apparently, one of the primaries on the case, your boy's boy, Tip, suspected Boppy for some time. He went to Boppy's house several times to talk to him, hoping to trip him up. One of those times, Tip offered to take Boppy's daughter outside to play on the swing set," Kate said, lifting the bun off her burger to adjust the meat. "What do you and that big fine cop of yours talk about anyway, or don't you talk?" Kate asked, lifting her eyebrows.

"We don't talk about anything that would compromise him, or me. I don't use him as a source."

"Tip is his best friend. He didn't let you in on what was happening? Next time you see homeboy, ask him why they call him Tip. Obviously, he hasn't given you anything."

"His first name is Tipton," Toni said defensively. "And the same applies, I don't compromise him either." *But he could have thrown me a bone, something to go on,* she thought.

"How did you know about Quinnterro anyway?"

"A little birdie told me."

Kate laughed. "You and little your birdies. Anyway," she continued, "under the pretext that the questioning might upset the little girl further, since she was probably already troubled with her mother, Boppy's wife, missing and all, Tip took her outside to play, while his partner, Stan, questioned her daddy. Sweet kid tells friendly Officer Tip that she and her daddy 'went to the beach with a pretty lady that couldn't talk, and Uncle Reek followed us. The lady stayed at the beach, and we went to another beach, and daddy and Uncle Reek burned the red car. Then we came back home in Uncle Reek's car.'"

"Uncle Reek is . . .?"

"Reechardo Quinnterro," Kate finished. "Some people call him *Crazy Q'* 'cause he ain't wrapped too tight."

Confirmation! Quinnterro is Crazy Q. Dr. Randall said they call him Reek.

"And the plot thickens," Toni said, looking around. The bar was getting crowded and loud, people were dancing

Kate laughed.

"So, the DEA agent, Quinnterro, wasn't involved with the actual murder, but helped dispose of the body, and the car?"

"Yep, and called in sick that day."

"Kate, what's Winston Frankland's connection to all of this? Why was he at the bail hearing yesterday, what reason would he have to be there?"

"Chief Frankland? I didn't see him in court yesterday. I don't think he's involved in this in any way, other than being a cop." She paused. "Toni, some things are bigger than you and me."

Some things are bigger than you and me? Trust no one? What the hell is going on?

"What does that even mean, Kate? What's bigger than you and me? The machine that let a murderer walk out of a courtroom, get on a plane and disappear to God's knows where, never to be seen, or heard from again on this island? The same corrupt machine that lets a double-dealing DEA agent that helped a drug lord dispose of a woman's body get off scot-free? Is that what's bigger than you and me?"

Kate dragged an onion ring through a glob of ketchup, but didn't eat it. She didn't answer the question.

"How old is Boppy's daughter?

"Six."

"Boppy and Quinnterro had to know that she saw what was going on."

"But neither one of them counted on the kid talking to the cops. People always underestimate kids," Kate said. "And besides, everybody knows that testimony from kids that young is often discredited. That's why the cops needed another witness."

"And a rogue DEA agent is a stellar witness?"

Kate laughed.

"Why would anyone take a six-year-old with them to dispose of a body, anyway? And if the cops know that he was an accessory, why hasn't Quinnterro been arrested?"

"That's what I was getting to earlier. When the cops pulled Quinnterro in for an interview based on what the kid said, ten minutes in he knew they had him. So, he cut a deal that will enable him to disappear to witness protection-land, in exchange for testifying against Boppy. We can't figure out why they took the kid with them. Not a smart move."

"Is he still with the DEA?"

"He's been suspended without pay, pending the outcome of an internal investigation."

"And what's to keep him from leaving the island, too?" Toni asked, pushing her plate away.

"Girl, what did your mama tell you about wasting food?" Kate asked, facetiously.

Toni laughed a dry laugh.

"There's nothing to keep him from leaving. He hasn't been charged with anything, and probably won't be. If he leaves on his own, he has to start over from scratch—no pension, no severance, no nothing. As a member of the witness protection program, he at least gets a new start on the government's dime."

"It's a wonder he's still alive," Toni said. "If, like you said, the lawyers would discredit the child, wouldn't Boppy and his legal team know, or figure out soon enough that the prosecutor had another secret weapon? Don't both sides, at some point, have to disclose their witness list? Wouldn't Quinnterro's name be numero uno on that list?"

"Hide in plain sight. Quinnterro thinks that Boppy and his crew will figure that since he has the balls to still be showing his face around the island, he can still be trusted. With a witness like him, we don't have to disclose it until very late in the game, to help ensure he lives to testify."

"And because we've probably seen the last of Boppy, there won't be a trial, and Quinnterro will never be called to testify. So, he gets off, too," Toni said.

"That's not necessarily true."

"Why not?"

"Because the judge set a trial date for Boppy. If he doesn't show up for his trial, we can try him in absentia, with Quinnterro as our star witness. As part of the deal, we can force Quinnterro to testify. And if that happens, membership in the witness protection program is no longer optional, he's gone," Kate said, shifting her position. "Toni, of all the things you *didn't* hear this evening, you *really* didn't hear that last part. There are only a few people who know about Quinnterro's deal."

"This is so jacked-up. Does any of this bother you, Kate?"

"Yes."

Toni moved her straw around her glass. Kate watched the dance floor.

"You're a good girl, Toni," Kate said after awhile, nervously tracing the rim of the beer bottle with her finger. "Don't let them change you. Don't let them compromise you."

"*Who* compromise me? All of the sudden you're speaking in some . . . it's like . . . all of the sudden everything is so cryptic. What's *really* going on, Kate?"

"There are things you don't understand."

"Make me understand. Kate, *help me* understand," Toni pleaded.

Kate hesitated. "Just be very careful. Things aren't always what they seem, and people aren't always who they appear to be."

Toni stared into Kate's eyes. Kate looked down at her empty plate.

"*Illusions of Paradise.*"

"*What?*" Kate asked.

"Everything on this island is so beautiful, and looks so perfect, but when you scratch beneath the surface, things aren't at all what they seem. I call it illusions of paradise."

They fell into an uneasy silence.

"Kate," Toni said after several minutes, "the woman in court yesterday, the half-naked, blinged-out chick sitting with Boppy's boys, who was that? Earlier, you said Boppy's wife was missing, was that her? Where's his little girl now?"

"That was his side-piece," Kate said. "And how did you know those were Bop's boys?"

Bop? Toni didn't answer.

"That's another strange thing about this case," Kate continued. "After the murder, his wife disappeared. Just vanished. The kid is with the wife's mother now."

Toni thought about the notes from last night. *Brady's . . . blank . . . missing . . . whereabouts unknown. Wife. Wife missing.*

"Any idea where she's at?"

"Maybe fled the island to avoid being implicated in the murder. Although, there is nothing to suggest that she was involved."

"Did the cops question the little girl about her mother?"

"Yeah, she said 'My mommy's gone.' Said she woke up from her nap, and her mommy was gone. Asked Officer Tip if he knew where her mommy was."

Toni looked at Kate. *I've filled in all the blanks,* she thought, wondering why the elation she'd expected to feel was eluding her.

Reechardo Quinnterro, a DEA agent working for a drug dealer on the side, helped the dealer dispose of the body of a woman he murdered, and then destroy the vehicle she was killed in. Soon after the murder, the dope dealer's wife disappears, leaving behind a small child. The same guy shows up at the chief of police's birthday party, and sends everybody, including cops, scurrying. No wonder Boppy has never been busted. The man had a DEA agent, and probably a high-ranking police official or two, at least one judge, and God knows who else on his payroll, she thought, eyeing Kate.

"Would one of you gals like to dance?" a big fine blond farm-boy type dressed in a checkered shirt, jeans that fit like a second skin, and alligator shit-kickers asked, breaking Toni's train of thought.

The meeting was over. Kate stood, gave Toni a smile, and headed for the dance floor. Toni watched Kate dance.

Once again Kate Marshall saves the day. This is one hell of a story. She gathered her things and headed for the door, blowing Kate a kiss on the way out.

"Thank you," she mouthed to Kate.

"Love ya," Kate mouthed back.

You really are a saint, Katherine, she thought, turning to take another look at Kate before pushing her way through the bar's swinging doors.

CHAPTER 12

I look tired. Toni closed her makeup compact and slid it back into her purse. She opened her notebook and flipped to a page secured with a large red paper clip, on which she'd made notes. *A few calls, coupled with the info I got from the court file, and from Dr. Randall and Kate yesterday, and I've got my front-page story for tomorrow's paper.*

She glanced at the clock on the opposite wall of the newsroom as she reached for the phone. A call to Quinnterro's boss at the DEA lasted all of five minutes, resulted in the expected string of "no comments," and ended with him hanging up on her. A call to Boppy's lawyer netted the same result, although she did get a laugh out of him before he hung up when she asked how Boppy's mother was doing. The D.A.'s office assured her that someone would call her back. *Fat chance, but I tried. And now, Baptiste,* she thought as she dialed his number.

"Mel Baptiste."

"Deputy Chief Baptiste, it's Toni Jackson, calling to ask you some questions about the Marie Doe case."

"There's not much new, Toni. We still haven't identified her."

What I'm calling about specifically is a DEA agent named Reechardo Quinnterro. I'm working on a story about the case, and his alleged involvement."

"Toni, let me call you back shortly," Baptiste said.

"How soon, sir? My deadline . . ."

He hung up. Her cell phone rang.

"Hey baby."

"Hey yourself."

"What are you up to?"

"The usual, ticking people off, gettin' in other folks' business, that kind of stuff," she said. "What are you up to?"

The land line rang. "Jamey, I gotta go. I'll call you back," she said, grabbing the other phone.

"Toni Jackson."

"Okay, Toni, you were asking about someone," Baptiste said.

"Yes sir, a DEA agent named Reechardo Quinnterro."

"What about him?"

"He's listed in the Marie Doe court files as an accessory after the fact. It's alleged that he helped Reynaldo Brady dispose of the body, and then helped him torch the car that was used to transport the body to the beach where it was dumped."

"Okay."

"His name is mentioned numerous times in the court files, but not in the police reports. Why is that?"

"I can't answer that, Toni."

"Why not?"

"It would compromise the investigation."

"He's been identified as an accessory, but he hasn't been charged, or arrested. Why?"

"I'm not at liberty to discuss that, either, Toni. I have been instructed not to discuss Agent Quinnterro. I'm sorry."

"Instructed by who?"

"People much higher up on the food chain," Baptiste said.

"Who? Chief Frankland, the DEA, who?"

"Toni, I really can't discuss it. And I've been asked to ask you not to write a story that addresses what you believe to be Agent Quinnterro's involvement in this case."

"It's more than what I believe, sir. I have official records, and other information to back this up."

"Toni, please, let this go."

"Deputy Chief Baptiste, is the San Saypaz' police department covering for . . ."

"I have to go. I will talk to you soon." After a pause, he added, "Toni, I would strongly advise you to be careful."

"Excuse me? Is that a threat, Deputy Chief Baptiste?"

The line went dead. She stared at the phone. *He hung up on me.*

She dialed Jamey's number on her cell phone.

"Hey."

"Hey yourself."

"So, what were we discussing?"

"Dinner. You've been working a lot of crazy hours the last few days. When are you going to tell me what the big story is?"

"Soon," she said.

"You know, I've been thinking, since we're engaged, you should move in with me."

"I'll consider it," Toni said. "Can we discuss it later? Right now, I need to get back to work if I want to get out of here at a decent hour."

His phone beeped.

"Hold on a minute baby, I need to take this call."

Baptiste's warning echoed in her head: "I would strongly advise you to be careful."

"I gotta dash, baby," Jamey said when he came back on the line. "I'll see you at the house."

"Okay," she said, not wanting to let him off the phone.

"Is there something else, Toni?"

"No. I'll see you later."

"You okay?"

"Yeah. I love you."

"I love you too, baby. See you later."

She turned her attention to the computer, forcing herself to focus on the words on the screen. The conversation with Baptiste had left her shaken. She read through her story one final time, making a few changes and inserting the words "no comment," and no comment-like comments from Baptiste and the others, then hit the print button. She read the printed copy, word-by-word, checking each word off with a red marker. The finished story would start with Old Yeller, then go through an exhaustive series of reviews by the paper's best editors. An article detailing a DEA agent's involvement in an alleged drug-related murder was so big, that even the paper's executive editor was going to be in on the editing process. And then it would get lawyered—there was a lot at stake. It would take a day, maybe more, for the article to go through the process. She scanned the hard copy one last time, turned back to the computer, hit the save key and waited.

"Done," she said aloud as she hit the send key.

***

"Hey, baby," Jamey said, greeting her at the door with a kiss and a lingering hug. "I missed you, girl."

"I missed you, too," she said, basking in the protective warmth of his hug.

"So, what are you up to?"

"It smells yummy in here. I'm starving."

"Turn around."

"What?"

"Turn around," he repeated.

Toni hesitated, then turned slowly, looking over her shoulder as she did. His eyes made their way down her body, stopping at her butt. He shook his head.

"Naw, you ain't starvin' gal. You might be hungry, but from what I can see, you ain't starvin'. Un un un. And if you are ever starvin', you call me, and I'll send you some biscuits, 'cause we don't want you to lose all that," he said, moving his hands up and down in an arc formation in the direction of her butt."

Laughing, she made her way back into his arms.

"You're silly."

He wrapped his arms tightly around her. "Dinner will be ready shortly," he said, kissing the top of her head. "In the meantime, what's going on with you?"

She followed him to the stove, positioned herself behind him, wrapped her arms around his waist and kissed the back of his neck.

"Ummmm. So, tell me about the story you're working on."

"Is there something specific you want to know?" she asked as she nuzzled his ear.

"I want to know about the article you're working on."

"Why are you so interested in what I'm working on? Want a glass of wine?"

"Yeah, sure."

She pulled two wine glasses from the rack above the kitchen counter.

"Earlier, when I put you on hold, Baptiste was on the other line asking, *no, ordering* me to his office ASAP. He wanted to discuss the story you're working on—the story about the DEA agent involved in the Marie Doe case."

"Okay," she said, pouring wine first into his glass, then hers. She added an extra splash to her glass.

"So, what's the deal with the article?"

"I finished it today."

"That's a problem."

"I gathered that. What, exactly, is the problem?" she asked.

"I don't know. But according to Baptiste, someone doesn't want you to write that story. Baptiste asked me to talk to you, and 'strongly discourage' you from doing the story," Jamey said, making quote marks with his fingers.

"Do you really not know, or are you just not going to tell me for some reason?"

He looked directly into her eyes. "This is very serious, Toni. If I knew, I *would* tell you."

"*Would you?*"

"If you'd seen Baptiste this afternoon, you'd know that if I knew I'd tell you, protocol or no protocol. He was a bundle of . . . I don't even know how to describe it. Nervous, scared . . . there was an undercurrent of something."

"What?"

"I don't know," he said, pulling silverware from a drawer.

"Here, I'll set the table," she said, reaching for the silverware after washing her hands. "Who doesn't want me to do the story? Who is he protecting?"

"I don't know. He said that certain people would be upset if you wrote that story."

"What people?"

"That's the thing, he wouldn't say who."

"When he said that to me—*that he was strongly advising me to be careful*—I asked him if that was some kind of threat."

"You went too far with that, Toni."

"Oh, and he colored between the lines?"

"Baby, this isn't a joke. I don't know why they want to kill that story, but the DEA guy, and apparently some other folks have a lot to lose if that story runs, and if they'd put a bullet in a young girl's head . . . these are very bad people, Toni."

"Something's going on, like you said, below the surface. Something bigger than Quinnterro, the DEA, and Boppy."

"What are you talking about, Toni? What do you know?"

"I haven't put it all together, but instinctively I know it's something big."

"You're not sure, but you wrote an article about it?"

"No. I mean, I verified everything that's in the article. But there's something beyond that, although, like I said, I don't have all the pieces. I'm pretty certain it involves. . ." her voice trailed off. She decided against telling him what she'd learned about Chief Frankland, what she suspected about his relationship with Boppy, and that she believed there was a cover-up going on.

"Involves *what*? What Toni?"

"I'm not sure, and I don't want to put something out there if it's not true. Okay?" she pleaded, hoping he would drop it.

"You know they don't know where Boppy is, right?" he asked, moving a pan off the burner.

"What, he's not by his dying mother's bedside?"

Jamey shook his head and laughed. "His mother has been dead for years."

"*What*? If you all knew this, how was he able to walk?"

"By the time we found out, he was in the wind."

"How is that possible? Tip didn't know?"

She handed Jamey a plate. He scooped some of the lemon butter and garlic Mahi-Mahi and peas and rice onto the plate, added some fried plantains, and handed it back to her.

"To say that Tip is livid is an understatement. He thinks that . . . well, let's just say he's not a happy camper."

She handed him the other plate. "What does Tip really think, Jamey?"

He gave her the look.

"Okay. Okay," she said, throwing up her hands in resignation. "But what about Chief Frankland?"

Jamey froze. "What about him?"

"Does he think I should leave it alone, too?"

"Don't know. He wasn't around today. He hasn't been around much lately. Why did you ask me that?"

He piled food onto the second plate, and handed it back to her.

"Just curious. You want more wine, or do you want something else to drink?" she asked.

"More wine, and some water. Toni, these aren't just some punks you're dealing with here. They're connected, and they've got resources," he said as he sat down and unfolded his napkin.

"So, are you trying to tell me to drop the story? Because it's too late for that, even if that was something I was willing to, or could do."

"No. I would never do that. We made a commitment not to compromise one another, and I honor that above everything else."

They joined hands as he blessed the food.

"Should I be scared?" she asked after a few minutes.

"You're getting in pretty deep. You should be . . . cautious," he said, struggling for the right word. "When is the story running?"

"I'm not sure."

He tilted his head.

"I promise you. It has to go through an extensive editing process, could be the day after tomorrow, or several days down the road."

"I see," he said.

She watched him as he shoveled peas and rice into his mouth.

There's no stopping it now. It, is about to hit the fan, she thought, picking at her food.

***

The clock read 3:37 a.m.

"Jamey," she whispered. He woke up right away.

"What is it, what's wrong baby?"

"Answer me truthfully. Am I in danger?"

He sat up and yawned. "I don't know. Boppy's organization, from what I hear, is falling apart. Quinnterro, that's another story. He's a loose cannon with a lot to lose. If this goes public, it'll bring a lot of heat on the DEA. Someone will have to take a fall for having a rogue agent under their wing. It'll cause the agency a lot of embarrassment. They would prefer that it go away quietly. He just wants to go on quietly with his life, knowing that if push comes to shove, he still has a deal on the table, and he can just disappear. On the other hand, once the story runs you're . . . things will settle down."

"What deal?" Toni asked, feigning ignorance.

Jamey hesitated. "Toni, this stays between you and me. Do you understand?"

She nodded her head vigorously.

"Quinnterro has a deal on the table. In exchange for testifying against Boppy, he goes into witness protection."

"Except, now that Boppy's gone, wouldn't that deal be null and void?" she asked.

"That's the question. That's the question Tip keeps asking. And he keeps not getting answers."

"Who is he asking?"

"His bosses, the D.A.'s office, Baptiste, and anybody else who will listen. Tip used his wits, and worked his ass off to build a solid case against Boppy, and now the powers that be just let Boppy walk. That doesn't sit well with Tip."

Toni repositioned the pillow behind her head. "What does Baptiste tell Tip when he asks?"

"He says it's a federal matter, that we should leave it to the feds."

"What does Chief Frankland say about it?"

"I told you, the chief hasn't been around much lately. Why do you keep asking me about him?"

"He *is* the chief of police. I mean, this is a big deal, where is he at on all this?"

"You keep making little remarks that lead me to believe that you know something about him. I'm coming clean with you, do the same for me. What's up?"

"Maybe some people are protecting other people."

"What people? And who do you think they're protecting?"

"Who has the power to offer criminals protection?"

"You think someone in the department is involved?" he asked. "The chief?"

"I didn't say that."

"You insinuated it."

"No I didn't."

"Yes, you did. Are we going to keep going in circles, or are you going to tell me what you're really thinking?"

"Jamey, sometimes, it's like, you know things, and see things, but pretend like you don't."

"There are things you don't understand, Toni," he said. He laid back down.

"Why does everyone keep saying that?" she asked angrily.

"Who else said that to you?"

"It doesn't matter. Just tell me what to do Jamey."

"It matters."

"No, it doesn't. Just tell me what I should do."

"About what?"

"Quinnterro. What should I do about Quinnterro?" She turned on her side and pushed her back tight up against his body. He wrapped his arm around her.

"Don't do anything out of the ordinary. Stay close to home, and your office. And listen to your gut, don't second-guess yourself. If something doesn't feel right, pay attention to it. Pay attention to the people around you. Look around, and inside your car before you get in. Keep your eyes open, stay alert."

"Okay," she said softly.

"Once the story runs it'll be out there. They won't have any reason to try to get to you, if there is even anyone thinking along those lines."

"I wish I knew who this *they* that you, and Baptiste, and everyone else keeps referring to is."

"I don't know who *their* they is, but it's better to be cautious until the story runs. And Toni," he said, pausing for emphasis, "do not go to any of those out-of-the way places you go to to meet your sources, until this all blows over."

"Jamey, I'm scared."

"I've got your back, baby. I can't tell you not to be afraid, but I can guarantee you, I've got your back."

"Okay."

"Now let's get some sleep. Good night baby."

"Good night."

She breathed deeply, trying to calm herself. Rather than reassure her, the conversation had left her even more unsettled.

He knows about Quinnterro's deal. Kate said that only a few people know about it. She could tell by the sound of his breathing that he had fallen back asleep. She felt her eyelids growing heavy, but the nervousness in her stomach wouldn't let her give in to sleep. She replayed the conversation again.

He told me not to go to any of the out-of-the way places I go to to meet my sources. But I never told him about those meetings, she thought as sleep overtook her.

CHAPTER 13

I'm missing something, Toni repeated to herself as she tapped the tip of an ink pen on her desk.

"Toni!"

Startled, she looked up.

"Please stop that racket."

"Oh, I'm sorry Danny. I didn't realize I was doing it. My mind is somewhere else. I feel like I'm missing something. It's gnawing at me, but I can't get to it. It's right in front of my face, but I can't see it."

"I don't think you have anything to worry about," Danny said, sliding his chair closer to the partition separating their cubicles. "I hear your story is the bomb."

"I'm not worried about that. That's not what's bothering me."

"Then what are you worried about?"

"Everything. I'm tired, my instincts are off. I didn't sleep well last night. There's something related to this whole Marie Doe thing I'm missing."

"Why don't you cut out early? Go home, get some rest."

I could call Jamey, and see if he can get away for a little pineapple afternoon delight, she thought, a smile crossing her face.

"I might just do that." She motioned Danny to come closer.

He slid his chair up to the partition.

"I think I'm just about ready to talk to Old Yeller about moving to the business desk," she said quietly.

"Why not just go straight to the business editor? Everybody knows you're a rising star. After your story about the DEA agent runs, you'll be able to write your own ticket."

"Yeah, but I don't want to tick Old Yeller off. I don't want to burn that bridge. I need to be strategic about this. And besides, I need him to vouch for me, and my ability to bring home the story."

"Why make the move now?"

"Because there are people who don't want this story to run, and who will probably shut me down after it does. That includes the police, the DEA, folks in the D.A.'s office, and the list goes on. It's going to make a lot of people look bad. It'll become pretty clear that there are some cover-ups going on. Plus, I'm tired of murder and mayhem, and blood and guts. A little white-collar crime would be a welcome change."

Danny laughed, and reached back to grab his coffee cup.

"Jackson!"

Toni turned to see Old Yeller approaching. Danny quickly spun his chair around and started typing.

"Excellent job! We're done, it's running A-1 tomorrow," he yelled. "You can take the rest of the day off if you want."

"I want, I want," she said. She dialed Jamey's number.

"Hey there," she said, swiveling her body slightly to make sure Danny couldn't overhear. "I'm headed home. Can you take the rest of the day off?"

"Yeah. Everything okay?"

"Yes. I'm just tired. I'm finished for the day. I'll stop at the grocery store and pick up something for dinner. Any requests?"

"I've been hankering for some pineapple. Some pineapple would be *rrrrreal* nice," he said.

She giggled. "I've been hankering for a piece of pineapple myself."

"I'll wrap things up here, and meet you at the house."

"Sounds delicious."

"I love you."

"Love you, too," she said.

"Toni, be careful. Stay alert. Keep an eye on what's going on around you."

"Will do!"

***

He was standing in front of her shopping cart when she turned to put the breadfruit in it. Distracted by her thoughts, she hadn't even heard him approaching. *So much for situational awareness,* she thought as they stared at one another. He was a smidgen taller than Toni, but built like a power pack. He had an unusually large Adam's apple.

"What's up, reporter girl?"

She didn't respond.

"You know who I am?" he asked, nodding his head up and down. "Let's me and you have a little talk."

"Okay, Agent Quinnterro."

He smiled. "Let's step outside."

Toni laughed, more from nerves than the absurdity of what he'd just said. "How did you know that I'd be here, considering I didn't know myself until thirty minutes ago?"

"What difference does that make?"

"Were you watching me?"

"You ain't asking the questions here."

She took a deep breath. *Stay calm Toni. Keep thinking. Keep him talking,* she thought, not sure what good it would do, but remembering that it always seemed to work in the movies.

"Why don't we play it this way, Quinnterro? You ask a question, I answer. I ask a question, you answer. How 'bout that?"

"You crazy. They didn't tell me that."

"They *who*? Who is this *they* everybody keeps talking about?"

"You don't know who *they* is? You seem to know everything else. Let's step outside, and I'll tell you all about them."

"*You're* crazy if you think I'm going outside with you."

He snarled. "I will dead you right here, right now, bitch. This ain't no game." He lifted his shirt to show her a gun.

They stared at one another.

"*Dead me*?" she asked, trying to keep her voice from shaking. "If you're gonna *dead me*, you're gonna *dead me* right here."

"Let's go outside, reporter."

"That's not happening," she said, shaking her head.

"I have a little friend here who says it will, mommee," he said, patting his waistband. He took a step back. "I ain't playing with you girl. Let's be up outta here."

She felt her body tensing.

"What is it that you think we need to talk about?" she asked, hoping her voice didn't betray her.

"You and me got a problem."

"Do we?"

"You workin' on an article about me?"

"Who told you that? Oh, wait, let me guess, *they*?"

"You funny. And you causing me problems. The agency just wants this little situation to go away. And with Boppy gone, it will. But if that story runs, I'm done."

"Yeah, you'll have to give up the good life, and disappear, because everybody will know you're a snitch!"

He glared at her. They fell silent as a grocery cart with a squeaky wheel approached from behind him.

"You called me a snitch?" he asked, adjusting his stance. "You a tough bitch, huh?" He swallowed hard.

She watched his Adam's apple move up and down. *That Adam's apple should have its own little set of legs.* She made herself laugh.

"What the *fuck* is so funny?"

Don't show fear, she heard her father's voice telling her.

"You! Are we done here, ree-*CHARD*-doe? I have an appointment."

He looked at her incredulously. "Look here girl, everybody and their brother on this here island is getting paid but you. Do you understand that? How the hell you think Boppy was able to walk? Let's me and you just go outside, and see if we can reach some sort of agreement."

Toni looked into his piercing eyes. *How could someone with such nice eyes be so vile?* She tried to look around on the sly. Quinnterro grabbed hold of the grocery cart and pushed it into her, hard. She stumbled back slightly, but quickly regained her footing.

If I was in the wine aisle, I could grab a bottle, break it, and ram it into that big-ass Adam's apple before he could get that gun out of his waistband.

"We're going outside, *right now*, or I'm gonna put a bullet in your fuckin' brain right here."

"Like you and Boppy did to the girl? That's in the story. Even if you drop me right here, it won't stop the story from running. The paper is being printed as we speak. The story is already on the Web site," she said, lying. "What you should do is walk out of here by yourself, right now, get on a plane, and get gone. Or get to the feds, so they can punch your ticket to witness protection-land before Boppy's boys get their hands on you. *Snitch!*"

He made a move toward Toni. He paused when he heard the squeaky grocery cart coming closer. She looked past him to sneak another peek at the person pushing the cart. The person was old and hunched over, and probably wouldn't be of much help when Quinnterro dragged her out of the store.

"Let's go," he said, lifting his shirt to grip the pistol.

Toni stared at the gun. The squeaky cart moved closer.

"So, dear," Quinnterro said loud enough to be overheard as he moved toward her, dislodging the pistol from his waistband, "what should we have for dinner?"

I gotta do something. Think Toni, think.

She jumped when the person wheeling the squeaky cart dropped a bottle, and it crashed to the floor. Quinnterro turned quickly, and was met with a forearm to the neck that knocked him clean off his feet. In an instant, the person pushing the cart, a plainclothes cop, was on top of him with his knee in his chest. Another cop ran up, and together they flipped Quinnterro over and handcuffed him. He glared at Toni as they snatched him up off the floor. Unable to quickly think of anything else to do, she grabbed a package of celery from her cart and whacked him across the face.

"Bitch."

Just then Tip appeared at Toni's side.

"Ooooooooh, that's not nice," he said, taking the celery from Toni to smack Quinnterro across the face again. "Anything else you wanna say?" he asked, holding the celery in a threatening manner above Quinnterro's face. "I didn't think so, tough guy. Get him the hell out of here," he said to the two cops.

They hustled Quinnterro out of the store while Mirandizing him.

"You okay, baby girl?" Tip asked, putting his arm around her.

She nodded. His radio beeped

"She's okay, J," he said into the radio.

"I'm on my way," she could hear Jamey saying. "Tip, tell her I'm on the way."

"You heard that, baby girl? Your man is on the way."

"Thank you," she said weakly.

"Come on, I'll stay with you until J gets here," Tip said, placing his hand on her back to guide her toward the door.

"Wait, I forgot something." She walked unsteadily back to the shopping cart, reached in and pulled out a pineapple. She hugged it tightly to her chest.

"Ready?"

She nodded as the tears she had been holding back streamed down her cheeks.

CHAPTER 14

"You scared?" Danny asked.

"Of what? What can he do to me now?"

"Nothing, I guess. They'd better get here soon. It's getting close to nine. The judge doesn't like it when people show up late."

"Yeah, we should probably get in there soon, too. Security is tight, and there's a big crowd," Toni said, looking out at the sea of faces surrounding the courthouse steps.

"I'll be right back," Danny said.

Scared? No. Tired? Yes, Toni thought as she watched Danny walk away. It had been several months, and she was still reeling from the Quinnterro incident. She'd decided that once the trial was over, she was going to make her bid to move over to the newspaper's business desk, and get to work planning her wedding. She fanned herself with her hand. It was another uncomfortably muggy day on the island. The rainy season was about to start.

A black four-door sedan rounded the corner, and headed into the underground garage. A rumble went through the crowd. Toni quickly realized that it was only the team from the prosecutor's office, and not the star of the show, Reechardo Quinnterro. After her story ran, the powers that be decided they needed to get rid of the embarrassment known as Reechardo Quinnterro. The most efficient way to do that was to try Boppy in absentia. When the trial was over, Quinnterro would disappear into the witness protection program.

I wish they'd hurry up and get here, this heat is oppressive.

She looked up to see Tip and his partner Stan headed her way.

"Hey baby girl."

"Hey Tip. Good morning, Stan."

Stan, looking as uncomfortable as always, nodded in Toni's direction.

"So, you ready for this?" Tip asked.

"Yeah, can't wait. He'd better get here already."

"Who, Crazy Q?"

"Who else? We, well, Danny, is waiting for the motorcade to arrive so he can get some color for his story. He's covering the trial. I'm second string today—you know, conflict of interest and all."

"Color?"

"Description, drama that sets the stage. You know like, '*At 8:45 a.m., a motorcade of black SUVs yada yada yada.*"

"Yeah, well, that's probably not going to happen. He's already here."

"Really?" she asked as she watched Stan make his way down the stairs, and disappear into the crowd.

"Been here all night. The feds were determined that this clown was going to make it to court today. They weren't taking any chances on this one. They housed him off island. When they brought him back, they didn't let him stay in one place too long. He spent the night here. He wasn't allowed to eat or drink anything. If he took a shhh . . . if he went to the bathroom, someone stood right outside the door. Word is he has some sort of bowel condition that keeps him in the bathroom."

"What are they so scared of, I mean, with Boppy not even being here for his own trial? Do they think he could order a hit on Quinnterro from wherever he is?"

"This is bigger than Boppy, baby girl. Quinnterro knows where the bodies are buried, literally, and figuratively. And he knows who had a hand in making sure they were in burying condition, if you get my drift. There are a lot of reasons, besides the fact he embarrassed the DEA, and threatened you, that the D.A. and the feds pushed to hold Boppy's trial in absentia. Quinnterro is the key to everything. I think he's gonna make like a canary on the stand."

"He already did that, didn't he? Isn't that why he got a deal in the first place?"

"He told *some* of what he knows," Tip said, scanning the crowd. "I suspect there might be a few more verses to the song he already sang for the feds. He's going to wait until he's on the stand, with a room full of witnesses, to start singing them."

Their eyes met. "What's up, Tip? Talk to me."

"I gotta go. You better get your boy Danny, and get inside."

"Tip," she called behind him as he started down the stairs when he spotted Stan.

He turned and winked at her. "Get ready for fireworks, baby girl."

***

"Are you sure he's already here?" Danny whispered.

"Trust me, he is," she said, looking around the packed courtroom.

"All rise," the bailiff said.

Everyone stood as the judge entered. "You may be seated," he said after taking his seat.

The judge gave spectators instructions on how to behave in the courtroom. He then instructed the defense and prosecution teams to make their opening arguments in the case of "San Saypaz' Commonwealth of the United States of America, versus Reynaldo Alexander Brady." Boppy was being tried in absentia on charges of murder in the second degree, desecration of a body, and arson. There was no jury—his fate would be decided by the judge.

"Bailiff, please secure the courtroom," the judge instructed.

A slew of people, male and female, guns clearly visible, rose from their seats and posted up around the courtroom. The prosecution called its one and only witness, Reechardo Octavio Quinnterro. A door cracked open and a phalanx of men in dark suits escorted Quinnterro into the courtroom. Quinnterro looked around the room. Toni felt uneasy when her eyes met his.

He can't do anything to you now, she reminded herself.

Just as Tip predicted, Quinnterro proved to be a canary with an extensive repertoire. Over the next three hours, he testified about the murder, and made revelations that would change lives forever. Toni listened intently while Danny scribbled notes. In exacting detail, Quinnterro described how he came to be associated with Boppy, and what happened the night Marie Doe was killed.

"Boppy said the girl's boyfriend sent her to the island to pick up some Yayo," Quinnterro testified.

"Yayo, Mr. Quinnterro? Please explain," the D.A. asked.

"Dope."

"Thank you, Mr. Quinnterro. Please proceed."

"She met up with Boppy at a bar in Centro Island Square, and he took her back to his house. They was just sitting in the car kickin' it for a minute. Boppy wanted to get with her," Quinnterro said, laughing, "but she wasn't havin' it."

Asked to clarify the terms "kickin' it" and "get with her," Quinnterro said that Boppy and the girl were sitting in the car talking, and that he wanted to have sex with her, but she refused.

"Boppy wanted to do a little sumthin' sumthin'. She said no, and that she was going to tell her boyfriend. He said, 'She made me mad, so I shot the bitch.'"

He looked around the courtroom, gauging the crowd's reaction.

What a bum. How did he even get into the DEA, Toni wondered?

"Mr. Quinnterro, I advise you to watch your language in my courtroom," the judge said.

"I'm just quotin' the man, Your Honor," Quinnterro said, raising his hands. "You asked me to tell you what happened, and that's what I'm tryin' to do here."

He added that Boppy called him about two in the morning, telling him to get to his house immediately. "He hit me up on the cell. I was sleep. He said, 'Get yo ass up, I need you to dump sumthin'. I thought he meant some dope."

"What was it that Mr. Brady wanted you to dump, Mr. Quinnterro?" the D.A. asked.

"The girl's body," he answered, swiveling his chair slightly to face the judge. "Can I have some water, Your Honor?"

"No," the judge answered, to everyone's surprise.

Danny gave Toni a puzzled look. She took the pen out of his hand, wrote the words "poisoning risk" in his notebook, then handed the pen back to Danny.

"Oh," he mouthed.

"Continue," the judge said in the direction of the D.A.

"I asked Boppy what the dead girl's name was, and where she came from. He said, 'The less you know, the better your chances of not havin' to join her motherfffffff . . .' I couldn't stop staring at her. Man, she was pretty. Boppy was just sittin' there smokin' a blunt next to this beautiful woman with a bullet in her head. He was actin' like it wasn't nothin'. Like he hadn't just killed a girl. *A girl*," he repeated.

"Objection, Your Honor," Boppy's court-appointed public defender said. "Mr. Quinnterro did not witness the murder. Therefore, he cannot testify as to who killed the woman," he added. It was one of the few attempts he even made to pretend to be defending Boppy. Boppy's high-powered legal team had withdrawn from the case after he fled the island.

"Overruled. The witness testified that the defendant told him that he shot the woman," the judge said.

"Please continue, Mr. Quinnterro," the D.A. said.

"I told Boppy that he had screwed up bad, that her old man was gonna come looking for her. Boppy said he whatn't worried. He said, 'let him come. He shouldn't have sent no bitch to do a man's job no way.'"

"Mr. Quinnterro, I again advise you to watch your language. You are not above the law, you will respect this courtroom."

"Yes, Your Honor."

"Continue Mr. Quinnterro," the D.A. said.

"Boppy said his wife heard the gunshot, came out of the house, and saw the dead girl in his car. That's why we took his daughter with us when we went to dump the body. His old lady was spoutin' off. She was sayin' she was gonna call the cops, so we took the kid with us to make sure she didn't do nothin' stupid. The kid was kinda like a little insurance policy," Quinnterro said, smiling. "I followed Boppy to Sandset Beach in my car. When we got there, I helped him dump the body. Then he told me to go back to the car, and stay with the kid. Ten minutes later, he's walking back to the car smilin', and zippin' up his pants."

The courtroom grew quiet.

"Mr. Quinnterro, please explain the significance of that last statement—that Reynaldo Brady, aka Boppy, was zipping up his pants when he returned to the car."

"I don't know for a fact, and I didn't ask him 'cause that would have been way too freaky. But I think Boppy did the dead girl."

The courtroom erupted. Boppy's boys were yelling out that Quinnterro was a rat, a liar, a pervert, and a punk-ass snitch.

"Order, order," the judge yelled, banging his gavel again and again. "I will have order in this courtroom. Now!"

When the room settled down, the judge nodded his head at the prosecutor to signal him to continue.

"Please explain, Mr. Quinnterro, what you meant when you said, 'Boppy *did* the dead girl?'

"He screwed her. I mean . . . he had sex with the body. Maybe he just took a piss, but that smile on his face, and that little extra bop in his step . . .naw, I think he did the girl 'cause that's what he wanted to do from the jump."

A rumble went through the courtroom. Toni felt the same sick feeling in her stomach she felt when Dr. Randall told her that the body had been violated. She looked around the courtroom. People were shaking their heads, had their hands over their mouths, or were whispering to one another. Boppy's crew was a mix of awkward smiles, and disbelieving looks.

"Order," the judge said, banging the gavel hard.

The D.A. took a seat at the prosecution table. Toni looked at the two assistant prosecutors sitting at the table. *Where are Kate and her boss? Maybe this trial is such a slam dunk they decided to let the second-string team handle it.*

"What happened next, Mr. Quinnterro?" the D.A. asked from his seat.

"I followed the Mercedes to Southshore Beach. When we got there, Boppy took a can of gas out of the trunk and poured it all over the car, inside and out. Then he stuffed a piece of cloth in the gas tank, and lit it. I couldn't believe he did that shhhh . . . stuff, 'cause he loved that car. It was his pride and joy. We watched it burn for a minute, then it exploded. Then I drove him and his little girl back to his house."

"What was the make and model of that Mercedes, Mr. Quinnterro?"

"It was a candy apple red Mercedes SLS AMG. Man, that car was sweet. There were only two like it in the world with that custom package. That car had everything but a stove. Boppy owned one, and he gave the other one to . . . a special friend as a gift."

Toni thought about what Frankland's wife told her about the red Mercedes in his garage. *He gave the other one to the chief of police, Your Honor,* she wanted to yell out.

Boppy's attorney didn't even bother to try to create doubt by raising the question that maybe it was the other red Mercedes, not Boppy's, that was found on the beach.

"To clarify, Mr. Quinnterro, Reynaldo Brady, aka Boppy, set his car, a red Mercedes, on fire on Southshore Beach? And he did this after dumping the body of the woman known as Marie Doe, on Sandset Beach. Is that accurate?" the D.A. asked.

"Yes sir."

"Mr. Quinnterro, was Mr. Brady's wife, Estella Brady, known as Essie, at his house when you drove him home?"

"Yeah. She ran up to the car, snatched the door open, grabbed the kid and ran into the house."

"What did Mr. Brady do?"

"He just laughed. He said, 'that bitch is crazy.' Then he told me to go home, and get some sleep. He said he would call me later."

The prosecutor rose and walked slowly to the box where Quinnterro was sitting. It was a calculated move.

"Mr. Quinnterro," he said, standing next to the box but looking out at the courtroom. He paused for effect. "Indications are that besides Reynaldo Brady and his daughter, you were the last person to see his wife. Do you know why that is?"

"Yeah. 'Cause Boppy killed her, too." The courtroom erupted again. Quinnterro sat back.

That explains the mystery of the missing mommy.

"Order, order in this court. If I have to bang this gavel again, I am going to clear this courtroom," the judge said over the noise.

"How do you know this, Mr. Quinnterro?" the D.A. asked.

"He told me. He said his old lady went on and on about the dead girl, and about him putting their kid in danger. He said he got tired of her mouth so he 'murked her.'"

"*Murked her?*"

"He killed her," Quinnterro said. "He said he turned on cartoons for the kid, real loud, and then took his old lady in the bedroom and choked her. Then he dropped the kid off at her MawMaw's house, put his wife's body on his boat, took her way, way out, and dropped her overboard. Boppy said he hoped the sharks enjoyed eating her as much as he used to," Quinnterro said, laughing like it was the funniest thing ever.

Nervous laughter rippled through the courtroom. Toni and Danny looked at one another. He scribbled something, and held it so only she could see it.

"What's a MawMaw?" the note read.

"Maternal grandmother," Toni mouthed.

"Mr. Quinnterro, please tell the court how you came to be employed by Mr. Brady, and what exactly you did for him," the prosecutor continued.

"We met when he was a pup in the trade. I busted his little butt. He was quick, whip smart, one of those people you know has got the goods to do whatever they want to do. A couple of years later, I'm sitting in a bar by myself, and in walks the kid. When he was right up on me, I remembered clear as a bell who he was. He got the drop on me. But he just sat down and started talking. He had done his homework. He knew all about me. He knew I was drowning in alimony and child support, and that I had a shhhh . . . a load of debt my ex ran up before she split."

The prosecutor sat down.

"That was Boppy's M.O. Find guys in trouble, make 'em an offer they can't refuse. One day you're drowning in debt, and you don't see no way out. The next day Boppy throws a life preserver your way. I didn't jump at his offer right away. I did *my* homework. He was going places, I liked him. I needed the money."

Drowning in debt—that's Chief Frankland's story, Toni thought. *Boppy threw him a life preserver, too. Wonder what he threw Boppy's way in exchange?*

"So, I started doing little things for him, looking out for him. He could trip sometimes, but that was okay once you got to know him, and figured out what *not* to do to make him mad. He had a stupid hair trigger temper."

'What kind of little things, Mr. Quinnterro?"

"Like, protection stuff."

"Protection stuff? Please tell the court what that means, Agent Quinnterro."

"Like, when we were getting ready to do a raid, I would tip him off," he answered, lowering his head.

"*We*? Who are you referring to, Agent Quinnterro?"

Quinnterro snarled at the prosecutor. "You know who I'm talkin' about."

"Again, Mr. Quinnterro, please tell the court who you're referring to."

"The agency I work, worked, for, the DEA."

"You mean the United States Drug Enforcement Administration?"

"Yes," Quinnterro said, looking around as if trying to read the faces of people in the room. "He let some of the smaller raids go down anyway, even though he knew they were coming. That was just for show—to throw people off so it wouldn't be so obvious he had people tipping him off. But he always let his boys know they were going down, and that he would take care of them. And he did. His boys never spent more than a few hours in jail."

"Mr. Quinnterro, you said that Mr. Brady had people tipping him off, is that correct?"

"Yeah."

"That indicates that there were others in positions of power, or at least with access to restricted information, feeding him information. *Were there* others giving Mr. Brady information to help him skirt raids, and keep his enterprises running without interruption?"

"Oh yeah, Boppy had a lot of people on his payroll," Quinnterro said, laughing nervously. His gaze stayed focused on one area of the courtroom so long that Toni and Danny both turned to see who he was looking at. Toni's eyes met Tip's in the same moment that she realized Quinnterro was referring to the police. She and Danny looked at one another.

"I got names, dates, *and* bank account numbers, judge. Here," he said, reaching inside his suit coat. The bailiff and several of the men who had escorted Quinnterro into the courtroom made rapid moves in his direction, some with guns drawn. "Whoa, whoa, ain't nothin' but a magazine," he said, waving one hand while pulling a magazine from inside his jacket with the other. "Have a read, Your Honor," he added, handing the magazine to the judge.

The judge took it hesitantly, fanned through it slowly, and then fanned through it again. He stopped periodically to examine the pages closer.

"What you got there, judge, is a list of some of the upstanding citizens of this little island that Boppy was paying-off. Cops, lawyers, even some of your cronies, Your Honor. If you check the bank accounts of the people on that list, you'll find a series of large monthly deposits from the same source. That magazine is *my* little insurance policy."

The court erupted again. The judge banged his gavel repeatedly hollering, "Order, order in this courtroom." He took his glasses off, rubbed his eyes, then scanned the magazine again slowly. "Good Lord!" He looked at Quinnterro with disgust, then out at the courtroom spectators, and shook his head. "How was this allowed to happen?" the judge demanded, looking in the direction of the federal marshals. "Get his man out of my courtroom. Now!"

"What just happened?" Danny whispered to Toni.

"I'm not positive, but I think the trial just ended, and all hell just broke loose," she whispered back.

"Once this man has been secured, the bailiff will clear the courtroom," the judge said as the marshals hustled the laughing Quinnterro out of the room. "I will see the members of the prosecution and defense teams in my chambers, immediately," he added.

When Quinnterro was out of sight, the judge banged his gavel, rose and left the courtroom.

Toni looked around the courtroom, careful not to make eye contact with anyone, including Tip. The bailiffs were going row-by-row ordering people to leave.

"What was in that magazine?" Danny asked Toni.

"He must have somehow stuck a list of the names of the people Boppy was paying off in that magazine. And apparently, he slipped it right past the marshals."

"Clever."

"He just punched his ticket," she said. "Stay here, I'll be right back." She walked over and held a quick conversation with a bailiff standing on the opposite side of the courtroom.

Toni and Danny were among the last to leave. They took the stairs down six flights, exiting through a door at the bottom of the stairwell. They crossed a driveway, huddled in a small doorway, and waited.

"What are we waiting on?"

"I'm not sure."

"I need to get back to the office, make some follow-up calls and write my story."

"I know," Toni said, peering around a corner. "Just stay real close to this door for a few more minutes."

The echo of the roar of the first one of the vehicles zooming by caught them off guard.

"Five," Danny said as the last of the SUVs with blackout window tint sped past. "There he goes, and there's the closing color for my story."

Toni grabbed Danny's arm. She held one finger to her lips to signal him to be quiet, and then held it up to signal him to wait. They moved in unison when they heard a helicopter ten minutes later. They hit the sidewalk in front of the courthouse just in time to see it land on the roof. Toni looked around. The streets were pretty much empty, the crowd having dispersed after the motorcade passed. She and Danny crossed the street to try to get a better view of the courthouse roof.

"That's the real color," she said, pointing toward the roof. They could only see the rotor blades, and a small section of the top of the unmarked helicopter. Within minutes it lifted off, and roared away.

"What was that?"

"The motorcade was a decoy, in case someone had a mind to *murk* Quinnterro," Toni said, making quote marks with her fingers. "He's in that helicopter, headed to one of the neighboring islands. There's a plane waiting there to take him to his new life."

"How do you know that? More important, how can I confirm it?"

"When you call the feds and the judge, start with the judge, act like you know. Instead of asking *if* Quinnterro was in the helicopter, ask which agency owns the Bell206 helicopter that whisked him away. They'll be caught off guard, and impressed that you know what kind of helicopter it was. They won't doubt that you know for a fact that he was in it."

"Wow! I'm impressed you know what kind of helicopter it was. How *do* you know that?"

"I used to date a pilot."

"That must have been fun."

Toni laughed and shook her head. "Lot of turbulence."

***

I need a glass of wine, and a good soak to wash this day away, Toni thought as she turned into the driveway at Jamey's house.

"But first the crazy," she said out loud when she spotted Tip in the driveway.

He was talking to Jamey, his head bobbing and arms swinging all over the place. She could tell from the rigidness of Jamey's body, and the way he was shaking his head, that they were in the throes of a heated discussion. She turned off the car and sat back, reluctant to get out. Tip lowered his arms and smiled at her. Jamey smiled but remained tight-shouldered. Whatever they were discussing had made him very angry.

"Get out," Tip mouthed, pointing to where she was sitting, and then to the outside of the car. "Get out."

She pointed to her ear and turned-up her palms to signal that she couldn't hear him, although she knew he was only mouthing the words. He pointed to her again, and balled up his fist. She laughed as Jamey approached the car. She hit the lock button. He motioned for her to unlock the door. She shook her head. He made the motion again, and waited. He put his hands together, as if pleading, and made a sad face. She unlocked the door. Their lips met when she emerged from the car.

"Hey."

"Hey yourself," she said.

"Crazy day, huh?"

"Nothing a bottle of wine, and a good hot bath won't cure."

He pulled her bags out of the backseat.

"Hey Tip."

"I'll put these in the house," Jamey said, holding up her bags.

"Thank you, baby. Bring me back a bottle of wine. I don't need a glass, I'm gonna drink it straight out of the bottle."

"Yeah, okay," Jamey said, laughing.

"So," she said, turning to Tip. "What was in that magazine?"

"Apparently," he said slowly, "Quinnterro had torn holes into some of the pages of the magazine. He filled them in with pieces of paper with names, dates and bank account numbers on them. I heard that before he even declared a mistrial, the judge took care of that magazine. He had the bailiff make three copies of the pages. He put two of them in envelopes he addressed to, well, we're not sure who they were addressed to. He had the bailiff change into street clothes, grab some other mail, put it with the two envelopes and get it to the post office ASAP. Don't know what happened to the third copy. Only the judge knows where that one went. He made everyone, including the folks from the D.A.'s office *and* the bailiff, hand over their cell phones. He also made all the attorneys wait in his office until the bailiff returned. I guess the judge was taking out a little insurance of his own."

"And I guess now we know what Quinnterro was doing when he was spending all that time in the bathroom?"

Tip laughed. "He used bar soap as glue. Ingenious, huh?"

"If only they'd use their powers for good and not evil," she said, shaking her head. "So, Tip, whose names are on that list?"

"Don't know, baby girl."

"*Really, Tip?*"

"I don't know."

Jamey walked up behind her, and put his arms around her waist. She leaned into him.

"You know Quinnterro was insinuating that some of you guys," she said, nodding her head in Tip's direction, "were on the take, working for Boppy."

"Yeah."

Jamey cleared his throat.

She waited for Tip to elaborate. He didn't. He locked eyes briefly with Jamey. She turned her head slightly, but couldn't see or read what was in Jamey's eyes.

"Quinnterro's gone for good?" she asked.

"You know it."

"And Boppy gets off free and clear?"

"Unless he comes back, or just happens to get arrested somewhere, and they run him through the FBI database. The judge said he wasn't going to waste taxpayer dollars to host another circus like the one we saw today."

"So it's a wrap."

"Far from it," Tip said. "That list is the proverbial can of worms, and Quinnterro busted it wide open. You heard the judge's reaction."

She stepped away from Jamey so that she could see both of their faces. "Is Chief Frankland's name on that list?"

"I honestly don't know, Toni," Tip answered.

Jamey sighed. She ignored him.

"Look, let's not pretend that we don't all know that your boss has a red Mercedes just like the one found on that beach. Quinnterro said that Boppy gave someone a Mercedes identical to the one he burned on the beach. That would imply that your boss was taking gifts from a known drug peddler. It would also seem to indicate that he was in Boppy's pocket, too."

Neither man said anything.

"*Nothing*? It's not of major concern to you all that your boss, the man entrusted to lead the island's police force, may have been one of the people doing favors for Boppy? That would undermine all the good that you two crime-fighters were trying to do."

"If he did get it as a gift from Boppy . . ." Tip started to say.

"Be careful, Tip," Jamey interrupted.

Her eyes met Jamey's. They stared at one another.

"Finish what you were saying, Tip," she said, irritation evident in her voice.

"If he did get it from Boppy, that is a problem. But can we prove it? Here's the thing you need to understand, Toni. I'm a law enforcement officer, that's who I am, and that's what I do. If my mother breaks the law, and I know about it, she's going down, *okay*? No one, *no one*, gets a pass. Because you don't see certain things happening, doesn't mean they're not happening behind the scenes. From the outside, where you stand, things may not be what they seem."

"What things? What exactly does that mean?"

"It *means* don't assume anything."

She looked at Jamey, and then back at Tip and shook her head.

"I'm tired," she said, rubbing her forehead. "I need a hot bath. Take care, Tip," she added, touching his arm before heading into the house.

***

She kicked her shoes off at the door. She spotted a glass of wine sitting on the counter. Next to it was a plate with a mound of papaya shrimp, crab and lobster salad, and some crostinis. Jamey had prepared the snack for her when he brought her bags in earlier.

I love that man, even though he gets on my very last nerve sometimes, she thought as she slid onto a barstool. She took a sip of wine. Wine glass in hand, she spun the stool around to face the window. She could see Jamey and Tip's outlines through the sheers. They had obviously picked up where they'd left off when she drove up. An animated Tip was doing most of the talking. Jamey was shaking his head as if Tip were trying to sell him something that he absolutely was not buying.

What is he saying, and why did Jamey discourage him from talking about Frankland and the car? She watched them going at it for a few minutes. *Tip seems to know a lot about what happened in the judge's chambers after the trial. In fact, he seems to have access to a lot of inside information. He knew that something big was going to jump-off in court today.* She swung back around and grabbed two crostinis. She used one to push a good amount of the seafood salad onto the other one, and stuffed it into her mouth. *Um.* She did it again, then turned back to watch Tip and Jamey.

Tip knows whose names are on that list. I think they both know. And the name at the top of that list is probably their boss'.

She topped off her wine glass, and headed for the bathroom. She set the glass on the edge of the tub. She turned the water on, dropped a handful of Sandalwood scented bath crystals in, and splashed them around with her fingers. She sighed as she eased herself into the steaming water. She couldn't relax. Her mind kept going back to the moment when Quinnterro focused his attention on Tip and Stan. The question was gnawing at her: *Are Jamey and Tip's names on that list?*

CHAPTER 15

"Why should I take you on?" Riley Cannon, the paper's business editor asked Toni. "You don't have any business reporting experience."

"I'm a good reporter. I know how to dig, and I'm good at cultivating sources. I can bring the story home. Old Yel . . . Jim can vouch for my ability to break a story," Toni said.

Riley's attention shifted from Toni, to the door of his office. She turned to see Danny and Myra, the paper's managing editor, standing in the doorway. Thomas, a new hire, stood just outside the door, behind Danny.

"Excuse us for interrupting," Myra said. "Toni," she paused, "we got a call from the police department requesting that you come to the hospital. There's been a shooting."

"Jamey?" Toni asked in a barely audible voice.

"We were only told that a couple of detectives were trying to apprehend a suspect, and there was a shootout. One of the detectives, and the suspect were wounded. We don't know who was shot. Thomas will drive you to the hospital," she added, extending her arm to encourage him to come closer. "It's going to be alright, Toni."

Toni wanted to stand up, but couldn't lift her body from the chair. Sensing her distress, Danny put his hand under her elbow to help lift her. She nodded her head in an expression of thanks.

"It's okay," Danny said.

"Let us know if you need anything, anything at all," Myra said, touching Toni's shoulder as she stumbled out of Riley's office. "It's going to be okay."

Toni looked into Myra's eyes. They betrayed her.

She doesn't really believe it's going to be okay, either.

* * *

A gauntlet of blue uniforms greeted Toni as she walked through the sliding glass doors of the emergency room. Mixed in among the uniformed officers were detectives and plainclothes officers she'd come to know—Jamey's "brothers in blue." They all turned in her direction as the doors opened.

Why are they all looking at me? Where is Jamey? Face-by-face, she looked into their red eyes. She couldn't find his eyes. Everything stopped. No one was moving. No one was talking. The world was perfectly still and silent. She wanted to touch one of the blue uniforms, to grab hold, and keep holding on. She wanted to turn, run out the door, and disappear. *Jamey where are you, where are you?*

"Come with me," a detective whose name she couldn't remember in that moment whispered. He held firm to her arm as she tried to head back out the sliding door.

"Where are we going?" she asked in a whisper as he led her gently down a long hallway to a room with stained glass panes in the door. "I don't want to," she said," shaking her head and trying to pull away. "I don't want to go in there."

"It's okay," he said, opening the door with one hand, and gently pushing her toward it with the other.

A man was sitting alone at the front of the chapel. When she recognized the shoulders, she ran up the aisle like an awkward child. He stood to greet her. His eyes were red and swollen. She paused.

Oh my God.

She raised her hand to her mouth. The word "Tip" escaped through her fingertips with the realization that his face was also missing from the faces lining the corridor. Jamey broke down and collapsed onto the pew. Toni sat next to him, cradling his head as they cried together under stained-glass images of heaven. They were both startled when the door of the chapel opened suddenly.

"They're here," the detective who'd escorted her whispered to Jamey.

Jamey dropped his head and took a deep breath. He used his hands to wipe his face, then wiped his hands up and down his pants. "Of all days to forget my handkerchief," he said, laughing through his tears.

She held his hand as they followed the man down the hallway. Toni spotted the police commissioner and Deputy Chief Baptiste talking to some of the other detectives as they rounded the corner. The uniforms were no longer slumped against the wall, or leaning on one another. Uniformed and plainclothes officers alike stood at attention in formation, ties straightened, shoulders back, chests out, arms by their sides, looking straight ahead. She turned in time to see a squad car stop in front of the emergency entrance. Two uniformed officers jumped out immediately. The one on the passenger side opened the back door, and extended his hand to someone.

Shannon. Toni imagined Shannon riding in the back of the patrol car, trying to convince herself that it was all just a mistake. She pictured Shannon alternately bargaining, and pleading with God to spare the life of the father of her children, including the child growing inside her—a child who would never know his father. She hesitated as she walked through the sliding doors. She looked past where Jamey and Toni were standing, to the sea of blue lining the hall. She searched slowly, deliberately, hoping against hope that her eyes would meet Tip's. There was no mistaking that moment in which the last flash of hope disappeared, and she accepted what everyone in that hallway already knew. Tipton Manley was gone. Jamey started toward her. It was too late. Her emotional collapse was slow, all encompassing, and unspeakably heartbreaking.

CHAPTER 16

Toni shook her umbrella several times, and leaned it against the front wall of the house. She stepped through the doorway and kicked off her left shoe. She was about to kick off the right one, when she noticed a pair of shoes already sitting by the door. They didn't belong to her, although they had been kicked off as if they, or at least their owner, lived here. She pushed them gently with her foot.

Those aren't Jamey's mother's shoes. Mrs. Tolliver is a sweet woman, but she has fat feet. Tina has long feet, and Yolee has little tiny feet. And even if Shannon could afford them, she would opt to put money into her kids' college funds before buying shoes that cost as much as these don't muck with me designer stilettos. These are the shoes of a woman in control!

She looked around. Designer luggage was haphazardly pushed into a corner. The shoes baffled her. The suitcases intrigued her. The sound of a woman's laugher coming from Jamey's bedroom concerned her. *What the . . .?* She hobbled to the bedroom. Jamey was sitting on the bed smiling. *I don't think I've seen him smile once in the weeks since Tip got killed.*

He looked like his old self, the before his best friend got killed self. He had shaved, showered, and put on fresh clothes—things he rarely did since Tip died. He spent most of his days staring into space. He had lost weight, and didn't work out anymore. They didn't go anywhere, and he didn't want to talk. They hadn't made love since before Tip's death. Baptiste had ordered him to take a leave of absence "to get himself together," but rather than getting it together, he had fallen apart. He stayed in close contact with Shannon, but would sink deeper into depression after each conversation.

Her eyes moved from Jamey to the woman who was making him smile. She was stretched out on the chaise like she was still married to the man of the house.

Jamey was right, she does have nice legs, but she's showing way more of them than is necessary, or appreciated.

"Hi. You must be Toni," his ex-wife said, jumping up to greet Toni with an outstretched hand. "I'm Karna. Where's your other shoe?"

"Nice to meet you, Karna." She turned to look at Jamey again. "Hey, you," she said, before turning her attention back to his ex-wife.

Toni and Karna stood facing one another. Toe-to-toe they were the same height, different builds. Except for her legs, Karna was thin and flat, like those size zero actresses. *If zero is nothing, and you're a size zero, do you really exist?*

She smiled at Karna. "So, what brings you back to the island?"

"I was in the final stages of a big project when Jamey called to tell me about Tip. I couldn't make it for the services, but I told him I would come and stay for awhile as soon as I finished. I wrapped it up, jumped on a plane, and here I am," she said, waving her hand with a flourish, like the prize girl on a television game show.

How long is awhile? "How long are you planning on staying?"

"A week or so, but I brought enough clothes so that I can stay longer if he needs me to," she added.

Toni sat down on the bed next to Jamey. *He won't need you to, honey.*

Karna sat back down on the chaise, and crossed her legs.

"We were just talking about getting something to eat," Jamey said in Toni's direction. "Karna was wondering if her favorite restaurants were still around." He rattled off the names of several restaurants while Karna ooohed and aaahed.

"Maybe I should put my things away before we leave," she said.

Are you kidding? "I imagine you still have friends on the island, Karna. Are you staying with one of them, or at a hotel?"

"I'm staying here."

Toni looked at Karna sitting on the chaise showing off her legs.

Has this chick ever heard of Woman Law, the code of conduct that females live by? I know it's not written down anywhere because we don't want it to fall into the wrong hands, but it's passed down from mothers to daughters. Did she not have a mother? Or maybe an aunt who told her when she was a little girl to keep her skirt down, and her panties up?' Or taught her about road-dawg etiquette—you come with your girls, you leave with your girls. Or that when you get a weave you don't go from damn near bald one day, to long, luxurious locks the next day. Or that if you've got more belly than booty, you should probably get a second opinion before venturing out in Spandex. Didn't she have an older sister, female relative, or good friend who schooled her on the slew of laws governing the care and feeding of the male species? Like you don't have sex with a man that your mama, sister, aunt, niece, best or oldest and dearest friend has had sex with. And you don't go into another woman's bedroom with her man, especially if she isn't home. Even if she somehow missed all the lessons, when a woman is in violation of Woman Law, a little voice in her head whispers 'you know you're wrong'!

"We should get going," Karna said, smiling at Toni as she rose from the chaise, went into the bathroom and closed the door.

Toni stood up, looked at Jamey, and back at the closed bathroom door.

This heifer is so breaking the law!

***

"We used to have such good times here, didn't we, J?" Karna asked, touching Jamey's back in an intimate way as she hovered under his umbrella walking from the car to the restaurant. Jamey didn't respond.

Karna did most of the talking during dinner. Toni told the waiter that they were having a reunion, and asked him to keep the sweet, delicious, locally made wine coming. Karna kept refilling her glass, and talking. Toni drank very little.

"Tell us about your life in New York, Karna," Toni said.

"I work so much that I really don't have time to meet a lot of people, so I haven't made a lot of friends. I get together with the people I work with for a drink after work, sometimes," she said. "I'm not seeing anyone special right now."

Translation: I don't have a man.

"I didn't realize how much I'd miss this little island. It feels so good to be back," she said, rubbing Jamey's back again.

I've got a repeat offender on my hands.

Toni watched Jamey, who nodded and laughed at the appropriate times, but didn't say much.

"I need to go to the little girls' room," Karna said, giggling. "Come on *gurlllll*, go with me."

"I really don't have to go right now. I'm saving up," Toni said, eliciting another set of giggles from Karna. "You go on, and take your time. We'll be right here waiting for you when you get back."

Now she has me breaking the law—everybody knows that women always go to the bathroom in pairs.

"Be right back," she said, touching Jamey's shoulder as she passed.

"So, you're feeling better?" Toni asked Jamey when Karna was out of earshot.

"I'm okay."

"Jamey, you know it's not appropriate for her to stay at your house, right?"

"Why? What's not appropriate about it?"

"It's kind of disrespectful to me," Toni said, taking a sip of water. "And how come I didn't know she was coming?"

"You're making this into something it's not. What could happen? You'll be there. And I didn't think I *had* to inform you."

"I'll be there at night."

He looked at Toni and laughed. "She's not a threat to you. You have no reason to be jealous. Stop being so insecure."

Oh, no you didn't!

"Jamey," she said, trying to stay calm, "for weeks you've done nothing but lay around. She comes to town and voilà, you're up and back to your old self. I come home from work and she's stretched out on the chaise in your bedroom. You can't see how you might be at least a little bit vulnerable, why I might be a little concerned, and why it might be a little inappropriate?"

"Nope."

Toni stared at him for a few minutes. *Are you purposely being obtuse?* "Put yourself in my place, Jamey. How would you feel if you walked into my house to find my ex-husband laying in my bedroom, like he lived there, using my personal bathroom rather than the guest bathroom? That wouldn't concern you?"

"Nope. I'm not that insecure."

This conversation is over.

"*Gurlllll*, you missed the meeting in the ladies' room," Karna said, laughing as she drunkenly fell into her chair.

So she does know Woman Law.

"Did I, *gurlllll*?"

"What's for dessert? You guys want some dessert?" Karna asked.

Karna ordered dessert. Toni ordered an espresso-like drink, Café Cubano, for each of them. *I'm not going to give you an excuse for any additional law-breaking behavior this night. Time to sober you up, girlfriend!*

Karna jumped into the front seat for the ride home. The wind and rain were brutal by the time they arrived back at Jamey's house. Toni climbed out of the car, said good night and headed for her car. Karna grabbed Jamey's umbrella and made a beeline for his front door. Jamey followed Toni to her car.

"Where you going? Come on, Toni, you're being silly."

She turned, ready to explode on him. Her anger quickly turned to sympathy as she watched him standing in the rain, clothes hanging off his body, a faraway look in his eyes.

"I'm tired, Jamey," she said as she began to cry, at the same time growing angry with herself for getting so emotional. "I'll see you tomorrow."

He stood looking helpless in the pouring rain as she drove away.

* * *

Toni kicked off her shoes as she entered her apartment. *This is my space.* She grabbed the throw from the couch, wrapped it around herself, plopped down into her favorite armchair, and quickly fell asleep. The ringing doorbell woke her from a deep sleep. Disoriented, she looked around to try to figure out where she was. She glanced at the clock. The bell rang again. She tiptoed to the door. She studied Jamey's gaunt face through the peephole.

"I'm sorry," he said as she unlocked the screen door and pushed it open. "I was wrong to call you insecure." He stepped inside. "I haven't been thinking clearly. For the past weeks, since," he hesitated, "since Tip . . . my mind has been all foggy. All I wanted to do was stay in the dark. Not think, not talk, not . . ." He looked around. "Can I sit down?"

She nodded. He sat in the chair where she had been asleep. She stayed by the door.

"I just can't believe he's gone. Tip was always so smart, besides you he has . . . had . . . the best instincts of anyone I know. I don't understand how the perp got the jump on him, and where Stan was when it all went down. Tip always said he'd tell himself before hitting the streets every day, that 'I'm going home to my wife and kids this evening, just the way I left them this morning—in one piece.'"

He slid his hands along the arms of the chair.

"After you left this morning, I got up and took a long hot shower. And then I shaved and put on fresh clothes. I went out on the lanai, and for the first time in a long time, I sat in the fresh air and just listened to the sound of the wind chimes. And I started to feel like me again."

He reached for Toni. She sat down on the floor in front of him. She realized he was working hard to keep himself from breaking down.

"I dropped her, Karna, off at a hotel. She said she'll probably stay a couple of days and take off. I have to tell you though, baby, I don't think her intentions were . . . straight up."

"No shit, Sherlock?"

He threw his head back and laughed a real laugh. Toni moved closer to him, and put her head in his lap. He stroked her hair.

"I love you, Toni."

"I love you, too, Jameyson.

"Yeah, then when are you going to marry me?"

She rose to her knees. "Saturday, October 21, at my church back home."

He smiled. "Saturday, October 21, at your home church. But, we have to have a second reception, or at least a party here, too."

"It's a deal," she said, reaching for his hand.

"Hey," he said softly.

"What?"

"I want to dance. Let's dance."

"Dance?"

"Yes, dance."

My Jamey is back.

He stood, and pulled her to her feet. She stepped away from him to grab her phone. He caught her by her arm.

"Music," she said, nodding toward her phone.

"Don't need it."

And there in the near darkness, he held her tight as they danced to a tune that only they could hear.

CHAPTER 17

Toni looked at the clock. Six-thirty. She laid still, listening to the rain. *Enough with the rain already!* It had been raining almost nonstop since Tip died.

"Good morning."

She loved the huskiness of Jamey's morning voice.

"Good morning. Did you sleep well?"

"I always sleep good when it's raining. What about you?" he asked, pushing his body into hers.

"I slept good. How could I not, laying next to your big fine self?"

He laughed.

"But Lord knows I've had enough rain to last me a lifetime. I see why it's called the rainy season, it really is a season of its own," she said.

"If you didn't have rainy days in your life, you wouldn't appreciate the sunny days."

"Blah, blah, blah, blah and blah," she said.

They both laughed as he swung his leg over hers.

"Besides, the tap tap tapping of the rain makes me want to tap tap tap you know what," he said, his body bumping against her back with each word.

She slid her body away from his, and laid on her back.

"It was raining the first time we made love. I'll never forget that. I wanted you *bad* girl."

"I'll never forget, either. After we made love you held me. Then you sang that song about being sweet like the rain on a summer day. That's when I knew you were the guy."

"The guy, huh?"

"Yep. You sang so sweet that I overlooked the fact that you tricked me into going to bed with you."

"Whaaaaaaa?"

"You know you tricked me. You took me to that beautiful place way back up in the woods, knowing it was going to rain, and we'd get wet. Then you said, 'we better get home and get out of these wet clothes'," she added, in an exaggerated deep voice.

"Is that what you're going to tell our grandchildren? You know that ain't true. You couldn't wait to drop those drawers, and meet big Willie here," he said, poking himself into her side.

"Quit it," she said through giggles. "You know you tricked me."

"I tricked you? *I tricked you*? I got your trick," he said, kissing her through laughter as he positioned himself on top of her, and slid his knees between her thighs to spread her legs. "I got your trick right here baby."

*   *   *

The peaceful slumber they had fallen into after their lovemaking session was shattered by the ringing of Jamey's cell phone.

Still raining, she thought as he answered the phone. She headed for the bathroom.

"Tolliver. *What?*" she could hear him saying through the bathroom door. *"Are you freakin' kiddin' me? Really?* Yeah, okay. I'll get back to you. Later."

He was standing in the middle of the floor reading the newspaper when she walked out of the bathroom.

"Did you know about this?" he asked, waving the paper in her direction. The house phone rang just as she was about to answer.

"Hello. Yes. Yes sir. No sir. Between eight-thirty and nine o'clock." He looked at Toni and shook his head. "Yes sir. Right away."

Toni sat down on the edge of the bed.

"I asked you if you knew about this," he said as he hung up the phone. "Did you know this was coming?"

"You mean did I know that Chief Frankland was going to be indicted, and that the paper was doing a story on it? I knew something was up, but you know I don't work that side of the room anymore."

"And you couldn't give me a heads-up?"

"You know we don't work like that. Besides, it's not my story. Was that Frankland on the phone? He knew it was coming." She yawned. "And even if you knew, what could you do with the information? Tell him? And what could he do with it? Believe me, they called him and gave him a chance to comment before that story ran."

"Amazing."

"What?"

"That the paper could be so careless with a man's reputation. It reads: 'Indictments are expected to be handed down this week, according to sources familiar with the case.' Expected, Toni?" he asked angrily. "Not that he's been indicted, but *expected* to be indicted. So, because some unnamed sources say it's going to happen, that rag you work for puts it on the front page as fact? Suppose it doesn't happen, then what? Do you backtrack and say oops, we made a mistake, the police chief isn't all the things we said he was in a previous edition? Is that the way it works?"

"That *rag* I work for?"

"I didn't stutter."

"It's going to happen, Jamey. Today, tomorrow or next week, he's going to get indicted. Those so-called sources are high-level, people in the know. That *rag* I work for wouldn't run that story front page, or anywhere else, if they weren't positive that it was going to happen. Read what it says. It says that the feds have evidence of fraud, corruption, money laundering, him taking bribes—a whole slew of RICO charges. And he's not the only one named in the article, although I'm pretty sure Winston

Frankland's name was at the top of Quinnterro's list. Which probably led to the indictment."

"Yeah? And what makes you so sure? Have you seen the list? Did one of your so-called sources slip you a copy."

"No, I haven't seen it. Frankland destroyed his own reputation. Did he stop to think about what he was risking when he was accepting cars and money from a drug dealer in exchange for looking the other way, or tipping him off when a bust was about to go down? The paper didn't charge him with anything, the feds are charging him. We just reported the story. And you know for yourself that he lives way beyond his means, although you choose to turn a blind eye to it. *Why is that, Jamey?* You've never once wondered how a man who makes $156,000 a year can afford to live in a nearly $750,000 house? He owns a fleet of expensive cars, sports $2,500 suits, pays alimony to three ex-wives, keeps the current trophy in designer clothes, *and* sends his kids to private schools. Do the math, Jameyson!" She paused, weighing her next words carefully. "Why do you insist on pretending that you don't see what's right in front of your face?"

"You certainly seem to know a lot about this, considering you're, as you say, on the other side of the room now. How is it that you, *you*," he asked, pointing at her for emphasis, "know so much about Chief Frankland's lifestyle, and his finances, exactly how much he makes, how much his house cost, and where his kids go to school? All of that information isn't in this story."

Screw it, I've already let the cat out of the bag.

"When I was still covering cops, I started looking into his life, his finances, his activities," she said. "When I moved to the business desk, I passed the information I'd collected over to the city desk team."

"Didn't you *just* tell me that you didn't know anything more than what was in the paper? Now, you tell me that you started this whole thing?"

"That's not what I said."

He laughed and shook his head. "Here we go with Toni's word games. Why were you looking into his lifestyle?"

"I got a call one day."

"A call from who?" he asked, dressing hurriedly.

"I don't know. They just said that I should look into Chief Frankland's finances, his lifestyle. That he seemed to be living way above his means, well, his legal means."

"Besides snooping around when we went to his birthday party, how did you get all that personal information about him?"

"I VitaTraked him."

He waved his hands back and forth. "Unh unh. I'm not buying that. How in the hell did you VitaTrak a cop, especially one that high-ranking? That kind of information isn't available to the public, it would put us in jeopardy. Try again Toni."

"The caller gave me a code . . . that . . . it allowed me to access Frankland's file."

He whistled. "Okay. What else did you learn?" he asked contemptuously.

"Beyond having a lot of debt, and several mortgages, he also has, *had*, a mysterious benefactor who deposited thousands of dollars into his bank account every month. He ran through that money like there was no tomorrow."

The house phone rang again. He ignored it.

"So, who was this mysterious benefactor?"

"I'm pretty sure it was Boppy. The deposits stopped when he left the island."

He stared at her. "And how do you know that?"

"Sources."

"It couldn't be just a coincidence that the money stopped when Boppy left?"

"Quinnterro testified that Boppy deposited money into the bank accounts of some of the island's 'most trusted citizens', people who had the power, one way or another, to keep him out of trouble. Come on, Jamey, think about it. Boppy showed up at Frankland's birthday party, and pretty much shut it down. A dope dealer at the chief of police's birthday party?"

"I told you that I didn't see him at that party, Toni. And you didn't see whoever it was either, at least not his face."

"That might be true, but you *know* he was there. You know it, and I know it, and Tip knew it, that's what he whispered to you before we hauled ass out of there. Even if you didn't see him, you know he was there. And there's no mistaking that pimp-daddy walk, and those little bitty feet."

"Oh, yeah, scientific proof," he said, nodding his head.

"You're trippin'," she said, heading to the kitchen to make herself a cup of coffee.

He followed her.

"Want a cup?" she asked, offering up her cup.

"No. Who called you, what exactly did they say?"

"I told you, I don't know who the caller was," she said as she poured cream into her coffee.

"How many times did this person call you?"

"A few."

"When?"

"It's been awhile since the last call."

"Was it a man, or a woman?"

"I don't know. They used one of those voice modulation devices. But I think it was a man. I'm pretty sure it was a man."

She headed back to the bedroom. He followed. She set the coffee mug on the nightstand, and took a seat on the edge of the bed. He stood in front of her.

"You suspect someone. You're no dummy, you have an idea of who it was that made those calls. And you still didn't tell me what they said."

"What does that mean, you're no dummy? What are you trying to say, Jameyson?"

"I'm just saying that you have good instincts, you're good at figuring things out, and I think you know who the caller was."

"I gave whoever it was my word that even if I figured out who he was, I would never tell anyone."

"Okay, so tell me what this mystery caller said."

"I told you, he just said that I should check Frankland out. He told me to take a look at Frankland's finances, and then figure out how a guy who earns so little, relatively speaking, lives so large."

Jamey backed awkwardly to the chaise, and plopped down. His body seemed to deflate.

He's heard those words before. They remained silent for several minutes.

"Toni, who was the caller?" he demanded. "I need to know."

She shook her head and took a sip of her coffee.

He stood up. "I need to know who it was," he yelled.

"Don't yell at me."

"Was it a cop?"

His cell phone rang. He checked the caller ID, and threw the phone down on the chaise. "Dammit," he said under his breath.

Toni shifted her position so that she could watch him as he pulled his gun and holster from the top drawer of the nightstand. He kept his eyes locked on her as he strapped the holster to his leg. He checked the gun's magazine, then slid it into the holster. He picked up his cell phone, and headed for the door.

"I VitaTraked you, too," she blurted out.

He stopped and turned to face her. They stared at one another. She stood up.

"What is it with you, Jamey? Are you just in denial, or," she hesitated before asking the question that she had been putting off asking for far too long, "were you . . . or are you, involved in all of this?"

He glared at her. "You tell me. Does money mysteriously appear in my bank account each month? And who the *hell* are you?"

"You know who I am. I'm just not sure I know who *you* are."

He started for the door again.

"Jamey, how did you know about the out-of-the way places where I meet my sources?" she asked, following him to the door.

"*What?*" he asked, his anger palpable.

"During the Quinnterro incident, you told me not to go to any of the out-of-the-way places I go to, to meet my sources. How did you know about that? I never told you about those meetings."

He started toward her, stopped, took a few steps backward, turned and headed for the door. She called his name. He stopped in his tracks, but kept his back to her. His shoulders indicated that he knew she was about to load the straw that was going to do the camel in.

"Jamey, what happened to the DNA evidence from Marie Doe's body? How could it just disappear?"

He stood stark still. When he turned to look at her, she didn't recognize him. He laughed, shook his head and walked out the door, slamming it so hard that two pictures jumped off the wall and crashed to the floor.

She went and sat back down on the edge of the bed, picked up the coffee cup and took a sip. It was cold, too.

***

"The sun," someone yelled from across the room.

Toni looked around the newsroom. People were rushing to the windows as if they were seeing the sun for the first time ever.

It has been weeks since we've had any sunshine, she thought as she rose from her desk and headed to the window. She laid her forehead on the glass. The sun's warmth felt good. She moved her arm so that she could see her watch without lifting her head from the window. *I am mentally exhausted,* she thought, reflecting on the past year. *Between the Marie Doe murder, the Quinnterro incident, Tip's death, and all this stuff with Frankland . . . I'm just tired. I need a break from this island. I feel like I'm losing myself.*

She looked at her watch again.

Almost five o'clock, and I haven't heard a word from Jamey since he walked out and slammed the door behind him this morning. It's not like him to not call and check in at least once a day. Guess he's still mad.

She had heard from soon-to-be ex-Police Chief Frankland, who called to demand that she come to his office to discuss "this indictment bullshit." When she politely refused, saying she wasn't involved in writing the story, he cursed at her. She held the phone away from her ear until he was quiet, then suggested he call the paper's executive editor. When he started cursing again, she gently placed the phone back on its cradle. *What a day!*

The newsroom had been a beehive of activity, with reporters scrambling to put finishing touches on their second-day stories on the impending indictments. The second-day stories would include full profiles of each of the officials slated to be indicted, reaction from other high-ranking officials, and plain-language explanations of the possible ramifications of the indictments. Although Toni had uncovered a lot of what was in today's paper, she didn't get a byline. For the sake of her relationship with Jamey, and his relationship with his fellow officers, she had also declined a "Contributed to" line. *All the guts, none of the glory.* She took a last look at the sun, and headed back to her desk.

I'm just glad I'm not covering cops anymore, she thought as she powered down her computer, and straightened up the desk.

"I'm out," she said, sticking her head in the business editor's office.

"See you tomorrow, Toni."

***

She stopped walking when she spotted him standing by her car.

"What are you doing here?"

"Let's take a ride," he said, walking past her toward his car.

"*A ride?*"

"Yes, a ride. We need to talk," he said over his shoulder.

She didn't move. He stopped when he realized she wasn't following him.

"Remember when we agreed that you're not supposed to say '*we need to talk?*'"

"We never agreed to that, Toni," Jamey said, walking back toward her. "Let's go."

"Where are we going?"

"I told you, for a ride. It's just a ride, to talk."

"That's what they told Jimmy Hoffa."

"You don't trust me?"

"I don't know you. I don't know the person you were this morning, Jamey. You know that what I was saying, what the paper said, is true. I don't understand why you won't accept what's right in front of your face. Why?"

"I was mad at . . . do we have to do this here," he asked, looking around, "in a parking lot?"

People were starting to pour out of the building.

"What about my car?" she asked.

"Leave it here. We can pick it up on the way back."

She took a few steps toward him, and stopped.

"Tell you what. Go tell someone you're with me. That way, if you should disappear, they'll know I was the last person you were seen alive with," he said.

She didn't move.

"What is wrong with you, Toni?"

"What's wrong with *you*?" She looked around to see if anyone had overheard. "You go off on me this morning, I don't hear from you all day, and then you show up and want me to take a ride with you. I don't know which side of the street you're working."

"You *mean* am I corrupt?"

"That's *exactly* what I mean."

"Toni, look at me," he said, walking close to her. "You know me. You practically live with me. Do you *really* think I'm crooked?"

"Nothing on this island is ever what it seems, Jameyson."

"I am the man that you see before you, nothing more, nothing less. Now let's go. Please," he added after a moment."

* * *

They rode in silence, with Toni sneaking periodic glances at him. His shoulders were still carrying anger. He drove to one of his beautiful secluded spots. She followed him along a short path to a clearing. The area was populated by boulders, looked out over the ocean, and had a sheer drop-off.

"So, you gonna choke me, or push me off the cliff?" she asked, looking over the cliff.

He walked close to the edge and peered over. "You might hurt yourself if I pushed you off," he said, turning to look at her.

"So, I guess it's choking, eh?"

"Will you stop?" He walked over to her and placed his hands on her arms. "I'm not the bad guy."

She touched his cheek. He hadn't shaved.

"I'm tired," he said, taking a seat on one of the boulders. She sat down next to him.

"Me, too."

"You were right. Nothing is what it seems. And people aren't who you think they are."

"Jamey," she said gently, "you had to know that something was up with the chief."

"I knew, but I didn't want to know. I purposely ignored what was, as you said, right in front of my face."

"Why?"

He went and looked over the edge again. He picked up a large rock, hurled it toward the ocean, and watched it make a splash.

"This feels good, try it. It's therapeutic." He threw another one. "Have you ever had so much faith in someone that you would trust them with your life? You put them on a pedestal, and then they fall, and it hurts like hell. That's how it was with Chief Frankland. The man was like a second father to me."

He picked up a very large rock, and with great effort, threw it over the side.

"You should probably stick to smaller rocks before you fool around and hurl yourself over the edge."

He laughed. "You drive too fast, Toni."

"What are you talking about?"

"You drive too fast. That's how I knew."

"Knew what?"

"Just like reporters make it a practice to know what kind of car people drive, so do cops. We look out for one another, we know what kind of cars other cops' family members drive, too. That's how I knew," he said, turning back to look at her, "about the secret source meetings. Every once-in-awhile one of the traffic cops would tell me he saw you speeding down Low Valley Fort Coast road, or some other road on one of the far ends of the island. He didn't flag you because you're my girl. Or because he had just seen someone like Kate Marshall, or some other official way out there, he figured you were probably meeting with them, and you were running late, so he gave you a pass. The next couple of days I paid extra attention to your articles. Not only did I know about the meetings, I can name a lot of the unnamed sources in your stories. Bet you didn't know that, did you?"

"Nope. Guess I'm not as smart as I thought."

"None of us is as smart as we like to think we are. You are smarter than most, though. I had to figure out why you were meeting people at out-of-the way locations. I figured out pretty quickly you weren't cheating on me. So, the question became, what *is* she doing? The process of elimination wasn't too hard. As for the DNA evidence, well, . . . some guy shows up at the medical examiner's office in a police uniform saying he's new on the job. Then he gets what he says is an emergency call that he needs to get to, and they let him walk right out of there with the evidence. It was an inside job. Someone on my team had a hand in it."

"Who?"

He shook his head. "Don't know. It could have been any number of people." He picked up a smooth black rock and rolled it around on his fingertips. "I'm sorry about this morning, Toni. I wasn't mad at you. I was mad at myself, and at the chief and at . . . Tip."

He sat down next to her.

"How does a guy who earns so little live so large? You don't have to say anything. Tip used those exact words on one of our fishing trips. He asked me if I'd ever thought about how well the chief lives, how a guy who earns so little, relatively speaking, lives so large? He said, 'I think the chief is on the take.' I told him that was a helluva accusation, and asked him if he had anything to back it up. He said 'J, just look at his lifestyle, the house, the clothes, the cars, the trips, the women. He's off the island more than he's on the island. Where is all that money coming from? It's not like he came into an inheritance. You know as well as I do that his daddy was too poor to pay attention, let alone leave him an inheritance.'" He swallowed hard. "The sad thing is, I knew. I *knew* that what Tip was saying was true. I guess I just didn't want to take the chief off the pedestal."

He scooted over to a boulder that was kitty-corner to the one Toni was sitting on, so he could study her face. "He said, 'J, if the chief has been corrupted, who else is? You know it doesn't stop with one guy, you know that one bad apple *can* spoil the whole bunch.'"

"What did you say?"

"I asked him if he had any concrete proof, and if he had talked to anyone else about it. That's what we were arguing about at my brother's wedding reception. He was late because he had been working on something he said would prove, without a doubt, that Chief Frankland was on the take. And something else, something even bigger. I told him I didn't want to hear it, that a wedding reception wasn't the time, or place."

"What was the something bigger?"

"Don't know. He never got the chance to tell me. We were going to meet the day he got...the day he died."

"Had he talked to anybody else about it?" she asked.

"He said he hadn't, but I think they knew what he was up to."

"Here we go with that *they* crap again. Jamey, who is they?"

"Whoever," he took a long pause, "whoever had Tip killed."

She stood up.

"What are you saying, Jameyson? You think . . .?"

"I think Tip walked into an ambush. I think they set him up. Tip wasn't that careless. No way in hell."

"Oh my God."

"The last time we talked about it, I told him that it was a no-win situation. I told him that if the chief is corrupt, and you turn him, you lose the respect of the other guys, and that puts you in danger on the streets. Who'll want to partner with you? If you're wrong, you can kiss your job, and maybe your career, goodbye. Either way you go, you're screwed. Cops know other cops in other places, so even if you did get hired somewhere else, they'd find out that you were the guy who ratted out a brother. You've got a wife and kids to think about, Tip. You can't save the world, save yourself. I told him to leave it alone." He wiped away a tear. "He was my best friend, and I wasn't there for him. I failed him."

"What could you have done?"

"I ask myself that question every day, Toni. He was hell-bent on doing the right thing, and it cost him . . . everything."

"Who do you think set him up?"

"That's a good question, one I don't have the answer to, yet. But the answer to that question, will answer a lot of other questions."

"Do you think the chief was involved, with Tip's death, I mean?"

"No. He's arrogant and egotistical, and even delusional, but he's not evil. I don't think he has it in him. I came right out today and asked him if he had anything to do with Tip's death. He said he didn't."

"You believe him?"

"Yeah. Tip knew things that someone didn't want him to know, so they silenced him. I'm pretty sure that someone wasn't Winston Frankland. But if I find out he had anything, anything to do with Tip's death . . ."

"Do you think Boppy's boys were behind it?"

"Naw. This goes beyond Boppy, too. Like I said, there are a lot of unanswered questions. When I went to clean out Tip's locker at headquarters, it had already been cleaned out, but nobody knew who cleaned it out, or what happened to the stuff that was in it."

"Jamey, I know you well enough to know that you have a theory. Give!"

"Baby, all I have is theories, nothing concrete. But I'll keep you posted," he said, throwing his Jamey smile on her.

"You think that little smile gets you a pass, don't you?"

"What? No," he answered as he stood and stretched.

"What about Stan, Tip's partner? Do you think he was involved?"

"No. Not directly. I don't know. I've been to visit him several times. I keep hoping he'll trip up and say something."

"Like what?"

"I'm not sure. I just know something is eating at him. I told you he took early retirement after Tip died, right? He moved back to the farm he was raised on. It's way out in the country, secluded, with not another soul for miles. He lives all alone. Baby, the man don't even have a dog! His hair has turned completely white. It's like he's living in a prison of his own making. I think he feels guilty about something. I like to think that he'll eventually come around."

"He's always impressed me as someone who's not comfortable in his own skin."

"Tip used to say that for all the hours they spent together as partners, he never felt like he ever really knew Stan."

"You ever notice that people with hearts like Tip's don't live to grow old? Why is that?"

"Don't know," he said, trying to wipe away a tear on the sly as he walked back to the edge of the cliff. "Too good for this world maybe?"

"What will you do if you find out for sure that somebody had him . . . killed?"

"I'm not going to let his death be in vain. I'm going to find out who killed Tip, if it kills me. It looks like the universe is going to take care of Chief Frankland, he's facing a lot of prison time. From what I hear, the case against him is ironclad—the feds have video and audio tape, pictures, bank statements, you name it. They'll have to ship him to a prison off island where his family won't be able to see him often, and because he's a cop, he'll have to do his time in isolation."

"He called me today," she said.

"What did he want?"

"He demanded that I come to his office immediately to discuss this 'indictment bullshit.' I told him I didn't know anything. I ended up hanging up on him. What happened when you got to his office this morning?"

"Nothing much—a lot of posturing, some threats, wanted to know what you knew about this mess. Just Winston Frankland being Winston Frankland at his slippery best."

"He threatened you? What did he say?"

Jamey laughed.

"He didn't threaten *me.* I'm not worried about him, and you shouldn't be either. The thing about the chief is that underneath it all, he's afraid of his own shadow."

"Tell me what he said, Jamey."

"It isn't important. This morning you said you pulled a VitaTrak report on me, too. What did it reveal?"

"That you were totally dull and boring before I came into your life. Now come and sit with me," she said, holding out her hand. He leaned over and kissed her, then took a seat beside her.

"Toni, if you really thought I was one of the bad guys, I mean, you slept next to me every night believing I was crooked? I don't get it. Do you love me so much that you were willing to just ignore it, if I was crooked?

"*Man*, ain't that much love in the world! If I truly, truly believed that you were a bad guy, I would have been gone long ago."

"So, are you convinced now that I'm one of the good guys?"

"Ah . . . about ninety-eight percent."

"I don't know if you're kidding or not."

"And you never will," she said, winking at him. They held hands in silence, enjoying the golden yellows, rusty oranges, bluish purples, and cotton candy pinks of sunset.

He kissed her on the temple. "I love you, Toni."

"I love you, too, Jameyson."

"What a totally beautiful end to a horribly ugly day."

"God, it's good to see the sun again. Funny how some of the most beautiful sunsets follow the rain. You know what you said this morning about needing rainy days in your life to make you appreciate sunny days?"

He smiled.

"It's so true!"

CHAPTER 18

Toni looked around the room, paying special attention to things hanging on the walls. *Wonder if I'm being videotaped. But that would be foolish on his part, since he's not supposed to be showing me what he's about to show me.*

Curious about what transpired between Jamey and Chief Frankland when Frankland summoned Jamey to his office the morning the indictment story ran, she'd asked one of her sources if she could view the tape of that meeting. Jamey would only tell her that Frankland had made some idle threats. Her instincts told her there was much more to it than Jamey let on.

Frankland and twelve other people were formally indicted three days after the story ran. The list included the judge who released Boppy on bail, and two other judges; Kate Marshall's boss and two of her co-workers; four vice cops, and two uniformed officers. Boppy and three of his lieutenants were named in a separate indictment. Two of Boppy's guys were found shot to death, the third one disappeared, and Boppy remained a fugitive. After the indictments were handed down, Frankland was arrested and released on bail, putting up the house he lived in as a surety bond.

"Toni, we're ready." She looked up to see a tall, thin, balding federal agent motioning for her to follow him to the back of the building.

"Have a seat," he said, pointing her to a worn rattan chair. "I pulled this for you," he added, waving a disc in her direction.

"Thank you for doing this for me, Pete."

"No problem. But I must warn you, Toni, some of what you're going to see is disturbing. Frankland comes for you hard."

"At *me*?"

"The real reason he wanted to talk to Detective Tolliver that morning was to find out what you knew. You ready?" he asked, loading the disc.

"Roll it," Toni said, sitting back in her chair.

He hesitated. "You never saw this," he said, looking into her eyes.

"Saw what?"

He smiled and hit the play button.

"Come," Frankland, sitting behind his big ornate desk, said as the tape starts.

"Chief," Jamey said, entering the frame. Toni could tell by the way Jamey was standing that he was angry. Frankland didn't seem to notice, or care. He was a bundle of nervous energy. He walked around the desk as if to greet Jamey, but stopped a few feet away.

"Lift your shirt."

"*What*?" Jamey asked, incredulously.

"Lift up your shirt," Frankland repeated.

"You think I'm wired? Want me to pull down my pants, too?"

"Jamey, lift your shirt," Frankland demanded.

Jamey pulled his shirt up.

"I had to be sure. What do you know about this indictment crap, what are you hearing? Can you believe they put that shit on the front page of the paper? I can't believe they put me out there like that. When this blows over, some folks at that newspaper are going to be sorry they ever heard my name," he added, laughing. "What have you heard?"

"I haven't heard anything. I don't know any more than what I read in the paper this morning."

"Sit down, man," Frankland said, slapping Jamey on the arm before walking back around to sit at his desk. "Take a load off."

Jamey remained standing.

Frankland was wearing a tailored suit, no tie, and a patterned pocket square that played off the colors of his custom-made striped shirt. As always, he looked freshly shaved and shorn, like he had just walked out of the barbershop. He flashed his high wattage smile.

"What about that bitch you're screwin', the reporter, she has to know something."

The federal agent placed his hand on Toni's shoulder.

"I'm okay," she said, touching his hand before turning her attention back to the screen.

"She doesn't know anything," Jamey said. "She doesn't even work that side . . . she doesn't cover cops anymore. She came off cops a good while back, after the Quinnterro incident. You know that."

"Yeah, but reporters talk. They're all nosey as hell, always into other folks' business. Have you asked her what she knows, J?"

"I told you, she doesn't know anything," Jamey said calmly. "Are you guilty, chief?"

"Man, you know how the feds are, how they gotta try to bring somebody important down every now and then to make it look like they're doing their jobs. And bringing down a cat like me is the easiest way to do it."

"Why you? Why not the governor, the mayor, the police commissioner, or somebody higher up?"

Frankland hopped up, walked around the desk and sat on the edge. "You think I'm guilty, son?

"Don't call me son."

Frankland stood up. "What's the matter with you?"

"We both know about grand juries, and how the indictment process works. There had to be some strong evidence against you for them to hand down an indictment. You know what we say, if it walks like a duck . . ."

"What are you trying to say, Jameyson? What's that bitch been telling you?"

Jamey looked Frankland up and down, slowly. They were standing just feet apart.

"What happened to the money in the survivors' fund, the money that Tip's wife has been waiting on for months?"

"Man, I borrowed it, temporarily," Frankland answered. "I plan to replace it next week, as a matter of fact. How do you know about that?"

"Where you gonna get $250,000 from?"

Frankland shrugged his shoulders and sat back down on the edge of the desk. "The money is gonna get back in there. Don't worry about it. And what does that have to do with anything, anyway?"

"Shannon is waiting for money she's never gonna see, isn't she? Back when you were a good cop, you used to tell us before we headed out to always do the right thing. Tip lost his life trying to do what was right. Now, his widow and kids are struggling because you didn't practice what you preached, chief."

"Come on, son, you know I'm gonna make good by Shannon. Tip was my boy, too. Just like you. I love you guys like you were my own."

"I asked you not to call me son."

"Okay, Jameyson," he said, standing up. "Forget about that right now. What I need you to do, find out what Toni knows. We gotta stick together, J, honor the code."

Jamey took a step forward and closed the space between them.

"Honor? You talk about honor?" Jamey chuckled. "I need to know if you had anything to do with Tip's death."

"I can't believe that you'd even ask me that," Frankland said, scrunching his face like he smelled something bad.

"I *am* asking."

"Absolutely not! What do you think I am, what reason would I have to hurt Tip? I'm a lot of things Jamey, but I'm not . . .," Frankland said, shaking his head swiftly back and forth.

"You need to take care of Shannon. I don't give a damn what else you do, but you need to take care of Shannon before the feds ship you off, and they are going to ship you off. You know it, and I know it."

"Here's the bottom line, kid," Frankland said. "I'm not going down. I've got friends in high, and low places. You hear me? When the smoke clears, I'll still be on top. You'll have to come through me, and that bitch you're screwin' won't be able to help you."

The federal agent cleared his throat. Toni kept her eyes on the screen.

"Hell, who knows, she could get hit by a patrol car tomorrow," Frankland continued. "I can just imagine her lying in the street, dead as a doorknob, that big juicy round ass sticking up in the air," he added, laughing loudly.

"Did he just threaten me?" Toni asked, turning to look at the federal agent. He didn't respond. She leaned closer to the screen to get a better look at Jamey's profile.

Jamey's going to hit him.

"Here's my take on it, *Money*," Jamey said sarcastically while repeatedly poking Frankland in the chest with his finger. "You've called Toni a bitch three times. That's three times too many. I realize you're under pressure, and not thinking clearly, but the very next time you call her a bitch, or anything other than her given name, let it be in your head. *Okay?*" He leaned in closer. Frankland leaned back.

Toni laughed to herself remembering that Jamey had stormed out of the house that morning without brushing his teeth, or shaving, washing his face, his pits, his balls or his butt.

"And you'd better pray to God that she doesn't get hit by a cruiser, bus or train, or that a house doesn't land on her, this afternoon, tomorrow, or any time within the next fifty years," Jamey continued. "If anything, *anything*, happens to her, I'm coming after your ass. You got that?"

Frankland started to say something, Jamey cut him off.

"You can't run, and you won't be able to hide. And even if you do, I'm gonna go after your family members one by one until you can't take it anymore, and you come out. Now, I realize that you," he said with a quick hard poke to Frankland's chest, "only care about you, and I may have to go deep into the family tree, but if anything happens to Toni, I'm coming for you, and I won't stop until I get to you. I'll make it my life's work."

The chief took a step back.

"You know me, you know that I'm a man of my word, and you know I'll find you," Jamey said. "And if I find out that you had *anything* to do with Tip's death, I'm gonna end you. And you can take that to the bank, *Money!*"

Then, with a swift startling kick backwards that made Frankland flinch, Jamey knocked the chair behind him out of the way, and backed out of the room.

Hood law, Toni thought. *Never threaten someone unless you absolutely plan to follow through, and never turn your back on someone you've just threatened, lest they put a knife in it.*

Frankland stood in the same spot, looking bewildered long after the door was heard closing. It was the first time Toni had seen the egomaniacal Frankland speechless.

"Thanks again, Pete," Toni said, rising from her seat.

Winston Frankland is a scared little punk, she thought as she opened the door. *But Jamey is the man. He stood up to Frankland, and defended my honor. He is so going to get some tonight,* she thought, smiling to herself as she exited the building.

***

Jamey cleared his throat and answered the phone.

Toni opened one eye to look at the clock. *That can only be bad news.*

"Tolliver."

She laid still trying to hear what was being said.

"*What?*" He sat bolt upright and swung his feet to the floor. "Oh no." He dropped his head. "Are you absolutely sure?"

Toni sat up.

"Where?" he asked. His shoulders slumped as if someone had placed something very heavy on them. "Okay, okay." He shook his head as the person on the other end spoke. Although she couldn't make out what was being said, she could tell the person was speaking rapid fire.

"Ohhhh no."

The bad news just took a turn for the worse.

He turned and looked at Toni, then turned his back again.

"Okay," he said. "I'm on the way. Cordon off the area—big perimeter. Don't let anyone, *anyone*, including the crime scene techs in until I get there. *Is that clear?*" He paused, waiting for whomever was on the other end to respond. "Is Baptiste on the way?" He stood up, then quickly sat back down. "Find him," he ordered. "I'll be there shortly."

He sniffled and cleared his throat. Toni held her breath.

"Winston Frankland is dead," he said, his voice breaking. They found him in a car out near Dolphin Leap, shot in the head."

"Oh my God."

"Toni," he said, turning to face her, tears glistening in his eyes. "He wasn't alone. Katherine Marshall was with him."

"What do you mean?"

"Katherine Marshall was with him."

"She found him?"

"No, baby, she was with him."

"She was in the car when he got shot?" she asked, pulling the covers tight around her.

"She's gone, Toni," he said softly. "They were together. It appears to be a murder-suicide, he shot her, then killed himself. We won't know for sure until . . ."

"Kate's dead?"

"Yes."

"That doesn't make any sense. Why would Kate Marshall be with Winston Frankland in a car in the middle of the night Jamey?"

"She was his mistress."

Toni shook her head swiftly.

"I thought you knew?"

"Kate?"

She slid back down in the bed and rested her head on a pillow, pulling the covers up to her chin.

Oh Kate.

"I have to go baby, they're waiting for me," he said, reaching for a tissue.

Kate and Winston Frankland?

"Go," she said weakly, waving her hand.

"You gonna be okay? Let me drop you off at my mother's house, or Shannon's place."

"No. I'm okay. Go. Really."

Ten minutes later he was heading for the door. "You sure . . ."

"I'll be alright."

He gave her a quick kiss and headed for the door. A few minutes later he reappeared at the bedroom door.

"Toni, are you sure . . ."

"Go, Jamey," she said, waving her hand. "They need you. I'll be okay."

She sat on the edge of the bed.

Kate with Winston Frankland? She remembered the warning Kate had given her the last time they talked.

"Don't let them compromise you," she'd said.

She checked the clock and scooted to the other side of the bed. She picked up the phone, but slammed it back down as tears started to roll down her face. She pushed her face into a pillow and screamed into it. *This freakin island! I can't take much more. How could this place be so damn beautiful, and so damn deadly at the same time?* She took deep breaths to calm herself, then took a sip of water from the glass on the nightstand. She cleared her throat, picked up the phone again and dialed. She swiped her hand across her eyes and under her nose, and took another sip of water. A woman's sleepy voice answered after four rings.

"Hello."

"Mama," she said, bursting into tears.

CHAPTER 19

"Hey, can you come over to the governor's office at noon? It's really important."

"Yeah, sure, I think I can get away," Toni responded. "So, are you being promoted?"

"You'll have to wait and see," Jamey said. "And please don't be late."

"I won't."

"See you later."

"I love you," she said. The line went dead. She looked at her watch. *Guess this is it.*

Following Winston Frankland's downfall, Mel Baptiste had been named acting police chief. It was widely assumed that Baptiste would be appointed to the post permanently. It was also assumed that Jamey would be named deputy chief, since he was the senior-most detective in the department now.

So much for assumptions, Toni thought, watching shock register on the faces in the room at the press conference when the police commissioner announced that Baptiste was retiring, effective immediately. From the grimace on Baptiste's face, it was clear that it wasn't voluntary. The commissioner's next announcement was even more shocking.

"I am proud on this day, to name Senior Detective Jameyson Tolliver to the post of chief of police of the San Saypaz' Police Department," the commissioner said.

Confused, Toni smiled, looked around, and clapped along with everyone else.

Jamey? Police chief? No!

She watched with a nervous stomach as Jamey stepped, handsome in full dress blues, to the podium. She looked around the room again, and was surprised to see Shannon. They acknowledged one another before she turned her attention back to the stage. She was caught off guard again when Jamey introduced her. She stood, smiled and waved. He also had his parents, siblings and Shannon stand, and paid an emotional tribute to Tip. The press conference lasted thirty minutes that felt like hours. Afterward, people swarmed around Jamey to congratulate him. Mel Baptiste jumped off the stage and headed straight for Toni.

"Congratulations."

"I didn't get promoted. You should be up there, congratulating Jamey."

"I will. Later," Baptiste said.

"You okay with all of this? I mean, you *were* next in line for the throne."

"I'm good. You have to be able to deal with whatever life throws your way. And you have to know how to exit gracefully. I'm happy for J. He'll do a good job. He always said that he was going to be the chief of police of the San Saypaz' PD someday."

Jamey wanted to be police chief? He never told me that.

"So, what are your plans?" she asked Baptiste.

"I've stashed away a little something. I'm moving to one of the Spanish-speaking islands to make a fresh start."

"You speak Spanish, Mel?"

"Un poco."

"A little, huh?"

He smiled.

"So, when are you leaving?"

"In a few days."

"That soon?"

"I've been tying up loose ends and packing since the indictments were handed down, when the commissioner let us know that Jamey was his choice for police chief," Baptiste said.

He's known for weeks that he was going to be named police chief? He never said a word to me about it. Why wouldn't he share something that important with me?

"Well, I wish you the best of luck," she said, moving away from Baptiste. He grabbed her arm.

"Take a picture with me, Toni," he said, holding onto her as he looked around for someone to shoot the picture. "Take a picture of us," he said, handing his cell phone to a woman behind him.

"Sure," the woman said.

He put his arm around Toni. "Say cheese."

Just as the woman was about to snap the picture, Baptiste shifted, pressing himself into Toni's side.

"Got it," the woman said.

"Take another one," Baptiste ordered, holding Toni so that she couldn't move without some effort, and possibly drawing attention to herself.

"Got it," the woman said again, handing the phone back to him.

"I'm going to miss you," Baptiste whispered, loosening his grip.

At that moment, someone tapped Toni on the shoulder. She jumped.

"I'm sorry, ma'am. I didn't mean to scare you," a baby-faced cop said. "Police Chief Tolliver asks that you come to the governor's private office for pictures."

"Can I have a hug?" Baptiste asked as the young officer extended his arm to her.

"I have to go. Take care of yourself, Mel," she said, taking hold of the man's arm.

She hesitated as the man held the door for her. After several minutes, she took a deep breath and walked through the doorway.

***

After posing for pictures with Jamey, his family and assorted dignitaries, Toni excused herself and headed to the ladies' room reserved for the governor's special guests. She wet a cloth hand towel and pressed it to her face. She wet it again, squeezed it out, and sat down on a sofa in the lounge area of the bathroom. She pressed the cool cloth to her forehead. She didn't bother to look up when the door opened. She hoped that whoever it was would just do their business, wash their hands, and leave.

"You got a headache, or are you just trying to get out of all that limelight?"

"The latter," she said, looking up to see Shannon standing in front of her.

Shannon bent down and gave Toni a strong hug.

"Thank you," Toni said as she started to cry. "Don't ask me why I'm crying because I don't know. I spend of lot of time crying these days. In fact, it's my new hobby, and I'm getting really good at it."

"You know why you're crying."

Toni took the cloth off her forehead, unfolded it, then refolded it before pressing it against one cheek, then the other.

"It dawned on me that tomorrow my picture will be on the front page of the newspaper I work for, because I went overnight from being the fiancée of a detective, to the future wife of the chief of police of this island."

"That you did," Shannon said, pulling a paisley print bench over to sit in front of Toni.

"Shannon, this is not what I signed up for. I mean, I knew he was a cop when I walked into this, and I was good with that. But police chief? That's another story. And it happened with no warning, no discussion. And he's known about it for weeks. I feel like I got sucker punched. But then, I think I'm being selfish because it's not all about me."

"You're not being selfish, Toni. It *is* all about you. This is your life, too."

"You know, sometimes I feel like this island is . . ."

". . . slowly sucking your soul right out of your body," Shannon said.

Toni removed the cloth from her face and looked at Shannon, then looked for a place to lay the cloth.

"Here," Shannon said, reaching for it. She went to the sink, wet it and gave it back to Toni. "The coolness will help."

"Thanks."

Shannon sat back down.

"You've felt like that?" Toni asked.

"Oh yeah! But I did sign up for this. You and I are cut from different cloth, Toni. I fully expected, had Tip lived, that he would one day be chief. And I was okay with that. I wanted that man, and his babies, and a home, and everything that came with it. That was my ambition—to fall in love, get married, and have a passel of babies. That's not you Toni, at least not now, not at this place in your life. And you have to honor that. You know I love Jamey with all my heart, and would kill for him, but as your friend, I have to be honest with you. You have to be true to yourself, and do what's right for you. Listen to your heart. What is it telling you?"

Toni shook her head as she used the cloth to wipe her eyes.

"I don't know what I'm feeling anymore, Shannon. The past months have been so hard." She hesitated. "You know how it's been. I feel lost. I want to run away. Sometimes, I feel like, like, I want to just drive right out of my own life."

"Except we're on an island, so you'd just end up in the ocean."

They both laughed.

"Have you talked to Jamey about how you're feeling?"

"No. He's been so wrapped up in what's been going on with the department. Besides, I could tell him that I'm unhappy, but then what? He's not responsible for my happiness. I hate to admit it, but I just don't want to be on this island anymore. I love Jamey, I really do, but it's just not enough. And I feel guilty as hell for dumping this on you, after all you've been through."

"I'm okay," Shannon said, reaching for Toni's hand. "I have my moments, but I'm okay, I really am. And I want you to be okay, too."

Toni squeezed Shannon's hand.

"Why don't you go home and spend some time with your mother and father, Toni? Nothing like family to help you remember who you are. Sometimes we lose our way," she added. "While you're at home, if it becomes clear that this is the life you really want, here with Jamey, on this island, then start putting things in place for the wedding. Find a wedding planner and book the reception hall. You know, get the process going."

"It's kind of telling that I haven't done any of that stuff already, isn't it?"

"Yeah, sweetie, it is. Most women start planning the wedding before they even get the ring. You've been engaged how long, and haven't started making plans yet?"

Toni sat back, folded her arms over her chest and ran her hands up and down her upper arms. "I guess I should probably get back out there," she said in Shannon's direction.

"You know you can call me day or night if you need me."

"I love you, Shannon."

"I love you, too. Now go fix your face girl 'cause you're kind of tore up right now."

Toni laughed and snorted, which made Shannon laugh. Shannon rubbed Toni's back as they hugged one another.

"No matter what, Toni, if you stay true to yourself, it'll be okay."

CHAPTER 20

Toni spotted Shannon standing near the baggage carousel on the lower level of the San Saypaz' airport. She waved.

"Hey."

"Hey Toni," Shannon said as the two embraced. "Welcome back. How was your flight?"

"Long," Toni responded.

"How was the trip home?"

"Great! There really is no place like home," Toni answered, looking around when the bells sounded to indicate the baggage carousel was starting. "Nothing like two weeks of good home cooked meals, and a mother's love and wisdom."

"Here, let me take something," Shannon said, reaching for Toni's carry-on.

"Thanks," Toni said, moving closer to the carousel.

"So, did you get with the preacher to finalize details for the wedding, and book a hall for the reception while you were home?"

"Uh, let's talk about that in the car," Toni said, pulling a large suitcase off the carousel.

***

"So, tell," Shannon said, looking over at Toni sitting in the passenger seat. "Did you get everything set for the wedding?"

"There's not going to be a wedding, Shannon. Being off the island, away from all the craziness gave me time to think about what I really want. From the beginning, I said that this was just a stopover. I wanted to believe, tried to make myself believe, that I could stay here. So much has happened. Before I left to go visit my parents, I was scared, and paranoid, and anxious all the time, always wondering what was going to happen next. When I got home I took a deep breath, and I realized that I was breathing. It was like I had been holding my breath, just waiting for something else bad to happen. Being back in the states made me realize how much I'm missing. There's so much world out there. I don't know that I could love Jamey any more than I do, but sometimes, sometimes love just isn't enough."

"I understand," Shannon said softly.

"I'm going to break-off the engagement. And . . . I'm leaving the island."

"I'm sorry to hear that, Toni. But I know that you have to do what you have to do. Have you told Jamey?"

"Not yet. I didn't want to tell him over the phone. That's one of the reasons I didn't have him pick me up, he would know something is wrong. I don't know how I'm going to tell him."

"You have to find a way, Toni. And you need to do it soon. It's going to break his heart. The sooner you make the cut, the sooner he can start to heal." She started to cry. They remained silent until Shannon pulled into a parking space outside Toni's apartment.

"Why don't you come up for awhile?" Toni asked.

"I can't stay. I have to pick up the baby before the kids get out of school. I'll help you carry your bags up."

"Thanks, but I can manage," Toni said as they both climbed out of the car. "And thanks again for picking me up."

Shannon nodded. "Toni, are you *sure* this is what you want?"

"Am I 100 percent sure? No. But it feels right."

"I'd better get going. I'll talk to you soon," Shannon said. They hugged one another tightly.

Toni waved, and watched until the car was out of sight. Shannon's words echoed in her head. "It's going to break his heart. The sooner you make the cut, the sooner he can start to heal."

I'm gonna take a nap, she thought, heading up the stairs.

*   *   *

"Hey baby," Jamey said, grabbing Toni as he entered her apartment.

"Hey, Jamey," she said as he pulled her into his arms.

"Welcome back. I missed you somethin' fierce."

She held him tight, prolonging the hug in hopes that it would delay the inevitable.

"I've got a lot to tell you."

"Yeah, what's up?" she asked as he pulled away.

He sat down in her favorite armchair. She yawned, still drowsy from her nap. She took a seat at her desk.

"What's going on?"

"I've got some big news about Frankland and Boppy, and that whole mess. But first," he said, a big smile crossing his face, "yours truly has been invited to be part of a panel discussion on protecting borders from drug trafficking at a national law enforcement conference in D.C. next month."

"Wow, that's great, Jamey. Congratulations. Quite an honor."

"Thanks. I thought so too, considering I haven't been police chief very long."

"How long is the conference?"

"Four days. You want to come?"

Toni hesitated. "We'll see."

Tell him.

"What do you have to drink?" he asked, just as she started to speak.

"Not much, since I just got back. There may be a soda, or some juice in the fridge, but check the expiration date on the juice before you drink it."

He headed to the kitchen.

"So, what's the news about Frankland and Boppy?" she asked as he walked back into the room, a can of soda in his hand.

He walked over and leaned down to kiss her. Still leaning over, he reached over her shoulder and picked up some papers from the desk. "What's this?" he asked, looking through them. "Why do you have your resume out?"

"I'm going to start sending it out."

He popped the can open, and sat down in the armchair. "Why are you sending your resume out? Did something happen when you went home?"

"I just . . . I did a lot of thinking about what I want."

He took several swallows of the soda. "Did you finalize the wedding plans?"

"It's just that things changed Jamey. You're really focused on your career and I just . . ."

"What's going on, Toni?"

She rubbed her hands together. "I'm leaving."

"What do you mean, *leaving*?"

"I'm leaving the island. I'm looking for a job. That's why my resume is out, I'm updating it."

He stood up and took a sip of the soda. His shoulders tightened. "I want to be sure I understand this correctly. You're looking for a job because you're leaving the island?"

"Yes."

"The last I heard, we were engaged, and you were going home to pick out a dress and a cake, book a hall, and finalize plans for our wedding. Now, you're sending out resumes, and telling me you're leaving? What did I miss, Toni?"

"I went home to clear my head, Jamey."

"I thought you were going home to make wedding plans. That's what I was led to believe."

"You were so wrapped up in what was going on with the department. I wasn't sure of anything, and I didn't want you to worry if there wasn't anything to worry about."

"But obviously, there *was* something to worry about. I mean, because my focus shifted from you for a minute, you're leaving me? *Really, Toni*?"

"That's not why. I'm just not happy here anymore. I feel like I'm suffocating on this island. And all of the stuff that happened—Tip and Quinnterro, and the chief and Kate. It's all just too much."

He turned the can up and drank the last of the soda.

"Jamey, you didn't even ask me how I felt about you becoming police chief. I was going to be the wife of a detective. Next thing I know, I'm engaged to the chief of police. You knew about it for weeks before it was announced, and you didn't even tell me. We didn't discuss this."

He sat down and absentmindedly twirled the can in his left hand. "Did we discuss it when you moved from cops reporter to business reporter? Did I have a say in the matter?"

"It's not the same. My changing positions doesn't impact your life, except maybe to make it easier. There's no longer any conflict of interest. We're supposed to be partners. Partners discuss things, especially life-changing events that affect the partnership."

He shook his head.

"So, I needed your permission to take the job? Is that what you're saying?"

"No. You know it's not. I just would have liked a heads-up, at least had a chance to discuss it, and what it would mean for me."

"What's the *real* reason, Toni?"

"Remember when I told you that this island was just a stopover for me? I never planned to stay. I told you that I had a plan, and that I wanted to travel and have adventures. I still want that. I just feel like if I stay here, I'll lose something."

"Something like what?"

"Like me. I feel like I'll lose me, my hopes, my dreams, all the things I want out of life."

"I thought that you wanted to be with me. You agreed to marry me, Toni."

"I got caught up. I shouldn't have agreed to marry you. I just got caught up. I'm sorry. I didn't mean to hurt you, Jamey, but I have to do what's right."

"What's right for you. To hell with me, huh?"

"Yes, what's right for me! If I stayed here for you eventually I'd start to feel regret . . . grow to resent..." her voice trailed off.

"Resent *me*? You resent me?"

"No," she said, walking toward him. "Jamey, I don't resent you, and I don't want to grow to resent you. I could stay here with you, and sacrifice my career and my dreams, but ultimately, I'd be sacrificing myself. I'd grow old resenting you and this place, but mostly angry with myself for knowing what I wanted, and not going for it. I don't want to grow old with regret. I need to chase my dreams, that's who I am. You know that. You told me when we first met that you thought I was searching for something."

"Funny, I thought I was what you were searching for," he said sadly. "And everything that happened seemed to confirm that."

"I'm sorry."

He disappeared into the kitchen. Toni heard running water, followed by the sound of the soda can hitting the recycling bin.

"There is no coming back, Toni," he said, walking out of the kitchen.

She couldn't meet his eyes.

"If you leave my life, you leave for good. Be sure this is what you really want. I'm not going to put my life on hold for you."

"I'm sorry," she said again. "I love you, Jamey."

"Don't. Just don't," he said, waving his hands furiously.

They stood in silence.

After some minutes, he went to her, put his hands on her cheeks and touched his lips lightly to hers, letting them rest there. In that kiss, she felt everything that he'd ever felt for her. The intensity of it made her shudder. His hands still on her cheeks, he pulled back to look at her. The sadness in his eyes was heartrending. She searched for something to say, something that would make it better, but there was nothing she could say. She walked over to the desk and pulled out the little red box containing her engagement ring. She placed it in his hand. He looked at it for a moment, then closed his hand tightly around it. He looked at her again, turned and walked out the door, and out of her life.

CHAPTER 21

Walking slowly up the stairs of the San Saypaz' airport lobby, Toni remembered vividly the giddy feeling she got the second time she saw Jamey. He was standing at the top of this very staircase. There was something almost appropriate about meeting him here today to say a final goodbye. He had always insisted on taking the first flight of the day, "when the pilots are well rested, and hopped up on caffeine," he'd say. After much begging and pleading, she'd convinced him to let her meet him here before he left for the law enforcement conference. She would be gone for good when he returned.

She spotted him sitting at a table close to a window overlooking the runway. He stood to greet her. Today, there was no hug accompanying the greeting. She sat across from him, watching him as he stared out the window.

"Jamey, you never told me what it was you'd learned about Boppy and Frankland," she said, breaking the silence.

"It's not important at this point."

"Sure it is."

"Really, it's not important. You're leaving, make a clean break. Forget about all this craziness."

"Jamey if . . ."

"Let it go Toni," he interrupted.

She looked out the window.

"I'm going to bury Marie Doe when I get back. I just wanted you to know that she'll have a proper burial."

"You can't do that. Suppose someone comes for her, comes to claim her, and you've already buried her?"

"I can, and I am. She's been in that drawer in the morgue for months, and no one has come to claim her. Maybe she didn't have any family. Maybe the guy who sent her here was all the family she had. If he really cared, he would have come looking for her. No one is coming for her. She's just taking up space."

"That's cold."

"It's true baby . . . Toni. Dr. Randall wants to lay her to rest, too."

"You're just going to bury her in a pauper's grave?"

"You think it's more humane to keep her in a refrigerated drawer? We'll give her a proper burial, and a grave marker. We won't stop trying to identify her."

Toni rested her head in her hand, sadness weighing her down.

"I miss you so much," he said, staring out the window.

And I miss you so much that . . . she started to say, but decided that it was best to leave it unsaid.

"I'm sorry things turned out the way they did, Jamey."

"I walked into this with my eyes wide open, Toni. I knew who you were, and I chose to take the ride."

"It was a good ride, wasn't it, Jamey?" she asked, her eyes filling with tears.

He didn't answer.

They sat in silence until it was time for him to make his way to his gate. She walked with him as far as she could. He hugged her tightly, and mouthed "I love you, Toni Jackson." He turned to walk away, stopped and turned back toward her. "It was a *damn* good ride," he whispered.

***

Toni looked around the parking lot as she walked to her car. Something didn't feel right. She turned and looked behind her. Her eyes scanned the cars in the lot. When she turned back around, there was a man walking toward her. His face was very familiar, but somehow unfamiliar. She studied the face.

"Deputy Chief . . . I mean, *Mel*? Mel Baptiste?"

"Hello, Toni."

"What are you doing here?" she asked, looking around the parking lot again.

"How are you?" he asked, ignoring the question.

"I'm okay. How are you? You look really different."

"Life is verrrryyyy good," he said.

He was no longer scruffy, or pudgy. He had a fresh haircut and shave. Straight white teeth replaced crooked yellow ones. He was wearing a crisp Oxford shirt, tailored slacks and Italian loafers. He could legitimately be described as handsome now. Her eyes were drawn to his very expensive watch.

"What brings you back to San Saypaz'?"

"I had to come back to take care of a little unfinished business," he said. "And you came here today to put your lover, the new police chief on a plane, didn't you?"

She started to tell him that she and Jamey were no longer together, and that she was leaving the island. She chose instead to focus on the uneasy feeling in her gut. Baptiste smiled at her.

"What unfinished business, Mel?"

"You and Jamey."

"What *about* me and Jamey?"

"You have to wonder, don't you?" he said, locking eyes with her.

She felt an urge to run.

"Wonder what, Mel?"

"How a guy who earns so little lives so large." He threw his head back and laughed, exposing his teeth.

She felt weak. She looked for something to hold on to.

"Poor Tip. Poor meddling do-gooder Tip. How often did he call you with that crap? Forget it, that's not important now," Baptiste said, shaking his head. "I knew someone was tipping you off. I knew it wasn't Jamey, he's too smart for that. Took me awhile to figure it out, though. Tip would still be alive if he'd just minded his own damn business. Always running his mouth, always questioning how Winston Frankland could afford to live like he did. He was shining light on things I preferred to keep in the dark. Do you know he kept that voice modulation thing in his locker—*who does that*? I found it when I cleaned out his locker. I took care of him, with a little help from my friends. I also took care of Boppy, and Frankland, stupid fuck that he was, and poor sweet needy Katherine Marshall."

"Kate? Kate was . . ."

"Naïve. Kate was naïve. Her mistake was screwin' Winston Frankland, and not having the good sense to jump ship when it started sinking. She just happened to be in the wrong place at the right time the night I killed him. I couldn't be sure what she knew, or what she was telling you. So, she had to go, too."

Toni shook her head and backed away from Baptiste.

"Yes, I killed Frankland. He got too close to Boppy, got too flashy, lived too loud. He was a punk. Sooner or later, he would have given me up to the feds to save his own ass. Kate was just collateral damage."

Just collateral damage. She searched Baptiste's eyes—they were the windows to nothing. She swallowed hard.

"You're surprised. You didn't know any of this? Jamey didn't tell you? He figured it out. I guess he was trying to protect you. Awww, how sweet. Fuckin' hero." Baptiste laughed. "Let me fill you in. Winston Frankland and Boppy didn't run anything. But they both had such big fuckin' egos that it was easy to persuade them to keep my role hidden. I just let people *think* they were running the show. But it was all my show. I ran the department. The drugs, the girls, the gambling, the payoffs—that was all me. They were just trained monkeys. I guess they weren't trained well enough, though. My bad!" He laughed again. "The monkeys got loose, and I couldn't get them back in order. So one-by-one, I put 'em down."

It was right there in front of my face this whole time.

"What about Marie Doe?"

"What about her?" he asked angrily.

"Who was she, how was she involved?"

"What the *hell* does that matter now?" He made a growling sound, like an animal gone mad. His face turned into a mask of rage. "I don't know who she was, or where she came from, and I don't give a shit," he said.

He closed his eyes. Toni watched as the rage disappeared from his face. He opened his eyes, looked around and smiled.

"That was Boppy's thing. I didn't even know anything about it until they found her body. That's when everything started to unravel," he said calmly. "It cost me a small fortune to get that little bastard out of jail. Everybody had their hands out, wanting to get paid. You know where Boppy is now?"

Toni shook her head slowly.

"I reunited him with his wife. He's fish food."

He's in the ocean.

"I took care of Boppy's boys, too. Except Quinnterro. The feds had him locked down so tight that I couldn't get to him, but that's okay. He really believed Boppy was the head of the organization. I'm not much worried about Quinnterro showing his face around here again. The feds sent him far, far away. Fuckin' canary!"

Without warning, Baptiste grabbed her by the scruff of her neck and turned her so that she was facing the airport. Instinct told her not to try to fight, or resist.

"I built this empire, me, Mel Baptiste," he said. "I have to admit, though, I made some strategic errors. But I've cleaned up most of my mess. Except for," he pulled her closer, "you and Jamey."

Terror gripped her stomach.

"You know, Jamey really is a good cop. He's one of the smartest cops I've ever met. And I've met a lot of cops, used to own more than a few," Baptiste said, a horrid laugh rising from him. "But I know him, and I know that sooner or later he'd come for me. Frankland told me how Jamey threatened to hunt him down if he ever found out that he had anything to do with Tip's death. He knows that I had Tip killed. He just can't prove it—yet. And I'm not going to spend the rest of my life wondering every day, if today is the day Jameyson Tolliver is coming for me."

He moved his face very close to Toni's lips, as if he was going to kiss her. She could feel the heat. His breath smelled sweet, and evil. She fought to keep from heaving.

"You're leaving the island soon. Yes? *Yes*?" he asked, nodding his head repeatedly, tightening his grip around her neck.

"Yes," she whispered.

"Yes. You will leave this little island and not look back, Toni, my love. Pretend this island doesn't exist. Forget what you know, and what took place while you were here. *Okay?*"

She nodded.

"That only leaves Jamey," he said, nodding toward the airport. "I'm going to walk away now, Toni. Don't turn around. I'm not Quinnterro, and I am not that punk-ass Winston Frankland. I *will* hurt you. I don't want to, God knows I don't," Baptiste said, resting his lips on her temple. "But I will if I have to. Do you understand?"

She nodded her head slightly. He clutched her chin gently, turned her face toward him and rammed his tongue into her mouth. She heaved as a wave of bile rose from her stomach. He loosened his grip, and walked away. She closed her eyes and breathed deep to keep from vomiting. She didn't dare turn around. When she opened her eyes, she saw a large plane taking off. The hairs on the back of her neck stood up when from behind her, she heard Baptiste start a countdown.

"Ten . . . nine . . . eight . . . seven . . . six . . . five . . . four. . ."

A feeling of dread knocked her to her knees. "Oh! God! No!"

The explosion was so loud that she couldn't hear it—a deafening loudness. She watched shooting flames make little spirals and fall to earth. They were beautiful orangey, bluish shimmering, silvery, fire-colored spirals of flames, metal and debris. *That engine is flying all by itself.* It was a spectacle like nothing she'd ever seen. *That's beautiful, prettier than fireworks against a cloudless midnight sky. But not prettier, not pretty, not pretty at all, not pretty, Toni. Airplane wreckage can't be pretty, silly.* She started to laugh uncontrollably.

"I'm tired," she said aloud as she eased herself, still laughing, into a sitting position on the ground. "I'm so tired."

She took one last look at the remnants of Jamey's plane falling to earth, laid down and curled herself into a fetal position. *I just need to rest. I'll be okay if I can just rest for a little while.*

PART II: Denouement

CHAPTER 22 - TONI

Toni watched as men and women in full dress blues moved into position when they heard the sirens in the distance.

I've seen this beautiful, sad show before. She scanned the crowd standing outside the church, and wiped a tear from her eye. *I hate funerals.* She reached into her purse and pulled out a tissue as the sound of the sirens grew closer. *Jamey would offer me his handkerchief if he was here. It would smell like him.*

The family would be arriving shortly. She had been invited to ride with them. "I'm not really family" she said, declining the invitation. The first motorcycles turned the corner. *It's time.* A contingent of twelve police motorcycles, two-by-two, led the procession, followed by police cars, the hearse, a series of stretch limos, and more cars than she wanted to count. When the motorcade came to a halt, officers in dress blues made their way, in formation, to the hearse. Toni marveled at their precision as they stepped in unison to the church, and up the stairs carrying the casket. They stopped on the landing at the top of the stairs, and waited.

She put her sunglasses on.

The funeral directors opened the doors of the family cars. Jamey's brother, Tank, was the first family member to emerge, followed by his wife, Yolee. His sister, Tina, her husband, Bertrand, and their children exited next, followed by Shannon. Tank moved quickly around to the other side of the car, and grabbed hold of his father's arm.

Mr. Tolliver looks so old and broken.

Three men Toni didn't recognize emerged from the second limo. *Bodyguards. Or to use Jamey's parlance, security detail.* The men did a quick visual sweep of the crowd. Her eyes saw him. Her stomach felt him. It had been months since she'd last seen him in person. He looked older, but he was still beautiful. He still moved her.

Thank you, again, God, for giving him the good sense to listen to his gut when it told him not to get on that plane.

He put his suit coat on and made his way to the stairs, keeping distance from members of his family for their safety. She recognized the sadness in his eyes, and knew the sadness he must be feeling in his heart. He'd been there for her, a friend offering her support when her mother died months before. Today, it was Jamey's turn to bury his mother, and she had to be here for him—no matter what the risk.

***

"Hello."

"I'm in the lobby."

"*You are?* Okay. Give me a few minutes. I'll be right down." Toni quickly brushed her teeth, washed her face and put on a dab of lip gloss.

Jamey was standing in front of the elevator when the doors opened. Her eyes traveled from his face to his shoulders as she approached him. He gave her a slight smile. She could tell he was holding back the smile that threatened to engulf his entire face.

"Hey," he said.

"Hey yourself." Her stomach was fluttering.

He gave her a stiff hug. She breathed him in.

"You want to get a drink?"

"Sure," she answered. She followed him into the hotel bar.

"Thanks for coming for the services," he said when they were seated. "My mother would have appreciated it."

"I promised her I would come. And I wanted to be here for you."

"Your phone calls meant a lot to her, especially during those last few months." He swallowed hard and cleared his throat. "How come you didn't come back to the house? Everyone was looking forward to seeing you."

"I guess I just didn't feel up to it."

"How long you staying?"

"A few days. I want to stop by the paper and see a couple of my former co-workers while I'm here."

"I see. So how have you been? How's the job?" he asked.

"I've been okay. The job is okay."

"Just okay?"

"Just okay."

"How's your fella? What's his name again?"

"His name is gone, as in no longer part of my universe. Thank you for asking though."

"Gone, huh? They don't seem to last long."

"Because they aren't you."

"*Me* didn't last long either," he said, laughing.

He ordered Campari for himself, a glass of Moscato for her.

"You look good, Toni."

"Thank you. How have you been, Jamey? And where are your bodyguards?" she added, looking around."

"My security detail is only with me when I have to be in large crowds, the commissioner insists on it. It's really a pain. Otherwise, I've been okay, considering everything."

She waited.

"I miss you. After all this time, I still miss you, Toni Jackson."

"I miss you, too, Jameyson Tolliver. That's why the others don't last long, because I'm still feeling you."

He looked away. She took it as a sign that he didn't want to go any further down that road. The waiter brought their drinks.

"Have you heard from him lately?"

"Mel?"

"Who else?"

"He still calls every now and then to taunt me," he answered.

She shivered.

"You cold, want my jacket?"

"No. I'm alright, although being back on the island again scares me a little. I keep wondering if he's somewhere watching and waiting."

"He's not here, believe me. He's far from here. I know where he's at, and I'll know if he sets foot on this island."

"How? How do you know?"

"It's not important how, but I know. You don't have to worry about Mel."

"That's what *you* say. He pulled the wool over my eyes once. I don't put anything past him. Just because he let me live doesn't mean he won't change his mind."

"Mel has a thing for you. That's the only reason you're still alive. We know from what happened to Kate," he hesitated, "that he has no qualms about . . . hurting a woman. If he wanted you dead, he would have killed you that day at the airport. He had ample opportunity. He didn't hurt you because he cares about you."

She took a sip of her drink. "If I had only seen what was right there in front of my face. I'll always regret . . . things might be different if I had just . . ."

"I should have figured it out sooner, too," he said, shaking his head. "It was right there in front of my face, too."

"He played us . . ." she said.

". . . like a finely tuned Stradivarius," he chimed in.

They laughed. They'd said that about Mel Baptiste so often that they'd developed a cadence. The laughter seemed to lighten his load.

"It's good to see you smile, J," she said, touching his hand.

"It's good to smile. It has not been easy. Tip, Chief Frankland, splitting from you, that plane exploding and all of those people dying, and then having to watch cancer ravage my mother's mind and body." He sipped his drink. "Sometimes, in those final days, I'd just watch her. I knew she was still in there, until the end there was a flicker of light, but she couldn't talk, and later she couldn't even write." He swallowed his sadness. "Let's stop talking about death. We're alive, and we should celebrate that. Ya hungry? Let's get out of here and go get some dinner," he said, rising from the table.

"What do you think I am, some girl you can just pick up in a hotel bar and swoosh, I'm off to dinner, and heaven knows where else with you?

"Um, yep."

"Okay then, let me grab a jacket."

***

After a dinner of jerk chicken and honey-mango glazed ribs at a restaurant near the hotel, they stopped at Jamey's parents' house, where members of his family were still gathered. Everyone froze when Toni entered. They stared at her, then rushed her, smothering her with hugs and kisses. They offered her food and peppered her with questions. She and Shannon found a corner where they could talk quietly. Their talk was interrupted by one of the two remaining elderly aunts—the touchy-feely one.

"Dare's dat gull with dem baby-making hips. Ya made any babies yet, Yunkee gull? Jamey, did she made any babies yet?" she asked Jamey, her mind clearly addled now.

"No, Auntie, no children."

"Sun of me brutha," the aunt said, "I taught you was gun marry her, and make sum babies! You ain't married her yet?"

"No, sweetie, she abandoned me."

Toni gave him the stank-eye and excused herself, saying that she needed to get something to drink.

"I *abandoned* you?" she asked as they drove back to the hotel. "Why did you tell her that, in front of everybody?"

"You did."

"I absolutely did not. You sent me away. You said that you didn't get on that plane because you felt in your gut that something was wrong. You came and found me in that parking lot, and less than twenty-four hours later you had me on a private plane and off this island. You didn't even give me time to finish packing my things. You sent me away. You *made* me leave."

"You were planning to leave anyway, *remember*? I just expedited things for you."

"I would have stuck by you, Jamey. I would have stayed."

"Before that all went down you broke off our engagement. You said you weren't happy. If you had stayed because of what happened at the airport, it would have only been a matter of time before you were overcome by the urge to run off again. Or you would have started resenting me. I just sped up your timetable." He gave her a sideways glance. "Mel told you to leave the island, didn't he?"

"But you said he left the island right after that plane blew up."

"He could have easily changed his mind, and come back for you. I couldn't risk that. Mel is a dangerous, unpredictable, murderous but brilliant sociopath. That's why I have to . . ."

"Jamey!"

"Okay, okay," he said, throwing up his hand in surrender. "So, what do you have planned for tomorrow?" he asked as they pulled into the hotel parking lot.

"I plan to stop by the paper tomorrow and say hi to everyone, and then have lunch with some of my former colleagues."

"And then?"

"And then you're taking me to one of your beautiful and

secluded spots for one of your famous picnics."

"*I am?*"

"Yes."

"Okay. And what time am I doing that?"

"Late in the day, so we can catch a sunset."

He reached for her key card as they approached her room. He unlocked the door, walked in and looked around, checking the bathroom and the closets.

"You forgot to look under the bed, that's where the boogie man usually hides," she said.

He got on his hands and knees and looked under the bed. "All clear," he said, standing back up.

"Stay awhile?"

He shook his head. "I'd better get going."

"Suppose Mel comes knocking in the middle of the night?"

"If Mel comes in the middle of the night, believe me, he won't knock."

"That's comforting, dear."

He smiled and shook his head. "Lock up behind me," he said, pulling the door closed behind him.

Toni quickly locked the door, securing all the locks, then kicked off her shoes. She went to the window and tested it, even though she was on the ninth floor. She had purposely requested a room with a view of the ocean, but no balcony. *If Mel is coming for me, he can't come through the window.* She stood at the window and looked around the room. She grabbed some books and magazines, and made two stacks behind the door. She placed a vase on top of one stack. She unwrapped three drinking glasses, laid one on top of the vase, and put the other two on the second stack. *And if he tries to come through this door, he'll make so much noise that . . .*

She took off her jacket and dress, propped pillows against the headboard, and laid back. She thought about Jamey and smiled. It was clear they still cared deeply for one another, even after all the time apart. They'd stayed in contact after she left the island, and toyed with the idea of getting back together. But the specter that was Mel Baptiste always seemed to be standing in the way. She'd just started to drift off when the phone rang.

"Open the door, please."

She tiptoed to the door and peeped out. "Just a minute," she said, putting the vase and glasses on the floor, and pushing the books and magazines aside. "Didn't want Mel to get me, *eh*?" she asked as she opened the door.

"What's all this?" Jamey asked, pointing to the floor.

"*My* security detail," she said, pointing her thumb at her body.

"Yeah, well, you won't be needing that now. I'm here to guard your body, baby."

***

The blue glow of the bedside clock was hypnotic. She watched time tick away. The tick-tocking of the clock, and Jamey's breathing formed a soothing rhythm. She looked over at him staring at the ceiling. His regular cell phone, the red cell phone that wasn't really red, and his holstered gun were on the night table next to him. Her cell phone, and her red, not really red phone, were on the table adjacent to where she was laying. Toni, Jamey, his family members, and bodyguards all carried identical cell phones they called red phones, although the phones weren't red in color. With the touch of a button, the emergency phones would alert Jamey, or a member of his security team if any of the people who carried one of them was in danger. Even though she left the island after the plane blew up, Jamey insisted that she carry one of them because Mel was still out there somewhere.

"Jamey, if you say the word, I'll go home tomorrow, give my notice, pack up everything, and run away with you. I'll give it all up tomorrow," she said, breaking the silence.

He turned his face toward her, looking at her as if he were seeing her for the first time. His eyes moved from her eyes to her nose and lips, and down to her chin. He looked back at the ceiling.

"Do you have a woman, a girlfriend, Jamey?"

"Lots of them."

She raised herself up on her elbow to look at him.

"No. I don't have anybody, and you know it. I'd take you up on that offer in a minute if he weren't still out there."

"Mel? Again? *Really,* Jamey? Why don't you just let this thing with Mel go? Let the feds take care of him."

"The feds haven't done anything, and I don't have a lot of faith that they ever will. They're not out there actively looking for him. I have to take care of Mel. You're not safe, we're not safe, and we could never be free to be happy as long as he's alive. I don't want to make you a young widow. That's why I'm going to . . ."

"No!"

"Yes! Stop it, dammit!" he said. He stood up. "Because you don't want to hear it doesn't make it any less real, Toni. I *am* going to kill that bastard. I can't rest until he's dead."

"If Mel was going to come back for you he would have done it after he blew up that plane, Jamey, when he realized that you weren't on it," she said, sitting up. "He's moved on with his life. Let's do the same. We can move somewhere—just pick a place and go. Someplace where we can watch the seasons change."

"And what, hide? As long as you have family, as long as I have family, there will always be a way for him to find us. The people we love would always be in jeopardy. I'm not running, I'm not hiding, and I'm not going to let him live. I promised my mother that as long as she was alive I wouldn't go after him. She's gone now."

"She wouldn't want you to do this, Jamey."

He exhaled loudly.

"He tried to kill me. And he'll try again. I have to end it once and for all. When it's done, if you still want to be with me, I'll come and tell your boss you quit, and pack you up myself. And we can go live happily ever after in a place where we can watch the seasons change."

"If you go looking for Mel, he'll kill you."

"I *know* where he is, but I'm not going looking for him. That would give him the home-field advantage. I'm going to make him come to me."

She fell back onto the pillow, frustrated.

"So, do you still want to have children, at some point?"

"Yes. But, you scare me sometimes, Jamey. It's like you're obsessed."

"You think I'm crazy?"

"I didn't say that," she said, shaking her head.

He went and sat in an armchair across from the bed, facing her.

"I wish I could make you understand Toni. When I saw you laying on the ground at the airport that day, my heart just stopped. I thought Mel had killed you. I can't go through that again, Toni. I can't. If anything happened to you . . ." he stopped mid-sentence.

"Jamey, you're a cop. For God's sake, you're talking about murdering someone."

"It's for the greater good. I'm sworn to protect the public, and that's just what I'm going to do."

"Is that what you tell yourself?" she asked.

He propped his feet up on the footstool, rested his head on the back of the chair and closed his eyes to signal that the discussion was over.

***

She sat on the bed watching him. The pain and loss of the past few years had taken a heavy toll. He was different. She walked over to where he was sitting, lifted his legs off the footstool and scooted in under them. She removed his socks and massaged his feet. She rubbed the balls of his feet with her knuckles, and kneaded each toe slowly between her thumb and forefinger.

He opened his eyes briefly. "That's nice. It's been a long time since I had anyone to do anything nice like that for me. Thank you."

She could feel his body relaxing. She slid from the footstool to her knees, moved in close to him and kissed him lightly on the lips. She kissed him again, and then pulled lightly on his bottom lip with her teeth. She planted butterfly kisses on his neck, and nibbled his earlobe. She ran her partially separated lips up and down his ear.

"Ummmmm."

She pulled his earlobe gently with her teeth, then worked her way back to his mouth. He lifted her face and looked into her eyes. He kissed her deeply, his tongue sliding in and out of her mouth. He sucked her tongue lightly, doing the signature humping motion that drove her crazy. She slid her right hand down, unbuckled his pants and released him. And then she made love to him. He lifted his head to look down at her. Their eyes met as she noisily pleased him. He watched her, smiling and licking and wetting his lips in a way that encouraged her, and made her hot.

"Yesssssss," he moaned as he laid his head back against the chair. He buried his hand in her thick hair. "Oh, babeeeee," he moaned, grabbing handfuls of her hair and releasing again as his pleasure mounted. She worked him and worked him, giving her all in an effort to make his pain go away.

"Oh baby. That's nice baby."

Just when she thought he would explode, he pulled her head up. He kissed her, then used his foot to push the footstool to the side.

She moved from her knees to a sitting position on the floor. He pushed her back gently, positioned himself between her legs and lavished her inner thighs with kisses. He moved up to kiss her face and eyes, her neck and ears. He concentrated on her mouth, taking ownership of her tongue again. He slid his right hand between her legs, crooked his forefinger and rubbed it up and down her through her panties. She swiveled her hips slowly and pushed herself against his finger, her wetness soaking through the fabric.

"Jamey," she panted, nipping at his ear. "Babeee, take care of me."

He rose to his knees, slid his hands under her and pulled at her panties. She lifted her hips so he could pull them down, and over her feet. He quickly slid out of his pants. He disappeared between her legs to taste her, and stayed there.

She moaned and grabbed his head. "Oh baby. Babeeee."

He moved back up so that he could look into her eyes as he slid into her.

"This is mine," he said in a raspy voice.

She gripped his butt cheeks tightly with both hands, lifted her knees and wrapped her legs around him.

"Yes baby."

"Say it!" he demanded.

"It's yours. Baby it's yours. Yes baby, yes baby, it's yours!" she gasped.

CHAPTER 23 - JAMEY

Jamey stepped through the doorway of his house, deactivated the alarm, and stood stark still, listening. Gun in hand, his eyes scanned the room slowly, searching for anything out of place. He squatted, scanning the floor for shoeprints, or anything that might have fallen from the bottom of an intruder's shoe. He stayed in that position, listening, for several more minutes. He rose and slowly made his way through the house, paying special attention to the windows and doors. His cell phone rang. He finished his visual sweep of the house before answering.

"What did you forget?" he asked, the smile evident in his voice as he entered his bedroom.

"To kill you."

He paused.

"You didn't forget, Mel, you just screwed it up."

"I was sorry to hear about your mother, J. She was a good woman."

"Needless to say, it didn't make her real happy that you tried to kill her baby boy. How did you hear about my mother?"

Baptiste hesitated. "I read it in the paper, online."

Jamey looked slowly around the bedroom again. Seeing nothing out of place, he headed toward the kitchen.

"Who forgot to tell you something, Jamey? Who did you think it was on the phone?"

"My brother," Jamey said, not daring to tell Baptiste that he thought it was Toni calling.

"Tank? How's old Tank doing these days? Still married to that sweet piece of . . .?"

"What do you want *now*, Mel? To what do I owe the pleasure of this call?" Jamey asked, taking a seat on a stool at the kitchen counter.

"I've been thinking about life. I guess death does that to us, makes us think about life, you know? And I've been thinking that we, you and I, should just bury the hatchet. Just let bygones be bygones. We can both get on with our lives."

"How can I do that, Mel? How can I forget that you killed my best friend? And Winston Frankland and Kate Marshall, and a plane load of innocent people? And you *tried* to kill me!"

"I feel bad about those people, Jamey, I really do. But as I remember, the final report listed the cause of that explosion as mechanical failure. Tip, well, that was about human failure—his failure to keep his nose out of my business. And besides, I didn't actually kill him."

"Oh, that's right, you just set him up to be killed. You didn't actually pull the trigger, no, but you might as well have." He grabbed a notepad and pen from the corner of the counter and made a note.

"He got what he deserved, J."

Jamey rotated his neck. *Just stay calm. He's baiting you.*

"Mechanical failure, huh? Mel, weren't you an aircraft mechanic in the service?"

"Man, you keep a file on me or what?" Mel asked, laughing.

"Yes. As a matter of fact, I do."

"Then you know that's what I did, don't you?"

Jamey grabbed a bottle of water from the refrigerator, opened it, and took a long swallow.

"You know, J, I have this theory about wars. Wars are never really about territory, religion, human rights, or even oil. You know what wars are really about?"

"No, Mel, what are wars *really* about, and what does your theory about wars have to do with anything?"

"You and I are at war, J. And wars are about egos, men's egos. Nobody wants to be the first one to back down, and consequently, needless blood is shed. So, I'm putting my ego aside and saying I give, I want to end the war between you and me. We agree I don't come after you, you don't come after me. What do you say, J?"

Jamey sat back down at the counter. "I say nice speech. Bullshit, but nice speech. What did you really call me for, Mel? I know that can't be it."

"You're still holding anger toward me after all this time? Your shoulders must be somewhere up near your eyeballs by now," Mel said, laughing.

"You're a funny man, Mel. Who told you about my mother? You still got moles in my department?"

"I told you I read it in the . . . online."

"You're lying. We purposely didn't put an announcement in the paper, or online," Jamey said, bluffing.

"I heard it somewhere."

Jamey made a note on the pad: Visit Stan, ask about Mel, mother's death. His mind drifted to Toni. He made a box in a corner of the pad and wrote the word picnic. He underlined it twice then wrote: brie, crackers, crab salad, grapes, wine.

"Be smart man, let it go," Mel continued.

"What?" *Stay focused Jamey*, Jamey admonished himself.

"I said let's let it go, Jamey. Just forget that you and I ever even knew one another."

"No can do."

"You don't want to play hardball with me, Jameyson. I could take the quick route and grab Toni to get to you."

Jamey didn't respond.

"You still there, J?"

"Yes, Mel," Jamey said, hoping Mel would pick up on the disinterest in his voice. "Still here, listening to you jerk-off."

"Speaking of which, you know, J, I'd know how to keep a woman like Toni happy. You apparently didn't have the balls, and obviously not enough bat, to keep her satisfied."

Jamey held the phone away from his ear as Mel laughed like a hyena.

"Keep it real, Mel. You and I both know that you can't get it up with a woman unless you beat her."

"Fuck you, Jamey. She liked me, you know it. She and I shared something. That girl is 360 degrees smart. Let me ask you a question, J, is she good in bed?"

Jamey massaged his shoulder and rotated his neck again. Between Mel, and a night of lovemaking on a cold, hard hotel room floor, he could feel his muscles getting tighter by the minute.

"I bet she's a tiger," Mel continued. "Girl that smart has gotta know how to keep her man smiling. Kept you whistling round the old station house. With a woman like that in my corner, I could conquer the world."

"World domination. That's your goal? Emperor Mel. No, doesn't quite have a ring to it, does it? Maybe you could be Mel the Great," he added, laughing.

"Or maybe I could blow your fuckin' brains out."

"Whenever you're ready, Your Highness. In the meantime, don't fool yourself. You wouldn't know what to do with a woman like Toni, even if you *could* pull a woman like that. Ego was Frankland's downfall, and it will be yours, too."

"You really think I give a damn what you think? I'm not Winston Frankland."

Jamey added an item under the word picnic on the notepad: extra gun.

"Did she come for your mother's services?"

"You didn't get a report from your mole?" Jamey asked, avoiding the question. "Let's take Toni out of the equation, okay?"

The phone beeped. It was Toni. He had forgotten to check-in when he got home. He let it go to voicemail.

"You know, Jamey, this really isn't personal. Things just went south when the commissioner fired me, and made you chief. That was my job. Then you figured out what was really going on."

"It's personal for me, Mel."

"You're really trying my patience, boy. Let me reiterate. I'm offering you an opportunity to get on with your life. Like I said before, you forget about me, I forget about you, or I come blow your fuckin' brains out. I got no beef with you, Jameyson."

Jamey added pineapple to the picnic list, and underlined it three times. He was only half listening to whatever it was that Mel was saying. His thoughts drifted to his mother. *She's gone*, he thought, sadness washing over him. *It's time. Gotta ratchet up the game, and set in motion my plan to lure him back to the island so I can end this, and get on with my life.*

"Speaking of beef, Mel," he said, "I'm working a cold case you might be able to help me with."

"Why the hell would I help you with anything?"

"The victim, Eduard Brinwyn, was brutally, and I emphasize *brutally* murdered in his home just about the time Tip and I joined the force. Brinwyn was the director of that orphanage near Lizette's Landing. You know the one I'm talking about?" He paused to let his words sink in. "Oh, wait, that's the one you were raised in, isn't it?"

"Leave it alone, Jameyson!"

"The guys that worked that case said it was the worst thing they'd ever seen. They kept saying they wondered what the victim had done to the perp to make him hate him so much."

He could hear Mel's breathing speed up.

"Brinwyn was accused of hurting the boys under his care at the orphanage—never charged, though. What a sick, sadistic . . . you know what's really strange to me, Mel? That you'd grow up to be just like him, a person who destroys other people. That's what he did to you, Mel, he destroyed any trace of anything you had that was remotely human."

"Fuck you, Jamey," Mel yelled into the phone.

"Not going to happen," Jamey said calmly. "Funny thing about that case, though. All the evidence seemed to just disappear."

"You think I did that? Come on now, you can do better than that."

"The killer assaulted Brinwyn, then assaulted him with a bottle. When he was done, the bottle still up the guy, the killer stumped that bottle again and again until it was shattered and coming out the guy's belly. Were you getting off when you were doing that, Mel?"

"You got a death wish, don't you boy?"

"How did it feel to hurt him? Did it feel good? Did you enjoy being in him? Did it feel good?" Jamey asked, rapid-fire.

"I tried," Mel said. "All I wanted was to end this on friendly terms, and let bygones be bygones. But I see now that that's not going to happen, is it?"

"One of the evidence technicians working the case was a newlywed. He was so eager to get home to his lovely bride that he decided to put the evidence he'd collected in his trunk overnight, rather than going straight back to the station. Women can really distract you," he added, laughing. "Anyway, the next morning, his bride switched cars on him, and went to work. She put all his stuff, including his evidence kit in the other car, but overlooked the bag of evidence from the Brinwyn case. And he totally forgot about it. Turns out that all the evidence didn't disappear. It was just misplaced."

He waited, listening as Mel's breathing began to speed up again.

"Are you taking all this in, Mel? Weeks later," he added, laughing, "he's cleaning out the trunk, and he comes across the bag. He felt so guilty, and was so scared that he'd lose his job, and not be able to support his little cutie, that he put the bag in his attic. When the guy got ready to retire, he wanted to go out with a clean conscience, so he brought the bag to me. In that bag were swabs taken from Brinwyn's various orifices, including a swab with the killer's semen on it." He paused to let what he'd said sink in. *I can almost hear the wheels turning in your head, Mel.* "Can you say DNA boys and girls?" he continued.

"When you retire, you should write fiction," Mel said after a long silence. "You're good at it. Un-fortunately, you're not going to live that long."

"Am I making it up, Mel?"

Mel laughed halfheartedly.

"Based on what I've learned about you, the way you get your rocks off, and the fact that you grew up in that orphanage, I started to wonder if you might be involved. *You* led that investigation."

"Even if that shit you're talking were true, you'd need a DNA sample from me to prove anything. Maybe I'll bring you one— when I come to kill you."

"Thanks, Mel. I appreciate the gesture, but I won't be needing it. I have a sample of your DNA."

"I don't have time for this crap," Mel said.

"Then why haven't you hung up the phone? Want to know where I got it?"

"Okay. I'll humor you. Where did you get it?"

"From your apartment. We went through that apartment with a fine-tooth comb. The guys kept saying your place was so clean that it didn't look lived in. That's when I began to realize just how insidious you truly are. You *didn't* live in that apartment. You only slept there on an old mattress in the corner. The reason your clothes always looked like you picked them up off the floor and put them on, was because you did. Besides that ratty old mattress, there was nothing that would even suggest that a human being ever even lived there."

Jamey took a big swig of water.

"You showered and shaved at the station, or not at all. That way your hairs mixed with the hairs of 55 other guys. You left as little of you behind as humanly possible." He stretched, and looked at his watch. "Even the way you cleaned out your office was out of character. It didn't fit the profile of the slob we'd all come to know and hate. You weren't cleaning it for the next guy, you were wiping away traces of the last guy—*you*."

Mel laughed.

"You find that funny, huh? Well, you know me, Mel, not one to give up. I went back through that apartment again. Still didn't find anything, so I took that mattress to the evidence room and went over it nano-inch by nano-inch. I found three little hairs imbedded between the end of the mattress and the piping, you know that seam where it's sewn together."

"I know what piping is, you stupid fuck."

"Caught you slippin', Mel," Jamey said in a singsong voice. "Caught you slippin'," he sang again, dragging out the word slipping to irritate Mel. "At some point, you made the mistake of sitting your big hairy naked ass on that mattress. Or maybe you left the hairs there when you were making love to the mattress."

"You're good at spinning a tale, J," Mel said. "I'll give you that."

"DNA from those hairs matched the DNA on the swabs taken from Brinwyn's body. Let's put this together, *shall we?* Follow along now, Mel. Abusive director of an orphanage gets murdered. DNA found on the victim matches DNA from one of his wards, who just happened to be the lead investigator on the case. *Coincidence?* I think not."

"I am really going to enjoy fucking you up, Jamey."

"You know where I am," Jamey responded, laughing as he pushed the button to disconnect the call. He hit the button to return Toni's call, and headed to the hall closet.

He bought the lie about the DNA evidence. He's scared. It won't be long before he comes for me, and this will all be over, he thought, holding the phone between his ear and shoulder as he pulled a picnic basket from the top shelf of the closet.

CHAPTER 24 - MEL

"You son-of-a-bitch," Mel yelled as he slammed the phone into the wall on the opposite side of the room.

Phone conversations with Jamey always left him wanting blood. He rose from his chair and kicked the coffee table as hard as he could. The intricate metal frame, pieces of glass, a Baccarat chess set, coffee table books and magazines flew every which way. He snatched books, including some rare first editions, from bookshelves and threw them across the room. He slammed a Lalique vase into the wall.

I'm going to make you suffer like you can't even imagine. Brinwyn got what he deserved, sick dog. But what I did to him is nothing compared to what I'm going to do to you, Jamey. I'm coming for you boy, and when I do . . .

He stumbled back to sit in the big leather office chair and closed his eyes. He felt the first stirrings in his groin. Like clockwork, anger triggered the urges. He ignored them, choosing instead to focus on what Jamey had said about the Brinwyn case.

A good cop can bluff with the best of them, and he is a damn good cop. He knows an awful lot about that case. Too much. Without any of my boys left on the inside it's hard to find out when he's telling the truth, and when he's bluffing. Stan is useless now. What a waste. When I finish with Jamey, I'm going to put Stan out of his fuckin' misery, too. I should have done it after I took care of Tip. Another misstep.

He went to the bar, poured himself a double shot of cognac, and finished it off in one tip of the glass. He didn't want to think about Jamey or Stan, and especially not Brinwyn. Even now, it was painful to remember life in that orphanage. When he allowed himself to think about it, really think about it, he always ended up depressed almost to the point of being non-functional. The urge was growing stronger. He poured himself another cognac, sipping it as he looked around the room. He congratulated himself on how well he had done despite his horrible beginnings, and how good his life was since he left San Saypaz'. Although his enterprise had come crashing down unexpectedly following the Marie Doe murder, the drugs, girls, gambling and other operations he ran on San Saypaz' had paid off handsomely.

His homestead on the island of Quattroportay was a walled compound on a secluded expanse of white sand beach, just steps from the ocean. His property included the main house, a large Mediterranean-style mansion, a guesthouse, an infinity pool, a spa, an outdoor kitchen and fire pit, a cabana, tennis and basketball courts, a climate-controlled wine room, and a multi-car garage. He had a penchant for Scandinavian-design furniture, fine crystal, abstract and contemporary art, unique pottery and sculptures, and rare books. He was a voracious reader, and loved architecture, and architecture magazines.

He surrounded himself with beautiful things, like the things in the pages he tore from magazines and stuffed under his mattress when he lived in the orphanage. In line with his rampant paranoia, the property also had an elaborate security system, with a slew of hidden features. He went to the bookshelf, reached under one of the lower shelves, and pushed a button. The bookshelf slid away to reveal a steel door. He pushed the light switch panel next to the door, then punched a series of numbers into a keypad hidden underneath. The door slid open. He stepped inside the beautifully decorated bedroom, looked around and smiled.

Toni will like it here. She'll appreciate that I created this for her, he thought as he smoothed the crease-free bedspread.

He opened the door of a closet that was as large as the bedroom. The right side and back walls were lined with rows of shoes and purses. The left wall was lined with beautiful dresses, from sundresses to formal dresses. Everything was grouped by color. Mel ran his hand along the dresses, stopping to gather a strapless sundress in his arms. He hugged it to his body. He opened a drawer and pulled out a pair of panties. He closed his eyes as he slid the silky fabric back and forth between his fingers before painstakingly folding, and returning the panties to the drawer.

She'll love this room, and these beautiful clothes. These are things that a woman like Toni should have, things that a man like Jameyson Tolliver can't give her.

The urge was too strong to ignore. It was time to tend to "the beast." He closed the steel door and pushed the button to slide the bookshelf back into place. He sat down at the desk, opened the top drawer and pulled out the silver-framed picture of him and Toni taken at the press conference announcing his "retirement." He stared at her face. He took a deep breath and imagined she was there with him. He touched himself through his pants.

Fuck what Jamey thinks! I could please a woman like Toni. I could make her happy.

He leaned back in his chair and imagined Toni sitting on his lap, her head close to his. He rubbed himself. He imagined for the umpteenth time that he was telling her about Brinwyn, and the horrible things he had done to him and the other boys. How he had been made to scream in the dark, and how no one came to rescue him. She would look deep into his eyes as he explained. He could make her understand. In his fantasies, she always understood. He adjusted his position. He ran his finger along the glass of the picture frame, down the length of her body. He imagined explaining how he had had to look out for himself, because until she came into his life, he had been alone in the world. She would listen intently, with love and empathy in her eyes, and she would understand.

She'll understand that I did what I had to do. And once she sees the world I've created for her, she'll forgive me for Tip and Frankland, and especially Kate.

He closed his eyes, unzipped his pants and unleashed the beast. *Toni would understand,* he thought as he manipulated himself. He imagined her planting little kisses on his face, and darting her tongue in and out of his ear. He mumbled to himself. He imagined Toni whispering nasty encouragement to him, whispering that she wanted him inside her as he slipped his hand under her dress. She would only wear dresses, those beautiful designer dresses in the closet, and high heels, when she came to live with him. And she would always beg him to make it rough, so painful that it would make her cry out.

Toni understands that pain is the pleasure.

He gripped himself tighter as he imagined standing her up, rubbing his hand between her legs and grabbing handfuls of her plump ass, squeezing until it hurt. He would call her names, debase her. She would laugh, and beg him to hurt her. He would tear her panties off. She would grab them from him and drag them across his face, stopping under his nose so he could smell them. He would inhale deeply. Then, she would plop them on his head to make a panty hat for him. He would laugh, grab her ass again, and squeeze hard until she cried out in pain. She would enjoy it because she understood that the pain is the pleasure.

Toni will understand. And she will love me.

He pumped the beast so hard it hurt. He imagined turning her around roughly, pushing her down over the desk and spanking her as hard as he could—so hard that he'd work up a sweat. She would moan, cry out in pain, and hump and grind herself against the desk because she knew it made him happy. He would stop spanking her, grab her by the waist, and slam the beast into her from behind, again and again, harder and harder. She would beg for it, the sound of skin slapping against skin as he rammed himself into her. She would egg him on, breathlessly begging him to hurt her because she understood the pleasure, and the pain.

My Toni, my Toni, he moaned, pumping himself faster and faster, harder and harder. The more it hurt, the harder he gripped and pumped. The pain was excruciating. The pleasure was mind-numbing. He let out a howl. He imagined slamming himself into her, again and again, her screaming his name, begging him to hurt her, begging him not to stop. A sound from the doorway startled him back to reality. He opened his eyes in time to see his housemate, Rayshell, backing away.

"How dare you spy on me," Mel yelled, pushing himself out of the chair, purposely leaving himself hanging out.

Rayshell looked into the pools of black nothingness that were Mel's eyes.

"How long have you been spying on me?" Mel screamed, growing angrier as he realized that Rayshell had likely overheard the conversation with Jamey. "How long, damn you?"

Rayshell started to speak. Mel slapped the words away. It was useless to try to explain, suicidal to try to fight back. With brute force Mel tore off Rayshell's silk top. Rayshell stumbled backwards.

"Look at you," Mel screamed. "I take good care of you. Dress you well. Feed you well. And you don't have the decency to appreciate it. You ungrateful bitch," Mel said, slapping Rayshell repeatedly. Mel dragged Rayshell to the bedroom, hitting the light switch as they entered.

"Strip," Mel ordered as he unhooked his belt, and yanked it loose from its loops. He threw Rayshell face down onto the bed. "When will you learn to respect me," Mel screamed as the belt rose and fell across Rayshell's bare buttocks again and again. "When will you learn to appreciate all that I do for you?"

Mel's voice grew guttural, his breathing labored. Sweat pouring down his face, insanity in his eyes, he switched off the light. The rustle of fabric could be heard as Mel snatched off his shirt and stepped out of his pants. Rayshell didn't make a sound as Mel pleasured the beast. Between horrific, animal-like growls, a single word escaped Mel's lips: "Toni."

CHAPTER 25 - RAYSHELL

Rayshell eased into the garden tub filled with a mixture of warm water, and an aloe concoction Mel's doctor had left for Rayshell after a previous beating.

"It promotes rapid healing and lessens scaring," the doctor, who Mel paid handsomely for home visits, and discretion, had advised.

But will it heal my soul, Rayshell wondered, shifting in an attempt to find a comfortable position.

Things had started well between Mel and Rayshell. Rayshell was almost twenty-four when Mel chose Rayshell over all the others tricking on the row that first night. Even a casual observer could see why Mel would pick the young, fresh and attractive Rayshell over all the others. Rayshell was born on the island of Quattroportay, and before meeting Mel, had never been off the island. Being with Mel meant having a place to call home, after what seemed like a lifetime of scratching out a living on the streets.

I was dumb enough to believe that good fortune had finally come calling, Rayshell thought, adding more of the aloe mixture to the water.

At first the relationship wasn't physical. It was more like teacher and student, with Mel schooling Rayshell about the finer things in life. Rayshell learned to cook gourmet meals, and how to pair food and wine. Rayshell enjoyed cooking for Mel, and after dinner some evenings, they'd take long walks on the beach, or a drive in one of Mel's beautiful cars. People stared at them as if they were movie stars when they passed. Mel taught Rayshell to drive on a road near the compound, and sometimes let Rayshell run errands alone to the grocery store, the post office, or the liquor store to replenish Mel's stash of specially imported cognac. It was during those errands that Rayshell heard the talk. People Rayshell had grown up with, some of them still working the row, started to say things, horrible things about Mel. They called him "la bestia," or the beast.

Jealousy, pure and simple, Rayshell reasoned, at first. Rayshell thought that they were just haters, jealous of Mel's wealth, and good looks, his beautiful cars, fine clothes, and ability to move like a tourist, dropping hundreds of dollars on meals, fine wines, cognac, and cigars in one sitting. Rayshell had found a home, while they still had to scrape by turning tricks on the streets of Quattroportay.

Rayshell shifted in the tub again.

How could they think badly of Mel, Rayshell had wondered? *Mel, who is so good and kind to me. Mel, who with sadness in his eyes, shares stories of how the people who came to the orphanage never looked his way, never made eye contact because they all wanted babies and small children. And how year after year, he languished in that orphanage, losing a little more hope each year, until all hope was gone. How could they possibly think badly of Mel?*

The Mel Rayshell had come to know wasn't real. Dressed to the nines one balmy evening, they went out to dinner to celebrate Mel's birthday. Mel ordered two bottles of a different type of wine—a sweet and intoxicating nectar that Rayshell would later learn was champagne. By the end of the evening, Rayshell was drunk, and had to be helped to the car. Back at home, Mel helped Rayshell into the house, up the stairs, and into bed. And then Mel helped himself to Rayshell.

The champagne clouded Rayshell's thoughts. *Why are you taking off your clothes here?* It was Rayshell's first encounter with the beast. It was brutal, painful, and life-altering. Afterward, Mel went about his days as if nothing had happened, inviting himself into Rayshell's bed whenever he felt the need. If the brutality of the act wasn't enough, after that first time it was almost always partnered with a beating—Mel's idea of foreplay. And Mel became very restrictive. Rayshell was still allowed to run errands alone, but that little freedom was always accompanied by the threat of what would happen if Rayshell didn't return, or told anyone what went on at the compound.

"Remember, we're family, Rayshell," Mel would often say.

Rayshell realized the stories were true. On those nights Mel said he wanted to be alone, was going for a ride, or to the movies, he was going to the row. Only the most desperate of the workers would climb into his car. He was a predator, and a sadist. He paid well, but after an encounter with la bestia, one could be out of commission for days, weeks, or forever. In a vain attempt to protect themselves, the workers developed a special whistle to signal one another when Mel came cruising. They had a rule that they would create a commotion before getting into his car, to make it appear that they thought they were special to have been chosen. It was their way of trying to ensure that there would be witnesses if they didn't return. It was all for naught. Some of them were never seen again. And soon, it was as if they had never existed.

Rayshell gingerly reached for the tap to turn on the water to warm up the bath.

All the witnesses in the world wouldn't mean a thing because you're a man of means, Mel, and they're just street hustlers that no one cares about. You can tell yourself you're not brutal and heartless like the man at the orphanage, but you are an animal just as he was. It is only a matter of time before the man from San Saypaz' destroys you. And I will help him.

Recently, Mel had stopped cruising, and often seemed troubled and restless. Rayshell wondered if it had anything to do with the man from San Saypaz', the man Mel hated. Rayshell adjusted the bath pillow, remembering the day that the man from San Saypaz' scaled the wall and came into the house. Rayshell had listened as "Mr. Jamey" detailed the horrible things Mel had done to people on San Saypaz', how he had murdered people and blew up an airplane. Rayshell had cried, and then apologized, explaining that the tears were tears of joy when Mr. Jamey said that he was going to make sure that Mel couldn't hurt anyone anymore.

"Please tell me about the woman named Toni," Rayshell had asked Jamey. "Mel stares at her picture, and calls out her name in the night . . . when he is doing things to me," Rayshell added, ashamed. *Mr. Jamey sure got mad then,* Rayshell thought, remembering how Jamey's body had stiffened.

Rayshell relaxed and smiled, soothed by the recurring fantasy of killing Mel. But it was just a fantasy, a failed attempt would mean certain death for Rayshell.

But Mr. Jamey will come back one day, and he will destroy you. And I will cheer. I hate you, Mel. Rayshell started to recite the litany of reasons for hating Mel. *I hate you for the damage you've done to my mind, and to my body and my soul. I hate you because you are evil, and because you hurt others. I hate you for the name.* "You are a ray of sunshine, as precious as a shell that glistens on the shore. I am going to call you Ray-shell," *you said to me the day you brought me to live with you.*

Rayshell released the stopper, climbed slowly out of the bathtub, and stood in front of the mirror staring at old scars, belt-buckle shaped welts and fresh wounds.

I hate you most of all for pretending in the dark that I am the woman named Toni.

He moved his face closer to the mirror, rubbing the stubble on his cheek with the back of his hand. He opened the medicine cabinet, took out his razor and closed the door. He stared at his reflection in the mirror.

Damn you to hell, Mel, my name is Rayf, not Rayshell! And no matter how much you beat me, or pretend otherwise . . . I AM A MAN!

CHAPTER 26 - TONI

Toni walked slowly through Jamey's house. He had changed some of the furnishings, but overall the place looked the same. Her favorite things, the red chaise and the wind chimes were still there, although some of the worn wind chimes had been replaced. In the distance, she could hear Jamey reciting numbers into the phone.

"Thank you," he said, hanging up the phone as she walked back into the room.

"We're set. Your return flight has been changed, my dear."

Toni walked over and threw her arms around him. "Thank you. Now, what are we doing for dinner? Sunset picnic in a secluded location? I think that's what you promised me yesterday."

"No, I think you came up with that," he said, heading into the kitchen.

She followed him into the kitchen. He transferred food and drinks from the refrigerator to a picnic basket on the counter.

"Picnic, picnic, picnic," she said, clapping her hands double time. She stopped when his land line rang.

Jamey walked over, looked at the caller I.D., and quickly turned off the answering machine. He picked up the receiver, then put it back down.

"What's that all about?"

"About nothing." The phone rang again almost immediately. He ignored it.

"Who's on the phone, Jamey? Somebody obviously wants to talk to you pretty badly. Why'd you turn off the answering machine? Is there something we need to discuss?"

"I'll tell you later," he said, rearranging stuff in the basket.

"Tell me now, I've got time."

"I'll tell you later. It's complicated," he said.

"I . . ."

"Trust me," he interrupted. "Please."

***

"You can always be counted on to find the most beautiful spots," she said when they arrived at a little grotto-like area. It was around a slight bend three-quarters of a mile down the beach. It was wide but shallow, and provided some privacy.

Jamey sat the picnic basket down, stepped back outside the enclosure and looked around. Backing in again, he reached into the small of his back and pulled out a small gun. Squatting down to look at her the way he used to when he was deadly serious, he nodded his head toward the gun.

"This is your new best friend. I don't expect anything to jump off, but, any hint of trouble, any sign of him, and you start firing. Shoot first, ask questions later reporter person. Got it?"

"*Him*? You mean Mel?"

He nodded. "We'll put this here," he said, placing it behind a rock. "You sit here." He motioned for her to scoot over so that the gun was within reach.

"What about that one?" she asked, pointing to his ankle. "If he shows up, won't that be the first place he'll look?"

"Yep," he said, with a wink. "It buys you time. Don't hesitate baby."

"I won't," she said with full conviction."

Jamey spread the cloth that would serve as their table, and placed items from the basket onto it. She reached in and grabbed the plates, glasses and flatware.

"Who was on the phone earlier, Jamey? Was that him?"

He opened the wine and filled the glasses. "I haven't been completely forthcoming with you about something," he said, recorking the wine. He sat down next to her. "I didn't lie, I just didn't tell you everything."

She waited.

"When you asked me if I ever hear from Mel, I said once in a while." He sat his glass down. "He calls me a lot, threatening me, trying to mess with my head, playing this cat-and-mouse game. He gets a kick out of it. He called this morning, and that was him on the phone this afternoon."

"Oh my God, Jamey. But how do you know it was him on the phone this afternoon? The caller I.D. box said unavailable?"

He laughed. "You checked, huh?"

She tilted her head and widened her eyes.

"How can you be so sure he's not here, on the island, watching, waiting for the right time to ambush you?"

"He's not here, baby, I promise you that he is not here. Unless he jumps off a boat miles offshore, and swims to an uninhabited corner of the island, he can't, and doesn't set foot on this island without me knowing it."

She sighed.

"Why do you live like this? If you know where he is, why don't you just go and arrest him?"

"The island he lives on is not a U.S. territory. We have no jurisdiction, and no extradition treaty. And besides, I don't have concrete proof that he had anything to do with those murders, or blowing up that plane. And what I have on the murder of the guy that ran that orphanage is circumstantial, at best."

"What about Stan? You keep saying you think Stan was involved in setting Tip up. Couldn't you make him testify against Mel? Wouldn't that be enough to make a case against him? He practically admitted to me, that day at the airport, that he had Tip killed."

"Stan definitely knows what happened, but he's terrified of Mel. He wouldn't testify, and even if he did, it's the word of a cop who helped set up his partner, against the word of the former deputy chief of police. He'd be a poor witness. I'm not a shrink, but I'm pretty sure Stan's mind is addled. He'd come off to a jury as a crazy, broken old man. Even though Mel was pushed out, he left the force with a clean jacket, not a blemish on his record. He might be insane, but he's a genius when it comes to covering his tracks. Despite what he told you, we can't even prove that he was at the airport that day."

She took a sip of her wine. "Ummmm. Good wine."

"Ever known me to serve *not* good wine?"

She laughed. He refilled her glass then leaned over to give her a quick kiss.

"Stan told me once that he wishes he had the guts to take himself out. He said he can't imagine where he'll go when he dies, because he lives in hell. He's reaping what he sowed. He knew it was an ambush, and he sent Tip in anyway. Then, he killed the guy that killed Tip. The guy Mel paid to kill Tip."

"You said you think Mel seduced Stan, then blackmailed him to get him to go along with the plan."

He nodded.

"It doesn't matter how Mel got him to do it, if Stan went along with it, he's as guilty as Mel is. He should pay, too," she said.

"Stan *is* paying. He's rotting away from the inside out. Unlike Mel, he has a conscience."

"He knows that you know what he did to Tip. Aren't you afraid that one day he might try to do something to you?"

"Stan is as harmless as a church mouse."

"Ever heard of the mouse that roared?"

He laughed. "Stan isn't innocent, by no means, but he's not the problem. I've learned so much about Mel, I could write a book about him. When the pieces first started to fall into place, I went and talked to people on the streets. They all knew Mel. He used to pick up prostitutes—male, female, it didn't matter. He beat them, and used them, then dared them to report him. He beat some of them pretty bad. One woman said she looked into his face when he was beating her. It was like he had turned into an animal, snarling and smiling this horrible smile. That's how he gets his rocks off."

"For goodness' sake, Jamey, this a small island. How come we didn't know this? How come no one ever reported it?"

"Report it to *who*? Law enforcement? People were terrified of him—he *was* the law."

"That's what Tip said, that he thought people knew something about the Marie Doe case, but were scared to come forward, scared of law enforcement."

"Can you blame them? The chief of police was best buddies with a homicidal drug dealer, the deputy chief of police was preying on prostitutes, and vice and patrol cops were taking bribes, shaking people down, and protecting the drug dealer."

Toni finished her wine, and studied the ocean. The sun had started its descent. "Enough about them," she said, rising to her feet. "I need to stretch my legs."

Jamey scooted over to sit in the spot where she had been sitting, near the second gun.

She had forgotten how much she loved the beach. She dug her foot into the sand until she got to the cool place. She looked back at him, walked over to the edge of the sand, and waited for the waves to roll in. She tensed herself, anticipating cold, but the water was surprisingly warm. She dipped her finger in the water and touched her finger to her tongue. She did it again. The natives believed that seawater had protective and medicinal powers. She didn't necessarily believe it, but always made it a point to taste the sea when she was near it. It couldn't hurt. Behind her, she heard Jamey laughing. She turned to look at him.

"What ya laughin' at, son?"

"The sea will protect you, the sea will heal you," he said, imitating an old woman's shaky voice.

She motioned him over with a little wiggle of her finger. He jumped up, looked around, walked over and stood in front of her with his hands behind his back.

She squatted, cupped her hand and let the water run into it.

"Open up."

"Silly superstition."

"Indulge me, *lover*," she said, seductively.

He opened his mouth. She dipped a finger into the seawater, then let the water drip onto his tongue.

"Repeat after me: "The sea will protect me."

"The sea will protect me," he said in a silly voice.

"Please, Jamey."

He looked into her eyes.

"The sea will protect me," she said again, dripping the saltwater onto his outstretched tongue.

"The sea will protect me," he repeated, serious this time.

She dipped her finger in again. "The sea will heal me."

"And the sea will heal me."

"Jamey, look at me," she said, searching his eyes. "Do not, *do not*, underestimate Stan. Promise me!"

He lifted her hand to his mouth and dipped his tongue into the drops of seawater that remained. He pulled her to him and kissed her, sliding his tongue into her mouth for a kiss that was both salty and sweet. He wrapped his arm tightly around her, and cupped the back of her head in his hand, their cheeks resting against one another.

"The sea will protect and heal us both," he whispered.

CHAPTER 27 - RAYSHELL

Rayshell wheeled the Range Rover out of the garage, parked near the front door, turned the engine off and waited. It would be twenty or thirty minutes before Mel emerged from the house. He liked to take long hot showers and sit in the sauna after his morning workout, which included a five-mile run, and a one-mile swim.

If I'm not ready when he is, he goes off, but it's okay for me to waste precious time of my life waiting for him, Rayshell thought, drumming his fingers on the steering wheel.

Twenty-five minutes later, Mel emerged from the house and climbed into the passenger seat. "Let's go."

They drove to the airport in silence, with Rayshell shifting positions periodically. It had been weeks since the last beating, but his butt cheeks were still sore.

"Be still, you're making me nervous," Mel ordered.

As was their routine, Rayshell parked curbside, near the luggage/ticketing area of the airline Mel was flying, so Mel could unload his luggage.

"Rayshell, look at me," Mel demanded. "Don't do anything stupid while I'm gone. And don't try to run away again. I will find you. You know that, don't you?"

"Yes, Mel."

"And when I do, I'll gut you like a pig," he said, flashing a sinister smile. "Be good," he added, climbing out of the pearl white vehicle.

"I won't run away again, Mel," he said, remembering the beating he took the time he tried to leave.

Mel tapped twice on the back of the vehicle to let Rayshell know he was done unloading. Rayshell merged into the airport traffic. He circled the airport once, driving slowly past the spot where he had dropped Mel off. He drove into the short-term parking garage, pulled a ticket and threw it away as soon as he reached the cover of the parking deck. He would do the same with the receipt.

I'd rather pay the full-day rate than risk accidentally leaving the ticket in the car for Mel to find.

When he reached the top level of the garage, he backed into a corner spot. He turned the engine off, trained his eyes on a green waste container fifteen-feet in front of him, and waited.

I wonder what Mel is up to now. He's been nastier than usual. Wonder why Mr. Jamey isn't taking his calls anymore. Ever since that last call, Mr. Jamey won't talk to Mel. I hope Mr. Jamey is alright. If anything has happened to him, I'll never be able to escape Mel. But if Mr. Jamey is the one who's making Mel so crazy, and it's Mr. Jamey that he's so mad at and wants to kill, why is he going to where the woman named Toni lives? Rayshell looked at his watch, a gift from Mel. *Won't be much longer now.*

One hour and forty-five minutes later, a man in gray workmen's coveralls with an airport logo appeared. He was holding a piece of green paper high above his head. Rayshell started the engine.

The man in the coveralls nodded subtly. Raising his other arm, he switched the green paper from one hand to the other, balled it up and tossed it into the green waste container.

Green means go! Rayshell pulled out of the parking space and headed for the exit. *The beast has flown.*

***

"Oh, hurry up," Rayshell said out loud, watching through the rearview mirror as the wrought-iron gates of the compound closed behind him. He parked the vehicle in front of the house and jumped out, making a mental note to wash it before Mel returned.

He bounded up the stairs, freed by the knowledge that he was home alone for the next several days. He was eager to make the call. He changed quickly, leaving his clothes in a pile on the floor. *Mel would have a hissy fit, but Mel isn't here, is he,* he thought, picking up the clothes and throwing them up in the air. *Don't forget the towel and the tape,* he reminded himself.

He ran along the beach at a steady pace, stopping periodically to run in place, just in case he was being followed. *Fat chance,* he thought. *In all the time I've lived here, I've never seen another soul besides Mel on this stretch of beach.* He stopped running and took a seat under a stand of trees as a precautionary measure. *Mr. Jamey told me never to take anything for granted.* He yawned and looked out at the ocean. He spotted a sailboat with blue sails on the horizon.

Blue sails? Who would have blue sails? That's too much like the color of the water, and the sky. If I had a boat, I'd have one with yellow sails, big bright yellow sails.

Twenty minutes later he stood up, walked further down the beach to another grouping of trees and looked up. The package was where he'd left it. He turned and looked out to sea. The sailboat was still there. He stared at it, and for a moment considered the possibility that someone on the boat was watching him. He quickly dismissed the thought.

They're too far out to sea. From out there I'd look like an ant crawling along the shore.

He took the roll of tape off his wrist and dropped it on the ground. He wrapped the towel around the tree, twisting one end of the towel first around one hand, then the other. Pulling his body tight against the tree, he used the towel and his feet to shimmy his small body monkey-like up the tree. Getting as close as possible, he reached with one hand and unwound the duct tape holding the package. Package in hand, he scooted carefully back down. He looked around slowly as he started to open the plastic package. He pulled out the cell phone and moved closer to the water. Holding the phone toward the west, he pressed two buttons. *Thank you, Jesus,* he thought as the signal bars flashed. The other party answered, but remained silent.

"Mr. Jamey?"

"Rayf?"

"Hi Mr. Jamey, it's me, Rayf."

"How are you, Rayf?" Jamey asked.

"I'm okay. He's on the move, Mr. Jamey."

"Is he headed this way, to San Saypaz'?"

"No. He's headed to her."

"*Her*? Who, Rayf?"

"The woman named Toni. He's going to where she lives. I dropped him at the airport this morning."

Jamey remained silent.

"Are you still there, Mr. Jamey?"

"Rayf, are you absolutely sure? Did you get confirmation that he boarded the plane? Did you wait for the signal?"

Rayf started to sit down in the sand, but decided against it, afraid of dropping the call. He looked out at the boat with the blue sails.

"Yes, Mr. Jamey. I waited for the man in gray to give me the sign to let me know that Mel's plane had taken off."

"You did good, Rayf. I have to go now. I'll put something extra in your account his month."

"Thank you, Mr. Jamey."

"We'll talk soon."

"Bye, Mr. Jamey, he said, not wanting to break his only real connection to the outside world. He returned the phone to its hiding place in the tree and climbed down. He searched the horizon for the boat with the blue sails. It was gone.

CHAPTER 28 - JAMEY

Jamey pushed the button to end the call, his shoulders tightening. He hit two buttons. A man answered on the first ring.

"What's up, J?"

"Porkpie, he's going for Toni. I can't leave the island right now. I need you to get to her ASAP."

"I'll catch the first flight out," the man on the other end said.

"No! He's got a head start, charter something—get there now! Take somebody with you, double tag him," Jamey said, pressing his back against the back of the chair.

"J, if he's there I can finish this real quick, and real quiet like. My treat."

"Not unless you have to. Just keep him away from her. If he gets within fifty feet of her, take him down. Don't hesitate. Call me as soon as you get there. Don't let anything happen to her Porkpie," Jamey pleaded, trying to keep his voice steady.

"I won't let you down, J."

Jamey laid the phone on his desk. He looked at his watch. *I should call her, but if I wake her up it'll make her suspicious. She'll hear it in my voice. No reason to worry her. Porkpie can handle it. God, please keep her safe.*

He pulled a small screwdriver from his desk drawer, walked over to the CD player and hit the button marked number one. The sounds of soft jazz filled the room. He unscrewed one of the hinge plates on the entertainment cabinet and pulled out a thumb drive. *Why now,* he wondered as he pushed the thumb drive into a port on the side of the computer. *Why is Mel going for her now, after all this time? Maybe because I stopped answering the phone when he calls. Maybe he found out we're back together, and that she came back to the island for my mother's funeral. Maybe that's what set him off. Oh, who the hell knows! I just need to keep her safe now that she's back home.*

He turned his attention to the computer screen, and shook his head. *This has gone on long enough.* He stared at the screen. The fuzzy words that were Mel Baptiste's life stared back. *I'm going to delete this file soon, real soon,* he thought, reaching for his reading glasses. *And when I'm done, I'm going to delete Mel Baptiste.*

CHAPTER 29 - TONI

"The usual, Toni? Toni?"

"Uh, yeah, Eddie," she said, her eyes scanning the room as she spoke.

She looked into the faces of people in line behind her, people seated at tables, and in armchairs around the coffee shop. She focused her attention on the door and the windows, people coming in, people passing, and people drinking their coffee al fresco. She recognized a few regulars, and a few faces from the neighborhood. No one seemed to be paying any special attention to her, but she couldn't shake the feeling that someone was watching her.

"Your Salted Carmel Frap, Toni."

"Thanks, Eddie," she said to the barista, handing him a bill and signaling him to keep the change.

"Thanks, Toni."

She stopped at a counter near the door to put a straw in her drink, and check her cell phone, again. She told herself that the feeling that someone was following her was just paranoia—a hangover of sorts from the five days she'd spent on San Sazpaz' with Jamey after his mother's funeral, and all the talk about Mel Baptiste.

But I've been back home almost three weeks, and this feeling just started the day before yesterday, she reasoned. She debated which phone to keep in her hand—the red not really red phone, or her regular cell phone. *Don't be silly girl. Knowing that Jamey's voice is just a touch of a button away is comforting, but his body is thousands of miles away on that island. If something jumps off, he can't come through that phone to save you.*

She put the red phone in her bag, stepped outside and looked both ways before starting the two-block walk to work. She thought about Jamey. She missed him like crazy. They talked three or four times a day, and for hours at night since she came back from the island. She hadn't told him that she thought she was being followed—she didn't want to worry him needlessly if she was just being paranoid.

He must sense something, though. He's been calling more frequently the last few days. Maybe it's something in my voice. He'd let me know if something was going on.

She took the elevator up to her floor, set her drink and cell phone on her desk, and sat down. She reached into her bag for the red phone. It rang just as she made contact with it—she jumped. She could hear Denise laughing behind her.

"Good morning, Denise. Go to the devil, Denise," she said over her shoulder.

"Good morning to you, too. You are really getting paranoid, Toni. Tell that man I said he needs to hurry up and get here."

"Burn, Denise," Toni said, holding up the middle finger of her left hand. She used her right hand to press the button to answer the call. She heard Denise walking away.

"Hey Jamey."

"Hey, baby. Everything okay?"

"Why are you asking me that?"

"It's just that you sounded tired when I spoke to you before you left your place this morning, that's all. I just thought I'd check back on you."

She paused. What he'd said didn't ring true, but she didn't want to make an issue of it now, at work. "I'm okay. Nothing that a good dose of you wouldn't cure," she said, trying to sound lighthearted. "You know I . . ."

Denise reappeared carrying two bagels in one hand, one with a bite taken out of it, and two bottles of water in the other. She laid a napkin on Toni's desk, put the unbitten bagel on the napkin, and then placed a bottle of water next to it.

"Thanks, Denise. Sorry about that, Jamey," she said.

"What were you about to tell me, baby, it sounded serious."

"It wasn't important. I was going to say I've been a little tired, but we can talk about it later. I'd better get going, Denise and I are going to a book launch event tonight."

"Okay. I love you."

"I love you, too, Jamey."

"Be safe."

"You too." She laid the phone down and took a deep breath.

"So why didn't you tell him? He'd want to know, Toni," Denise said, coming to stand by Toni's desk.

"There's nothing he can do from there but worry, Denise. And he has enough to worry about, trust me."

"You really should tell him that you think someone is following you. That's all I have to say. Even though I think you're just being paranoid."

"Denise, when you say, 'that's all I have to say', that's all you get to say."

Denise laughed. Denise was the first reporter Toni met when she started at the paper, months earlier, after a brief stint at the paper she hired on with when she left the island. She moved to this paper because it was in the Midwest. The location made it easier to travel back and forth to be with her mother, while her mother was fighting the cancer that ultimately won the battle. She had shared some of the Toni and Jamey saga, and some of the bad cop stuff with Denise, but not the darkest stuff, the stuff about Mel Baptiste.

Toni and Denise lived a couple of blocks from one another in a funky little artsy community, in lofts converted from warehouses. It was a trend that had taken hold in the Rust Belt—convert abandoned warehouses to lofts, add sidewalks, retail, restaurants, and green space for recreation, and voilà, a community is born. Within walking distance of Toni's loft were a good many of the things that made life worth living—a coffee bar, a bookstore, an upscale grocery store, a good deli, a liquor store with a wine bar, a park with walking trails, and a beautiful lake surrounded by Weeping Willow trees. For Toni, the only thing missing was Jamey. She took a bite of her bagel and looked over at Denise, who was texting.

"You really should get to work so we can get the heck out of here in time to get good seats at the book launch," Toni said, taking another bite of the still warm bagel, which was slathered with just the right amount of cream cheese. "You know, Denise, when it comes to cubicle mates, I could do a lot worse, but I'm not sure I could do much better."

"Toni, I think that's what they call a backhanded compliment, but I could be wrong. Just in case, thank you. I think."

***

Toni shivered. She gathered her shawl tighter around her shoulders. *I wish I had driven my car tonight,* she thought as they walked home after the book event.

"Let's take a cab," she said, turning to look at Denise.

"*A cab*? We're what, seven, eight minutes from home?"

"It's cold. I'll pay for it," Toni said.

Denise stopped and stared at Toni.

"Toni, girl, you have got to get a grip. Look around," she said, grabbing Toni's arm with one hand, making a sweeping motion with her other hand. "Seriously, look around."

Toni looked for a familiar face. She made eye contact with as many people passing by as possible, in the hope that someone's eyes would betray them.

"See anything?"

Toni looked at her. "No," she said, shaking her head, the uneasiness in her stomach growing.

"There's nothing to see. No one is following us."

Denise started walking. Toni reached into her bag, pulled out a ballpoint pen and clicked the button. She looked around again, then caught up with Denise.

"What are you doing?" Denise asked.

Toni didn't answer, staying focused instead on the people around her. She fought the urge to tell Denise to shut up. *You'll be home soon, just hang on,* she told herself.

Sensing Toni was only half paying attention, and trying to get her out of her head, Denise ramped up the chatter. The uneasiness in Toni's gut intensified, too.

Someone is following me!

Had she been able to focus on her instincts, she would have seen, or sensed him, maybe both, before he stepped out of the shadows.

"Hi, Toni. It's been awhile."

* * *

"Michael, what the *hell* are you doing here?"

"I saw you in the bookstore, Toni. I've been trying to catch up with you."

"You scared the crap out of me. What do you want? Why are you following me?" she yelled, clicking the ink pen nervously.

Every woman has a Michael in her past. Probably met him during a dating dry spell, wasn't really attracted to him, but dealt with him anyway because he was nice, smart, available, not bad looking, and gainfully employed. He was also dull, lousy in bed, and hard to get rid of. She'd met him shortly after moving to the city, and only dated him for a short time. He would never know how close he came to dying from ink pen to the eyeball when he stepped out of the shadows that night.

"Toni, calm down," Denise said.

"Shut up, Denise."

Denise took a step back, and was about to say something when a man wearing a hat interrupted.

"Are you alright, ma'am?" he asked in Toni's direction. "Is this man bothering you?"

Toni looked at him, and then at Denise, who shrugged her shoulders.

"I was passing by, overheard what was going on. I couldn't just ignore it. Seemed like you needed help."

He's lying. "Who are you?" Toni demanded.

"Like I said before, I was just passing by . . ."

"I *heard* what you said." She studied his face. There was something almost sympathetic in his eyes. Michael was saying something about meeting for coffee. Toni kept her eyes locked on the stranger.

"I think you need to move on, buddy," the stranger said, turning toward Michael so that Toni and Denise couldn't see his face. "Leave the lady alone."

"I'm sorry, Toni," Michael said, backing away. "I haven't been following you, I swear. I won't bother you again."

"Toni, let's just go," Denise said, pulling Toni by the arm.

Toni and Denise hurried away, looking back at the man in the hat frequently. He watched them, but didn't move.

***

Denise took the keys from Toni's shaking hand to unlock the door of Toni's apartment.

"I need to sit down," Toni said, throwing her messenger bag onto the couch.

"I need some alcohol," Denise said, heading for the kitchen.

Toni laid her cell phones on the coffee table. She plopped down in a chair just as Denise returned with a bottle of wine, and two glasses. She scooted to the edge of the chair to take the bottle from Denise, and just as she did, the phone rang. The bottle hit the hardwood floor, wine gushed out.

"Shit," Denise said, "I can't take much more."

"It's Jamey."

"Tell him I said his timing sucks." She sat the wine glasses on the coffee table. "I'll clean up this mess, and open another bottle of wine. My nerves won't be denied."

Toni took a breath and answered the phone.

"Hey, Jamey."

"Are you okay?"

"Why do you keep asking me that? Why *wouldn't* I be okay?"

He didn't say anything.

"Jamey? You know what happened tonight, *don't you*? What's going on, Jamey?"

"Are you okay?"

"You're talking to me, *aren't you*?"

Denise covered the spilled wine with paper towels, then went back to the kitchen.

"Calm down, Toni."

"*Calm down*? Jamey, do you *know* what I've been through tonight, and what I've been going through the past few days? *Do you*?"

"Take it down a notch, baby."

"*Excuse me?*

"I *said* take it down a notch, all of that attitude is uncalled for."

"*Uncalled for*? Jamey, I'm damn near positive that someone has been following me for the past few days. At first, I thought I was just being paranoid, but tonight I realized that it wasn't all in my head. And now I'm pretty sure that *you* know something about it."

Denise returned and filled the glasses. Toni emptied her glass in one tip. The warmth of the wine sliding down was like fuel.

"Who's following me Jamey?"

"Several people."

"*What?*" She realized she was yelling, and refilled her glass to try to calm herself. She took a big gulp.

"Mel is there, but I've got two guys following him to make sure he doesn't get to you."

"Mel is *here*?"

"Yes."

"Mel Baptiste is *here*?" She fell back in the chair. "How long have you known this?"

"Pretty much since he left Quattroportay."

Toni emptied her glass and held it in Denise's direction to signal Denise to refill it. She mouthed "Thank you."

"Slow down," Denise whispered.

"Jamey, you *knew* Mel was following me, and you didn't tell me?"

"I didn't want to worry you."

"You didn't want to worry me?" she repeated loudly.

"He's gone now."

"At least you *think* he's gone."

He didn't respond.

"The guy tonight, the guy in the hat. That was one of your guys?"

"Yeah. He works for me."

"So, he's been following me, too?"

"He and another man have been following Mel . . . who was following you. Believe me, you were never in any real danger. One of them had their sights on you, and Mel, the whole time," he said.

"Jamey, a man, who, thank goodness, wasn't Mel, walked right up on me tonight. If he wanted to harm me, he could have, and been gone by the time your guy got there. You should have told me what was going on."

"Maybe it wasn't the best call, Toni, but I was only trying to protect you. And I didn't want to alarm you."

"Not the best call? *Not the best call?*" she said, standing up. "You can never admit when you're wrong, can you? It was a bad call, Jamey—a *freakin' bad call, a really bad call!*" She could feel the wine taking hold. She sat back down. "When are you going to realize that keeping things from me usually doesn't work out well for either of us?"

"Why didn't you tell me you thought you were being followed? Huh? Maybe it's because you didn't want me to worry. I was trying to protect you, Toni, that's all."

"It's not the same, Jamey. I didn't want you to worry about something that I wasn't even sure was real. You *knew* that sociopath was following me around. It wasn't a perceived or imagined threat, it was a real threat, and you didn't tell me. *It's not the same!* If you were trying so hard to protect me, how come you didn't come yourself?"

She picked up the wine glass, then sat it back down.

"I have a job, Toni. And a responsibility to the people of this island, you know, the people who pay my salary. I wanted to come, and you know that if I could have, I would have. But I needed to be here. I sent not one, but two people to watch over you. The guy in the hat is former special ops, he's the best at what he does. *And you know what?* I'm not appreciating your attitude. I was trying to protect you. Maybe I didn't make the right call on this one, maybe I should have told you sooner, but my only intention was to protect you."

"And I don't appreciate you keeping this from me. This is not some game, Jamey. *This is my freakin' life.* If you and Mel want to play games, have at it, but count me out."

"Is that what you think I was doing, playing some game? I was trying to protect you."

"And by not telling me, you took away my ability to protect myself."

"What? What's that? Oh, thank you, Jamey, for trying to protect me. For sending not one, but two people to look out for me," he said.

"Oh, give me a break. I didn't ask you to."

"No, you didn't. I thought it was the right thing to do. Forgive me for trying to protect the woman I love. You a want break, Toni? Consider it broken. I'm done."

The phone went dead. "Hello . . . hello?" She stared at the phone.

"Did he hang up?" Denise asked.

"Yeah. You believe that?"

"Yes, considering you practically cursed him out."

Toni sat on the edge of the chair, reached for her glass then changed her mind. She was drinking on an empty stomach, and it was going straight to her head.

"He said he's done with me."

"Wow! So, someone really was following you?"

"Yeah. I think I might have gone too far with Jamey."

"Ya think?" Denise said, laughing. "He's not done with you, he's just mad at you, and at himself. He realizes in hindsight that he should have told you. You should have told one another."

"He was only trying to protect me. I went too far," Toni said as she started to cry.

"A crying-ass drunk? *Really, Toni*? No!"

Toni laughed. "I'm hungry."

"I'm hungry, too. What do you have to eat up in this joint?"

"Not a darn thing."

"Want to run out . . .?

"Are you crazy? I may never leave this loft again, *ever*."

"So, who was following you?"

Toni sat back. She pondered whether she should tell Denise about Mel.

"I need coffee, and I need to tell you something," she said, rising from her seat on wobbly legs. "Crap, I just remembered, I don't have any coffee, either." She sat back down. "Oh well, what I'm about to share with you is pretty sobering."

***

Toni refilled the glass with water, and took several rapid sips. She opened the refrigerator, shook her head, and closed the door. She drank the rest of the water, and put the glass in the sink. She looked at the clock on the stove: 5:45 a.m. She tiptoed to the center area of the loft, and looked at Denise sleeping on the couch. She looked at the front door, then at the almost floor-to-ceiling windows. Nothing seemed out of place.

It was only a dream, Toni. He wasn't really here, she reassured herself.

She'd dreamed that Mel Baptiste kidnapped her, and was holding her captive on his island. She was locked in a beautifully decorated room, and she could vaguely hear what she thought was the ocean. She could smell, and feel Mel's hot breath on her face as he described, in excruciating detail, all the twisted things he'd done to Jamey, before killing him. The dream was so real and vivid that she woke up screaming and disoriented.

Can you smell in a dream? If you can hear, have conversations, and see colors, it's possible that you can smell, she thought as she walked over to the door to check the locks again.

"What are you doing?" Denise asked, flipping the blanket back and pulling herself into a sitting position.

"Sorry I woke you. Just checking to make sure everything is still in the same place. The cans and the bells, I mean. That dream was so real. It was like he was here. I swear I could smell his breath."

"*Dream*? You mean that nightmare you had? You scared the sheeteezle out of me, you screamed so loud."

"Sorry."

"I need to get out of here. I've got that big interview today. I need to get home and get showered and changed. She stood and stretched. "Toni, I get the soup cans stacked by the door," Denise said, gesturing at the cans, "but what's the deal with the bells on the windows?"

"If someone tries to climb through the window, there's no way they'll get through without hitting the bells hanging from the top, or the bottom, maybe both. It's a primitive early warning system."

"When the cans get knocked over, or the bells start ringing, you do what, grab your gun?"

Toni scrunched her face. "I don't have a gun."

"After what you told me last night, you mean to tell me you don't own a gun?"

"Nope."

Denise folded the blanket, and laid it over the top of the couch. "I need to get out of here. After the night you had last night, I think you should call in sick."

"Yeah. I don't feel so good, and I didn't sleep much."

Denise started for the bathroom, stopped and turned to Toni, who was still standing in the middle of the floor looking confused. "Toni, it's a silly question, but in the dream . . ."

"Yeah?"

". . .what did his breath smell like?"

"Just like it did that day at the airport," she said as a shiver ran down her spine. "Sweet, and evil."

***

Toni rolled over and grabbed the phone.

"Hello."

"I'm back in the office now," Denise said.

"How did your interview go? You got everything you need for your story?"

"Went great! I'll tell you all about it later. How ya feeling?"

"A little better," Toni said. "I need to go get something to eat, and some coffee."

"Toni, are you sure you want to go out? You could order in, or if you can wait just a few hours, I'll stop by the store and pick up some stuff for you. Or, you could open one of your early warning system cans of soup," Denise said, laughing.

"Thanks, Denise, but I need to go out. For a lot of reasons, not the least of which is hunger. And those cans are so out-of-date that I'd probably die instantly if I ate from one of them."

"No word from Jamey yet?"

"Nope. Tried calling him on all his phones, he's not answering any of them. I can't believe that he could see my name come up, and not answer. I don't know where he is, I don't know where Mel is. Either Jamey is so done with me that he's never going to speak to me again, or he's. . ."

"He's okay," Denise interrupted. "He's just taking some time to cool off. You were brutal last night."

"I was half in the bag after all that wine, and fully scared after that encounter. He should understand that."

"If you haven't heard from him in a couple of hours, maybe you should consider calling his brother, or his assistant."

"Yeah, I thought about that. If I haven't heard from him by the time I get back from the store, I'll do that."

"I have to go, but call me before you head out so that I can keep track of you."

"Thanks, Denise. I'm going to take a quick nap. I'm exhausted."

"Okay, talk to you later."

"Denise," Toni said, bolting upright.

"Yeah?"

"Just in case, do you remember the name of Mel's island?"

"*Quatt tro poor TAY*," Denise said slowly. "Just in case of what, Toni?"

"Just in case something *has* happened to Jamey, and I disappear."

"Call me before you leave. Don't forget."

"Believe me, I won't." She hung up the phone and fell into a deep sleep.

***

Toni closed the bathroom door, then opened it again. *Closed or open? If I close it, I won't be able to hear if someone comes into the apartment. But then again, if it's closed they'll have to get through it to get to me. If I leave it open, I'm a sitting duck, or maybe a showering duck.* She laughed out loud. *This is ridiculous.*

She turned the water on, wet the wash cloth thoroughly, turned the water off and soaped herself up. She turned the water back on, checked the temperature, stepped in, rinsed off quickly, and stepped back out. She thought about Jamey as she dried herself. She checked the phone again. *He's okay,* she reassured herself. *If something had happened to him I'd know it, I'd feel it in my spirit.*

She thought about Denise's suggestion that she order-in. *The thought of a stranger coming here is more terrifying than the thought of going out. Even though Eugene is on duty at the door, you can't underestimate Mel. He could still be around. He could hijack the delivery, get past Eugene, and straight to me.* She decided that instead of ordering in, she'd run to the corner deli for sandwiches for later, and coffee and cheesecake for breakfast. *Under Woman Law, it's perfectly okay to eat cheesecake for breakfast, a pint of ice cream straight from the carton in one sitting, or a whole pie if you're PMS-ing, dealing with a broken heart, or have had a traumatic experience. I can check one, maybe two of those boxes.* She thought about Jamey again, and shook her head. *Why hasn't he called?*

She dressed quickly, then moved the cans away from the door. She looked around one last time before calling Denise.

"Hey."

"Hey. I'm heading out."

"Have you heard from him?"

"Nope. Denise, stay on the line while I ring for the elevator, okay?"

"Okay."

Toni looked around nervously, pushed the button for the elevator repeatedly, and tried to remain calm.

"I feel like one of those women in the scary movies. The audience is yelling at the screen, 'don't go in the basement. *Gurlllll*, don't go in that basement'! But you know she's going to do it anyway, and it's not gonna end well for her."

Denise laughed.

"I'm getting on the elevator. I just hope we don't get cut off. Hang on the line until I get to the lobby."

"I'm here."

"I sure hope this bad boy doesn't stop on any of the other floors. What's going on there?"

"Nothing much," Denise said. "SSDD."

"SSDD?"

"Same shit, different day," she said, laughing. "Come on, Toni, don't tell me you never heard that one before."

"I've always heard SOS, same old stuff. Leave it to you to put your own spin on it."

Denise didn't respond.

"*Denise. Denise,*" Toni yelled into the phone.

"I'm here. What happened?"

"I thought I'd lost you," she said as the elevator came to a stop.

"*Can you hear me now?*"

They both laughed.

"I'm in the lobby. Thanks, Denise."

"Okay girl, be safe. Keep your phone on, and be sure to call me when you get to the store, when you're leaving the store, when you walk back into your building, and when you're safely back in your apartment."

"Denise, are we going steady now?"

"Girl, shut up. Just call me, okay?"

"I will," Toni said, laughing as she ended the call.

"Hi Eugene," Toni said to the doorman as she stepped off the elevator. He was standing behind a large circular reception desk off to the left side of the lobby.

"Hey, Toni, I was just trying to call you on your cell phone, but the line was busy."

"I just now hung up from a call. What's up?"

"I have this package for you, and this gentleman . . ." Eugene started to say just as Toni heard footsteps behind her. A wave of cold terror hit her stomach. She turned just in time to find herself standing face-to-face with him.

CHAPTER 30 - MEL

Mel checked himself in the mirror one last time. *You look good, son,* he told himself, admiring his beige-colored Guayabera shirt, black Chinos creased to knife-edge sharpness, and beige leather loafers. He grabbed a Panama hat with a red band from the dresser and headed toward the door. He took a last look at the computer screen, which displayed information confirming purchase of a round-trip plane ticket to San Saypaz'. He smiled and placed the hat on his head.

Rayf was waiting in the driver's seat of the Maybach when Mel emerged from the house.

"So, Rayf, what are you going to do while I'm gone?"

"Relax, exercise, swim, and watch movies."

"Yeah?"

"Yes, Mel," Rayf said, turning to look at Mel.

Mel pushed a button and music filled the car. He hummed along to it for the remainder of the drive.

"Be good while I'm gone, Rayf," Mel said as Rayf pulled the car to the curb at the airport.

"I will."

Mel opened the car door, turned, looked into Rayf's eyes and flashed a bone-chilling smile. *Liar.* He put his sunglasses on, climbed out and slammed the door.

***

Mel made his way through security and headed to his gate. He checked in at the ticket counter, glanced at his watch and took a seat. It was 10:10 a.m. At 10:30 the alarm on his phone beeped loudly and repeatedly, drawing attention to him. He stood slowly, took his time silencing the alarm, then headed toward the men's room. He made note of the location of a janitor dressed in gray coveralls as he passed. Midway down the corridor, he glanced over his shoulder, dashed past the entrance of the men's room and darted into a small room just beyond it.

"Boo," he said, startling the man waiting inside.

"You crazy like shit, man."

"Did I scare you?" Mel asked, laughing.

The room, slightly larger than a closet, was empty except for stacks of old in-flight magazines. Mel laid his hat, sunglasses, keys, ticket and boarding pass on one of the stacks, stepped out of his shoes, unbuckled his belt and stepped out of his pants. The man, dressed in a blue sweat suit, followed Mel's lead, laying his baseball cap, tinted eyeglasses and keys on another stack. He stepped out of his shoes and sweatpants.

Mel turned his body so that the man could see his nakedness full-on. The beast grew hard as Mel watched the man bend over to step out of the sweatpants.

"Let's just do this thing, man," he said as he and Mel exchanged pants.

Mel used his foot to push his shoes toward his doppelganger. The man handed Mel his sneakers. Mel promptly slid his feet into them. They exchanged shirts, and quickly finished dressing. Mel slid his Girard-Perregaux watch over his wrist, and handed it to the man. "Take care of this."

"Nice," the man said, drawing the word out. "I always wanted one of these."

Mel ran his eyes slowly up and down the man's body, and licked his lips. "Play your cards right, and you could have as many of those, and anything else you want," he said, rubbing himself to underscore his message.

The man kept his eyes focused on his wrist as he slipped the watch on. When they finished dressing, Mel looked him over carefully, then handed him his ticket, boarding pass and sunglasses.

"Put these on, keep them on," he ordered. "Did you park the motorcycle where I told you to?"

"Third floor, number seventy-three." He handed Mel the keys.

Mel put on the man's baseball cap and eyeglasses. He picked up the Panama hat, put it on the man's head and pushed it down.

"Don't take it off. Don't make eye contact with anyone. Get on that plane as soon as you can."

"Roger," the man said, giving Mel a mock salute.

"Enjoy San Saypaz'. Don't fuck up," Mel said, pointing his finger at the man. "Oh, and be sure to hit me up as soon as you get back. I'll have a little something extra waiting for you, for your trouble."

The man smiled big, opened the door slowly then moved quickly through it.

I've learned my lesson about leaving witnesses, Mel thought as he watched the door close. *I've got a little something extra for your ass alright—a bullet with your name on it.*

He waited twenty-five minutes before walking back into the boarding area, adopting a stooped posture that made him appear much older. He kept his gaze down, took a seat several boarding gates down from the original gate, and waited.

That has to be the cleanest area of carpet in the whole fuckin' world, he thought, noting that the position of the janitor in the gray coveralls and his carpet sweeper hadn't changed much from when he'd passed earlier. He watched as his body double boarded the plane for San Saypaz'. When it was airborne, the janitor quickly picked up his carpet sweeper and headed toward the main terminal, pulling something green from his pocket as he went. Mel waited another forty minutes before heading back to the main terminal of the airport. *Time to get to work.*

CHAPTER 31 - JAMEY

Toni positioned herself behind Jamey near the edge of the bed, and wrapped her legs around his body. She rubbed his chest and shoulders.

"My hero," she said, kissing his shoulder lightly. "You came to save me,' she added, laughing.

"Yeah, yeah. I should have just dropped everything, and come myself in the first place," he said.

"You're here now. That's all that matters. You don't know how happy I was when I turned around and it was you, not Mel, behind me in the lobby."

He remained silent.

"Jamey, I know you, and I know something's up. You've been quiet since you got here. What's up?

He relaxed slightly and leaned his body into hers, but didn't say anything. She wrapped her arms around him tightly. His red cell phone rang.

"Rayf."

"Hi, Mr. Jamey. I wanted to let you know that Mel is coming to your island. His plane left a little while ago."

"Are you sure he got on the plane, Rayf? Did you wait for confirmation?"

"Yes, Mr. Jamey."

"Rayf, is there something else going on? You sound . . . different."

"I'm scared, Mr. Jamey."

"Sacred of what?"

"There was something about Mel. Something in his eyes, the way he looked at me. And he's been calling me by my given name lately."

Jamey hesitated. "What did you see in his eyes, Rayf?"

There was a long silence.

"Death."

Jamey's sense of foreboding grew stronger. He wanted to ask Rayf whose death he saw in Mel's eyes, but decided against it. He wanted to say something reassuring, but couldn't think of anything to say.

"Are you still there, Mr. Jamey?"

"Rayf, I think you should get off that island as soon as possible. Go home and throw a few things in a suitcase. I'll have a ticket waiting for you at the airport. Do you have any family or friends somewhere off that island that you could go stay with?"

"No. I don't have any family, and no friends, except here on the island."

Jamey shuffled his feet around the cool floor. It felt good. His mind was fuzzy. *Something's off.* He climbed out of the bed and walked to the window. *I need to get home. But first I need to get Rayf off that island.*

"Mr. Jamey?"

"Give me a minute, Rayf. I'm thinking." He looked out over the lake. It was beautiful and peaceful. *It's not hard to understand why Toni loves it here so much,* he thought. *I could live here. When this is all over . . .* He rubbed his forehead. "Rayf, is there anywhere you'd like to go? Eventually, if you want to move to San Saypaz' to make a fresh start, but as long as Mel is . . . where would you like to go, in the meantime?"

"I've always wanted to see the Statue of Liberty. I'd like to see New York before I die, Mr. Jamey. All of those tall buildings."

"You're not going to die. Get that out of your head."

"Mel said that if I ever tried to run off again, he would find me, and gut me like a pig, and he will, Mr. Jamey. He'll do it."

"I'll wire you some money. I'll wire it ahead so it's waiting for you when you arrive in New York. And I'll make reservations at a nice high-rise hotel in New York City. But are you sure you want to go to New York, all alone? It's a big city."

"I've always been alone, Mr. Jamey."

Jamey swallowed hard and rubbed his forehead again. He suddenly felt very tired. "You're a good person, Rayf," he said, not knowing what else to say.

"Thank you, Mr. Jamey."

The way he said it reminded Jamey just how young and innocent he was. *I should never have gotten him involved in this.*

"Rayf, take the phone with you his time, don't leave it in the tree. Call me as soon as you land in New York. I'll have someone in law enforcement waiting to escort you to your hotel."

"Okay."

"Be very careful."

"I will. Thank you for everything, Mr. Jamey."

"Thank you, Rayf," Jamey said, his eyes misting.

"Goodbye Mr. Jamey."

"Goodbye, Rayf," he said. He pushed the end-call button, then stared at the phone for a few minutes. He took a deep breath before turning to face Toni.

"That was Mel's housemate. Mel is on his way to San Saypaz'," he said, walking over to sit next to her on the bed.

"Why did you say, 'you're not going to die'? Why does he think he's going to die?"

"He's scared," Jamey said with a nervous chuckle. "He said he saw death in Mel's eyes."

Toni placed her hand on his chin, and turned his face toward her. "Jamey, why did you laugh when you said that he said he was scared?"

He looked deep into her eyes, then looked away. "For the first time, I have to admit something to myself," he answered.

"What's that, baby?"

"I'm scared, too." He intertwined his fingers in hers. "You know, it's not one thing I'm scared of, it's everything. I've had this shakiness in my gut since I learned Mel was on his way here. I was so scared that he was going to get to you. I'm scared for you. I'm scared for Rayf. I'm off my game, and that scares me. Or maybe being scared, is *putting* me off my game." He moved their intertwined hand up and down, as if weighing something. "Chicken or the egg?"

"The age-old question," she said.

"I've got to go home, Toni. It's time."

"Time for what?"

"Time to end this thing with Mel."

"Jamey, you just said you were off your game. Stay here. Relax, build yourself back up. You're vulnerable now, and that gives Mel the advantage. It's like walking into battle without your armor. Just because he's on the way to San Saypaz', so what, let him go. Have your guys arrest him as soon as he gets off the plane. They can just make up a charge, and hold him until you get back. You're not his pawn! He doesn't get to dictate your moves. Stay here for awhile, at least until you're feeling better about things."

He lifted her hand to his lips and kissed it. "I'm afraid that if he goes to the island and I'm not there, he'll get crazy and do something to someone in my family. If that happened . . . I could never forgive myself."

"That's the problem, Jamey. You blame yourself for everything, you can't forgive yourself. The guilt is going to get you killed. You've got to let it go. You're not responsible for his actions."

"Don't you understand, Toni?" he asked quietly. "I can't let it go until Mel is dead. I love you, Toni. I've loved you from the minute you walked into that room at police headquarters, and I know now that I'll never stop loving you. Believe me, I've tried," he said with a little laugh. "But I've got to do what I've got to do."

"I should have married you when I had the chance," she said. "Maybe things would be different now."

"Yeah, maybe we would have had some kids. That way, there would be something concrete, something real, when I'm gone, to serve as a reminder that I really existed. The way it stands now . . ."

"That you loved, and were loved by so many people, is verification that you lived."

"*Is it? Is it really?*"

"Yes," she said softly.

They sat on the bed holding one another.

"I could use a shower," he said finally. He stood and extended his hand to her. "Wash my back?"

CHAPTER 32 - MEL

I've got to get one of these, Mel thought as he accelerated the motorcycle. *If I didn't have to take care of things at home, I'd spend the day riding this baby around the island, but first things first.*

Two miles from home he slowed the motorcycle and pulled to the side of the road. He climbed off the bike and walked it deep into the brush, keeping the helmet on to protect his eyes and face from low-hanging branches. He laid the bike on its side, and walked back toward the road. He glanced back periodically to make sure it wasn't visible. Near the side of the road, he tied a thin orange string on a low branch to mark the spot where he hid the bike. He took the helmet off and started to jog. Minutes later he was scaling the wall of his compound. He entered the house through a pool door he'd unlocked before leaving for the airport this morning.

Where are you, you sneaky little bastard?

"Rayf, Rayf," he called, walking through the house. He checked the game room, the theater room, the kitchen, and all the other rooms on the main floor. He took the stairs two at a time, and headed straight to Rayf's bedroom. Rayf wasn't in the house. *I know where you are, you ungrateful son-of-a-bitch. You're the only one who could have tipped Jamey off that I was going for Toni. And Jamey is the only one who could have sent those two men to follow me around when I got there.*

He walked into his bedroom and straight to his closet, pulling the borrowed sweatshirt over his head as he entered. *I had enough of wearing other people's clothes in that orphanage,* he thought as he stuffed the sweatshirt into a small waste can. He did the same with the pants. He pulled a navy track suit with red and white stripes off the closet rack, then hesitated. *Too nice for what I have to do.* He put it back on the rack. He opened a drawer and pulled out a gray sleeveless sweatshirt and matching shorts. He considered a quick shower, but decided against it. *First things first,* he told himself again. He put the sweats on quickly and headed for the front door. A few steps down he snapped his fingers, turned, and headed back up. *Almost forgot.*

He went back the closet and pushed the light switch plate on an interior wall. The wall slid away. He scanned the shelves slowly. *Um, which one?* He closed the wall and exited the house, creating a mental to-do list as he walked along the beach. He spotted a sailboat with multi-colored sails on the horizon. He stopped to study it.

Nice, but not nearly as nice as my boat. Blue, like the water and the sky—that's the best color for sails. I'm going to use that boat more in the future, when this is all over. Maybe I'll even build a dock behind the house, and keep it here. Maybe I'll paint the dock blue, to match the sails. Or maybe I'll walk away from all of this, and Toni and I can just sail off into the sunset after I get rid of Jamey.

He started walking again, his pace quickening until it became a trot.

CHAPTER 33 - RAYSHELL

Rayf sat down in the sand, looked at the phone, and then out to sea. He watched a bird glide low over the ocean. *That must be what freedom feels like—like a bird flying wherever you want, whenever you want, with no one telling you where you can, and can't go. That's what life will be like for me in New York,* he thought, suddenly feeling giddy.

He scooped up a handful of powdery white sand and let it run through his fingers, then did it again. *I'm gonna miss this beach. Good thing I brought a plastic bag to collect sand and shells since I'll never see this island again.* He grabbed handfuls of sand and threw them in the air. He stood up and did a little song and dance. "I'm going to New Yo-ork, I'm going to New Yo-ork." He thought about Jamey's directive to be careful, and stopped dancing. *I'd better get back to the house and pack, and be there in case Mel calls.*

He started for the house, traveling a few feet before turning back to the tree. He wanted to take a last look out over the island he called home. He climbed up and looked around. He positioned himself so that he could see the top of Mel's house just around a sharp bend, barely visible over the trees. Securing his grip around the tree with one arm, holding tight to the cell phone, he used his other hand to shield his eyes from the sun as he gazed out at the horizon. He was about to reposition himself, when out of the corner of his eye he spotted something moving along the beach. His heart raced. He pressed his body tightly against the tree and closed his eyes, hoping that when he opened them again, the figure on the beach would be gone. His ears confirmed what his eyes, and mind, tried desperately to deny.

"Ray-af, Ray-af," Mel called out as he approached. "Ray-af, where are you? Come out, come out wherever you are," he sang.

He walked very close to Rayf's tree, then turned and walked back to the shoreline. He turned and walked back to the trees, squatting to look between them, all the while calling Rayf's name. He stopped and studied the horizon, quiet and still. He stayed that way for a long moment, as if frozen, then turned and started walking toward home. He walked a distance, turned sharply and made a beeline for Rayf's tree. He looked up, his soul-less eyes meeting Rayf's terrified eyes.

"Well there you are," Mel said. "What the *hell* are you doing hiding in a tree?"

Rayf didn't respond, and didn't break eye contact with his tormentor.

"Cat got your tongue, you little bastard?" he said, smiling up at Rayf. He paced back and forth. "Surprised to see me? I bet you thought I was on a plane on my way to San Saypaz', didn't you? How did you know where to drop me off this morning? I never told you what airline I was flying, or where I was going. When I went to the states, two guys started tailing me almost as soon I got there. It was like they knew I was coming, like someone had tipped them off. There's only one person who could have tipped them off. Wanna guess who that might have been?"

Rayf stared down at Mel.

"Come on boy, fess up. You betrayed me, didn't you? Come on down now. Climb your ass down out of that tree, and come down here. Now!"

Mel stopped pacing. Rayf remained motionless.

"Is that a cell phone in your hand? Who gave *you* a cell phone? I'm losing my patience, Rayf," he said, backing away from the tree. "Tell you what I'm gonna do. I'm going to go and cool off, and when I come back, I expect answers. Okay?"

Mel walked to the water's edge and took his shoes off. He let the water run over his feet. He squatted to let the water run through his fingers. He lifted his fingers to his face, tilted his head back, and let the water drip onto his tongue.

"The sea will protect me," he said. He let more seawater drip onto his tongue. "The sea will heal me." He stared out at the ocean. "Rayf," he hollered over his shoulder, "did you know that the elders believe the ocean's waters can protect *and* heal you? Did you know that? You should come down out of that tree, and get some of this protection before it's too late."

He stood and walked back to the tree.

"Come down," he demanded. "I'm not coming up, but you are coming down." He pushed the tree hard with his foot, trying unsuccessfully to shake it. "I was good to you," he said, reaching behind him to pull out the gun he had chosen from the shelf in his hidden closet. Elongated by a silencer, at first glance it could be mistaken for a rod. "You look scared, Rayf," he said, shutting one eye as he aimed the gun in Rayf's direction.

Rayf closed his eyes, and tried to remember the images of New York skyscrapers he'd seen in magazines. Hard as he tried, he couldn't bring any of the images to mind. *I'm never going to see the tall buildings.*

The bullet went clean through Rayf's wrist, and into the tree limb, splitting it lengthwise. Rayf let go of the cell phone, but managed to regain his grip on the tree. He didn't make a sound.

Mel looked at the phone on the ground, then back up at Rayf. Their eyes met. Rayf thought about the prayer an old whore had taught him when he was just a small boy living on the streets.

"Boy, when you ain't got no hope left, you say dis, and everything'll be alright," she told him.

Rayf closed his eyes. "The Lord is my Shepherd; I shall not want," he began to recite out loud. "He maketh me to lie down in green pastures: He leadeth me beside the still waters . . ."

"Rayf," Mel said calmly, trying to get his attention.

Rayf spoke louder to drown out Mel's voice. "He restoreth my soul; He leadeth me in the paths of righteousness for His name sake."

"Rayf," Mel repeated.

"Yea, though I walk through the valley of the shadow of death, I will fear no evil," Rayf said with a conviction, and a sense of peace like none he had ever known.

He was dead the instant the bullet slammed into his brain. Eyes wide open, his body landed near Mel's feet with a dull thud. Mel stepped over it, and picked up the phone. He dragged the body to the edge of the water, leaving a trail of blood in the sand. He plopped the body face down in the surf.

"The sea won't heal *or* protect your ass now," Mel said aloud, laughing. He watched without emotion as blood pouring from Rayf's head turned the frothy white surf pink. He hit the redial button on the phone. The "No Signal" message appeared. "One down," he said, turning in a wide circle until he finally got a signal. He hit the redial button again, and waited. "And one to go."

"This will be over soon," Jamey said. "And when it is, I'm coming for you. We can live here, or anywhere else you want. But I don't want to live without you ever again."

"For true?" Toni asked.

"For true," he said. He kissed her deeply, then laid down beside her. They laid in silence, side-by-side, holding hands. The sweet, but poignant lovemaking session in the shower had lightened his mood. "I have to leave soon," he said after some time.

"I know."

He climbed out of bed, went to the closet and pulled out his duffle bag. He stepped into his pants, and was about to put on his shirt when his red phone rang. He studied the caller I.D.

"Be very quiet, okay?" he said in Toni's direction.

She nodded. He pushed the button to answer and remained silent.

"Jamey, is that you, buddy?"

Jamey sat on the bed. Toni grabbed a blanket, scooted over next to him and wrapped it around them both. He placed his finger to his lips to remind her to remain quiet. He nodded to make sure she understood. She nodded back.

"Jamey, this is your old buddy, Mel. What, cat got your tongue? That damn cat has been very busy today. He had Rayf's tongue, too."

Jamey remained silent as the feeling of dread returned. *There's only one way Mel could have gotten that phone.*

"Come on boy, I know you're there."

Jamey continued to listen, trying to decide if he should say something, or hang up. *If I respond, and Rayf isn't already dead then. . .*

"I bet you think Rayf was good, don't you? He was a piece of shit. You're a piece of shit, Jamey. I was good to him, he betrayed me. He was up in a tree when I found him, J. A fuckin' tree! What fool hides in a tree?"

He said he was. Rayf is gone.

"You know what I can't figure, Jamey, is how you got to him, and when? Did you come to my island, Jamey, *to my home?* Were you in my home? You knew every move I made, didn't you? Every time I left this island you knew about it. The two guys following me around when I went for Toni, those were your boys, weren't they? That tag team thing was pretty good, and would have worked, except for that stupid hat your boy was wearing. That was amateur hour. What are the chances that in a strange city, I'd see the same guy in the same hat every day? Stoopid, stoopid, stoopid," Mel said, laughing. "Come on, Jamey, say something."

Jamey turned to Toni and put his finger to his lips again.

She nodded.

"Where's Rayf?"

"Surfing," Mel said, laughing again.

"Surfing?"

"He's dead, and it's your fault. You couldn't leave me be, could you? And you *had* to get him involved. Well, now he's dead. And guess what, Jamey, my boy, you're next. I'm gonna enjoy killing you as much as I enjoyed killing that freak Brinwyn. Get ready, I'm coming for you boy. I'm coming to San Saypaz' one final time—coming for you. Then I'm going to go get Toni, bring her back here, and fuck her brains out every day, two or three times a day. Do you hear me, Jamey? And you'll be dead, so you won't be able to play hero."

Jamey felt his anger rising. He forced himself to remain calm.

"I'll be here when you get here, Meleva," he said, not letting on that he was with Toni, and not on San Saypaz'.

Mel remained quiet for so long that Jamey began to think that the call had been dropped. He listened closely, and finally heard Mel breathing, along with what sounded like the roar of the ocean. He let the silence hang in the air knowing that he had gotten under Mel's skin.

"You there, *Meleva*?"

"What . . . did . . . you . . . call . . . me? What did you call me?" Mel yelled into the phone so loud that Jamey had to move it away from his ear. "Don't you fuckin' call me that!"

"Meleva. Wasn't that your name when you were with Brinwyn? Isn't that the name Brinwyn gave you? You know what I think, Mel? I think Brinwyn called you that so he could somehow justify, in his warped mind, what he was doing to you. But you understand that, *don't you?* It's the same thing you did to Rayshell, I mean, Rayf."

"I'm going to fuck you up, Jamey," Mel said calmly. "I'm going to mess you up *real* bad, son, and I'm going to enjoy every single minute of it."

"I'll be waiting for you. Bye, Meleva." Jamey hung up the phone and immediately pressed two buttons to dial out. He rested his head in his hand.

"Hey. He's on the move, headed your way," he said when the person on the other end answered. "That last call was a false alarm. He didn't get on that plane this morning. He apparently doubled back on his housemate. He's coming this time, I have no doubt. He doesn't know I'm not on the island. I'm headed back, ASAP. How soon can you get me a charter flight out?" He grabbed his watch from the night table, checked the time, then strapped it to his wrist. "Good. I'll be on it. Put things in motion immediately. Make sure my family, and Shannon and the kids are secure. Instruct the team to be extra careful, he's out for blood. If he steps foot on that island, this time, when he leaves, it'll be in a box."

He ended the call, and laid the phone back on the nightstand. He turned to face Toni just as the first tear slid down her cheek. He brushed his fingers lightly across her face, then pulled her into his arms.

"Jamey, there's something I never told you."

"What's that, baby?"

"The first time we met, that day at police headquarters, when I walked out of that room I was weak in the knees. You took my breath away," she said.

He smiled at her.

"I'm telling you this now, just in case . . ."

"*Shhhhhhh,*" he whispered, tightening his arms around her. "*Shhhhhhh.*"

CHAPTER 35 - JAMEY

From up here, San Saypaz' looks like paradise, Jamey thought as he scoured the island from his perch high up in a tree overlooking Stan's farmhouse. *Toni would say it's just an illusion.*

He took a sip of water and re-capped the canteen. He raised the binoculars to his eyes again, taking a moment to look around the inside of Stan's house. He spotted Mel sitting in an armchair thumbing through an exotic car magazine. He had his back to the wall, the front door in plain sight. *Good strategic positioning Mel—if I was going to come for you through the front door.* Stan sat, zombie-like, on the couch staring off into space.

Jamey tugged hard on the rope attached to his safety net again, to ensure it was secure. Another trick he had learned from Tip. Tip had taught him so much about life, and survival. He taught Jamey how to tie the safety netting so that it wasn't visible, but secure, in case you fell into a deep sleep, or got disoriented from lack of sleep, and tumbled out of the tree. It was Tip who'd originated the idea of "high-top surveillance"—a stakeout conducted from a tree.

"The bad guys are always on the lookout for dark-colored Crown Vics, or white vans with some laundry service or air conditioning company logo on them. They never think to look up in the trees," he'd told Jamey.

Tip also taught him about subsisting on bites of protein bars, taking only small sips of water, and wearing adult diapers so that you don't have to climb down as often to take care of bodily functions.

"But bury those diapers deep, and far away from the tree. You don't want to attract animals to you. And you don't want the smell of those funky diapers coming back at you in a strong wind. Man, that'll knock you right out of your tree. And when you have to do the big one, make like a bear in the woods," he'd added, laughing his silly Tip laugh.

I'll never stop missing that boy, Jamey thought, laughing to himself. He took a bite of protein bar, wrapped it up, and put it back in his backpack. He had been in the tree almost two and a half days now. From his perch, he'd watched as Mel made his way from the beach to Stan's house. He guessed that Mel had flown to a neighboring island, secured weapons, and rented a boat for the final leg of the trip to San Saypaz'. He'd anchored offshore, swam ashore, and walked through the brush to Stan's house with his wetsuit, weapons, and other gear stuffed in a buoyant backpack.

Jamey had been monitoring Mel's movements closely—a miscalculation could be fatal. He watched as Mel hid weapons throughout the house. Paranoid, and obviously scared, Mel checked his stash of weapons every hour. He also kept two guns and a knife strapped to his body. In the evening, Mel and Stan watched television, with Stan downing cans of cheap beer back-to-back, then crushing the cans in his hand. Mel limited himself to one Cognac, and one long skinny French cigarette. He kept the cigarettes, and a gun, in a drawer next to his strategically positioned chair.

Afraid of the dark, Stan slept with a light on. The first night in the tree, Jamey saw Mel enter Stan's bedroom. He watched as Stan tried to fight Mel off, and as Mel beat Stan into submission. The beating, and what followed, was a level of brutality he never wanted to see again. He grew angry as he thought about

Rayf, and the horrible things that Mel had probably done to him. When Mel entered Stan's room the second night, Jamey climbed down from the tree to stretch.

When the time was right, he would slip out of the tree, and enter the house. He knew the land surrounding Stan's farm like the back of his hand. He'd walked the property a hundred times, in all sorts of weather, including during hurricane watches and major storms. He wanted to be ready for anything when the time came. Instinctively, he always knew that it would all end here, on this stretch of land. He checked his watch. There was nothing to do now but wait. He had the element of surprise on his side, but he knew that the lack of real sleep would soon start to work against him.

In the evening of the third day, Stan and Mel got into Stan's car and drove away. Nothing they did before leaving indicated where they were going, or how long they'd be gone. *It's now or never*, Jamey thought as he watched the car drive out of sight. He threw his backpack to the ground, quickly climbed down from the tree, and raced for the farmhouse.

* * *

"Welcome back, Mel," Jamey said, stepping out of the shadows as Mel entered Stan's house nearly two hours later.

"Jamey, my boy, so good to see you. I've been waiting for you. What took you so long to get here?"

"Just waiting for the right time to pop in," Jamey said.

Mel started to turn around.

"Stop! I don't want to shoot you in the back, Mel, but I will if you make any sudden moves. And please know that I mean the back of the head. Now lock your hands together behind your head."

Jamey heard Stan approaching and called out to him.

"Stan, it's me, Jamey. I'm in the house, I've got a gun trained on Mel. Please come in."

Stan walked through the door slowly, alternately looking from Jamey to Mel.

"It's good to see you, Jamey," Stan said.

"I need you to do something for me. Walk over to Mel and pat him down."

He didn't tell Stan where to look for the weapons, opting instead to see if Stan could be trusted. Stan pulled a gun from the small of Mel's back, and the one that was strapped to his ankle.

"Thanks, Stan. Now put them in this chair," Jamey said, motioning with his head to a chair beside him.

"Yeah, thanks, Stan," Mel said.

"Shut up Mel," Jamey said. "Stan, unbuckle Mel's pants."

"Jamey," Mel said in mock horror. "I had no idea."

"Stan, that bulge in the front of his pants isn't all him. He has a knife hidden in his cup. Get it."

Stan looked at Jamey curiously.

"Get it, Stan," Jamey ordered.

Stan walked toward Mel.

"Wait," Jamey said. "Turn slightly toward me, Mel.

Mel shuffled his feet.

"Now, Stan."

Stan unbuckled Mel's pants, reached in and pulled out the knife.

"In the chair," Jamey said to Stan.

"Well, now that you've stripped me of all my weapons, can I get a cigarette? They're in that drawer," Mel said, nodding his head toward the table.

"Sure," Jamey said.

Mel went to the table and pulled out the drawer. It was empty. He let out an almost inaudible sigh.

"Smoking is bad for your health," Jamey said. "And you with the gun that was in that drawer would be bad for *my* health. And don't waste my time, and what little you have left, trying to get to the other weapons you stashed around this house. They're not there anymore."

"Jamey, have you been watching me?"

"Yeah, Mel, I've been watching you."

"From where?"

"A tree."

"*A tree*? Are you fuckin' *kiddin'* me? Is that why you smell like an animal? You know you smell like an ass monkey, don't you?" Mel asked, laughing heartily.

Jamey ignored him.

"Stan, why are you helping *him*?" Mel asked. "Don't you know that when this is all over you're going to prison? You know what happens to ex-cops in jail? You don't want to go to jail, Stan."

Stan looked at Jamey.

"He's baiting you, Stan. You have my word that you will not be arrested. I'll make sure you get to spend the rest of your days here on this farm."

"He's lying to you," Mel said. "You killed his best friend. You think he's just gonna let you spend the rest of your days here at Happydale Farm? Don't be stupid Stan."

"I didn't kill Tip," Stan said. "Jamey, you know that I didn't kill Tip."

"I know, Stan. I know what Mel did to you, and what he did to Rayf, his housemate. I know what he still does to you here in this house, late at night, when he thinks no one is watching."

Stan lowered his head.

"You watched that, too, Jamey?" Mel asked. "Did you enjoy it?"

"I told you to shut up, Meleva."

Mel made a sudden move toward Jamey. Jamey didn't flinch.

"Come on," Jamey said, opening and closing his free hand to encourage Mel to keep moving toward him.

Mel stopped.

Before Jamey could grasp what was happening, Stan pulled a gun from the small of his back. He pointed it at Jamey.

The three men stared at one another. Mel moved in Stan's direction. Stan backed up.

"No, Mel," Stan said.

"What's up, Stan?" Jamey asked. "Right now, I can't tell whose side you're on."

"He's on my side," Mel said. "Otherwise why would he need his own gun? Wouldn't *your* gun be enough if he was on *your* side?"

"Stan, I need you to put that gun down," Jamey said slowly. "I've got this. You don't need the gun. And you don't need to spend the rest of your life in fear of this man. I got this, Stan," he added, trying to keep his voice calm. Stan had thrown him a curveball.

"Stan," Mel said, "you know that I can afford to give you whatever you want, and certainly everything you need. You fight me in the night, but you know you like what I do to you. You *know* you like it. You even like the fight. Admit it, Stan, it feels good when I'm in you," he added, rubbing himself teasingly. "I can give you whatever you want, whenever you want it, however you want it. We can leave this island today, and disappear, and they'd never find us. We'll spend the rest of our lives traveling, living like kings. Together, just you and me. All we have to do is get rid of this piece of shit," he said in Jamey's direction."

Mel took a step toward Stan.

"One more step, and I'm going to kill you, Mel," Jamey said. "Regardless of whatever else happens, next step, you're dead."

Stan looked at Jamey, then back at Mel.

"Stan, go to the mirror and take a good look at your face, and those bruises on your body. That's what Mel will give you until you're of no use to him anymore, and then he'll kill you like he killed the man that lived with him, and Chief Frankland, and Boppy, and all the others."

Stan pondered what Jamey said, then turned to face Mel.

"Anything I want, Mel?"

"Anything!"

"Stan, you know you can't trust this psycho," Jamey said.

"Be quiet Jamey," Stan said.

Concerned about Stan's unpredictability, Jamey reached for his second gun just as Stan pulled the trigger. The pain, and the reality of what had just happened hit him at the same time. *This must be what it feels like when someone pours gasoline down your throat, then throws a match in after it,* Jamey thought as explosive pain radiated deep into his chest. He looked at Stan, then at Mel, who was grinning from ear-to-ear. Toni's face flashed through his mind as he clutched his chest, and fell to one knee.

"Jamey, my boy, looks like you lose," Mel said, his voice fading.

Jamey looked up at him. He saw Mel's lips moving, and heard garbled sounds, but couldn't make out what Mel was saying. He looked back at Stan. *It's over,* he thought as a second gunshot rang out, and his world faded to black.

He looked around slowly, his radius limited by the ventilator that had been helping him breathe.

"Hey you."

She read the confused look on his face.

"Thought you were dead, didn't you?" Toni asked. "You don't get off that easy."

He smiled weakly. She kissed his forehead. Jamey raised his trembling arm slowly, the I.V. cord moving with it. He felt around his chest, wincing when he got to the huge bruise that covered the area between his breasts. He felt again, pressing down slightly this time. His eyes questioned her.

"You didn't get shot. I mean, you did, but you didn't. The bullet didn't pierce your body, but the force of it stopped your heart. Stan revived you, and called for the EMTs. He said he knew you'd be smart enough to be wearing a vest. He left a note asking you to forgive him for Tip. He killed Mel. Mel is dead, Jamey."

He shook his head. His eyes expressing doubt.

"Yes. He's dead. After Stan shot you, he killed Mel. He waited with you until your guys, and the EMTs arrived. When they arrived, he walked out his front door and told them that you were inside, hurt, and that Mel was dead. Then he walked toward them, pointing a gun at them. They shot him. Stan is dead, too, Jamey."

Jamey made a writing motion with his hand.

"Okay. I'll get you some paper and a pen, but first let's ring for the nurse. They need to know you're awake."

Toni pushed the red call button. She told the nurse that Jamey was awake, and asked her to page his family. She handed Jamey her notebook and a pen. Hands trembling, he wrote: how long sleep?

"Three weeks."

He wrote: family ok?

"Dad is at home resting. Tina and her family, and Shannon and the kids are fine. Tank and Yolee are in the cafeteria. The nurse is paging them."

Just then Tank burst through the door, followed closely by Yolee.

"Man, you had us scared," Tank said. They both gave him big wet kisses on the cheek.

Jamey's parched and cracked lips broke into a smile as he wrote: get Daddy, Tina, Rev. Branford, Shannon.

"Rev. Branford?" Tank asked.

Jamey nodded and started writing again. He held the paper so that only Toni could see it.

"Yes. Yes, absolutely," she said excitedly. "Get the reverend," she said, turning to Tank. "Get everybody, and hurry, please."

"What did he write?" Tank asked.

Jamey held up the piece of paper for Tank and Yolee to see.

It read: *MARRY ME. RIGHT NOW!*

THE END

Dear Reader,

Thank you for taking the time to read my book!

I sincerely hope you enjoyed it, and will recommend it to family, friends—real and virtual—and "Followers" via social media.

Please take a moment to visit my website illusionsofparadise.net to read my blog, and leave a testimonial. Be sure to let me know how you want to be identified, first and last name, or first name and last initial, profession or job title, and contact information.

Thanks again!
Sincerely,

Pat